THE RETURN

by Herbert Mitgang

SIMON AND SCHUSTER, NEW YORK, 1959

ALL RIGHTS RESERVED
INCLUDING THE RIGHT OF REPRODUCTION
IN WHOLE OR IN PART IN ANY FORM
COPYRIGHT © 1959 BY HERBERT MITGANG
PUBLISHED BY SIMON AND SCHUSTER, INC.
ROCKEFELLER CENTER, 630 FIFTH AVENUE
NEW YORK 20, N. Y.

FIRST PRINTING

LIBRARY OF CONGRESS CATALOG CARD NUMBER: 59-7266
MANUFACTURED IN THE UNITED STATES OF AMERICA
BY AMERICAN BOOK-STRATFORD PRESS, INC., NEW YORK

To Shirley

Hard by the Sicilian coast rises an island, steep with smoking rocks. Beneath it thunders a cave and the vaults of Etna, scooped out by cyclopean forges; strong strokes are heard echoing groans from the anvils—the home of Vulcan and the land Vulcan's by name. In the vast cave the Cyclopes were forging iron. They had a thunderbolt, which their hands had shaped, such as full many the Father hurls down from all heaven upon earth, part already polished, while part remained unfinished. Elsewhere they were hurrying on for Mars a chariot and flying wheels, wherewith he stirs up men and cities. . . .

—THE AENEID

THE RETURN

Part One

CHAPTER ONE

ONE AUTUMN, in the years after youth, I returned to Sicily. It was a later season now: all over the island a fine rain fell, misting the hillsides of the country and delicately enveloping the cities. The weather did not disturb me because I knew that, in good time, this vibrant place would again be radiant with light reflected from her seas. I remembered it that way.

New events and old dreams had transported me here again. At the moment I could think only of the dreams. I made my excuses that first morning after coming to Palermo and descended from the Company's villa into the streets. I said innocently: A little walk of recognition among old haunts, and the others had nodded and smiled. I turned a corner and found myself on the Via della Libertà, the wide boulevard leading this way toward the older part of the city. Twice taxicabs pulled close to the sidewalk, but I shook them off. I wanted to feel these streets underfoot. Walking at my own pace, clutching the buildings and squares to my willing memory, I savored the thought of our encounter.

The name and address were in her hand. I had asked her to write them in this old address book, crumbling now. Franca Florio. Below, she had written Corso dei Mille and, in parenthesis, translated the street as Course of the Thousand. She was always so proud of her growing knowledge of English. The page in the address book was curled from handling; I would open it often to wonder at her writing. Corso dei Mille, 72. She had made one of those funny little European sevens with a cross through its center, and sometimes, playing with a pencil, I would imitate its gracefulness. The street was on the other end of Palermo, in an area of baroque houses beyond the railway station. I had no idea if she lived there, but it was morning and strangely pastoral, the air fragrant with mimosa and bougainvillaea, and I found myself drawn in that direction.

The main landmarks of the city looked unchanged. On the pedestals of the old marble monuments there were new slogans and political advertisements. In the early blush of day only the people who had work to do were around, cartmen and peddlers and the omnipresent policemen under awnings, motionless, as I had left them more than a decade ago. I turned away from someone seeking a light for his pipe, tossed him a matchbook, and quickened my step near the railway station. Here once more was Julius Caesar Square, fronting on the railway station, and a few blocks on, her street, the Course of the Thousand. I wanted to be calm and matter-of-fact, and I told myself the tightening in my chest was immature, this coldness in my finger tips not sensible. That was past; this was now.

I forbade my eyes to glance at once up her street; instead, I sought my reflection nervously in the store front of a souvenir shop. The shadowed doorway glass dwindled my nearly six feet in elusive silhouette. Behind the shop's showcase a tilted mirror acted to double the quantities of reflected trinkets. One open space, surrounded by strands of tourist coral, revealed my angular face in prism. I ran my fingers across the sides of my head, flattening the loose hairs. From here the speckled gray did not show in the dark brown hair; but it was there. I placed my forefinger between my neck and shirt collar, trying to loosen my appearance. After all the post-war years of working in the Company's main office in New York, I could not bring myself to walk tieless in the street, not even this familiar one. If anything, I had acquired a deceptive formal look.

I turned the corner, and stopped abruptly. The low houses on the street, sand-colored blocks of stone, stood in their places. Only at the far end of the street a new taller apartment building with terraces broke tradition. Her building, with its courtyard behind the massive wooden door, emerged boldly. I hesitated for a moment, thinking of what to say, the casualness of a polite approach. Suddenly it only mattered to see her face and self. A few children were beginning to appear on the street, escorted by the black-robed grandmothers of Sicily. One young girl came out of No. 72, and I wondered. But I went up to the wooden door, whose shadows in the evenings had concealed our embracing, and yanked the rope bell. I waited for someone to answer, my heart pounding.

From within the courtyard came the shufflings and mutterings of an impatient woman. A smaller portal, opening almost secretly from within the larger door, revealed a buxom, rouged figure wearing a man's loose bathrobe.

I asked, "Does the Florio family still live here?"

She replied by feeling my pockets for a cigarette. I handed her one.

"All the rooms are taken," she said, blowing smoke in my face.

Looking at my clothes suspiciously, she asked, "Are you from the police?"

I said, annoyed, "Of course not; I'm an American."

"So that's how you got my address," she said. "From your consulate."

"Look, madam," I replied, "I am looking for the Florio family who lived here during the war, right off this court-yard."

"Foolish," she said, laughing. "No families live here any more—those pompous Christian-Democratic politicians have raised all the rents."

She regarded me closely, taking my measure, and then took out a business card from her bathrobe and pressed it into my hand.

"All my girls are taken now," she said, motioning obscenely in my palm, "but you come back tonight, call first on the tele-phone, and bring along some of my American friends."

She grinned slyly, her heavy tongue moistened her thick lips, and she slammed shut the door within the door. The heavy musk of her perfume remained.

I stood there with the mocking card in my hand. The Course of the Thousand, as I looked along its length, seemed a strange, alien street.

I should have known that I could not pick up the thread this easily. And this address, at this portal of love, seemed part of someone else's life. On an impulse, I had gone to the Italian consulate the day before embarking for Palermo again, and in an embarrassed voice asked if they had the overseas telephone books. Which cities? the woman behind the recep-tion desk asked. The books from Sicily. They had one. I ran down the names quickly but could not find hers; I knew her father's first name, but he was not listed. I tried looking up the name in other ways, through the business part of the book, through the advertisements and schools, but there were no hints. Yet even examining this Palermo book had stirred the fires.

Turning my back on No. 72, I walked to Caesar Square, watching the city move through the railway station's arcades. I had no plan, only a fresh desire to see Franca. I determined to comb our old haunts for a clue. If only through the magnets of sentiment, she would be drawn back occasionally to the places where once we had known only ourselves.

This time I signaled a taxicab. The driver turned toward the center of the city, down the noisy Via Maqueda, and as we drove by I looked at the university where she had studied. The logical starting point would be the language school next to the once-requisitioned offices my outfit had occupied. Berlitz, of all things, seemed out of place in wartime, but it had been attended by some Italians who desired to know English in a more scholarly way than they could pick it up on the streets from the swarming troops. I had signed for some Italian lessons. As one classroom emptied, another filed in— and one day our lessons and paths had crossed. Bolder hearts beat beneath khaki—I introduced myself in halting Italian. Franca had replied, politely, in halting English. We thrust our feelings forward with groping words. In the rush of days that followed, we discovered that our best common language was French, which we had both studied in college and, later, we spoke all three languages at once.

Now I climbed the familar steps to Berlitz's. I went to the office and said I was an old pupil, looking around; that I had taken a brush-up course in the States a month ago, too, before returning to Sicily.

The office director was a wise man. He asked me if, for old time's sake, I would like to see my name in their wartime records. He looked pleased when he found it. I asked him if he kept a record of the whereabouts of all former pupils.

"Do you have a particular one in mind?" he asked.

I said, "A Miss Franca Florio, an old friend who studied English here about the same time."

Her name turned up in his yellowing files, too, but the address was the same as the one I had just left. No, he was sorry but that was her last address, and he did not know where she lived.

As I left, he told me that I was not the first American or Englishman who had requested the address of an old friend.

5

Of course her main school links would be with the university in Palermo. She had graduated with honors as a teacher. Once we had visited the college together during one of the celebration weeks and she had told me what all the symbols on the tricornered student hats meant. I imagined they would have records, too, and class meetings and old club groups, that this university kept track of its graduates with the same persistence as an American college in pursuit of alumni contributions.

I looked at my watch and the passage of a few hours frightened me. The thought entered my mind that time would fly, the work which had brought me here for the Company would overtake all my free movement. I signaled another taxicab and told the driver to take me to the middle of the city quickly.

The prefect at the university was a short, bearded man who appeared to have difficulty hearing or, at least, understanding what I wanted. The record clerks in his office, behaving with the tired formality that made them a universal brotherhood, looked on in bored amusement as I attempted to explain slowly that I was after the latest address of a former woman student.

I thought that one of the working students would be of help, and I called toward the group. One fellow broke away with great effort.

I asked him in Italian, "Do you keep records of old graduates?"

He replied in English, "American?"

And I said eagerly, "Yes, I am an American."

He looked at me and said, "Old girl friend?"

I said, resenting the intimacy, "An old friend."

He grinned. He asked me to tell him the name and year, and I hesitated, but finally did so. After a moment he returned and said that he found no such party, and anyway, it would be better if I wrote a letter to the prefect, and then it could be studied more carefully because, as I must understand, being

6

an American and knowing such things, the university could not give out information to anyone who came in off the streets. His sarcasm was too apparent.

"Thank you for your trouble, you son-of-a-bitch," I said, smiling, and he glowered. I trusted that his English was perfect.

I walked out of the building, past knots of students talking and flirting animatedly. The men seemed younger than the women, and I wondered how I appeared to them. I noticed one of the young women among the others: she had Franca's slim body and the same deep-set eyes. But one of the men danced before her and they whirled away together down the crowded street.

It was near lunchtime, and I felt the need for a drink—a reassessing drink. I passed up the brassy student hangout across from the university that advertised local drinks and Coca-Cola. At a bar near by, I drank a small glass of red wine and, almost automatically, I began to ask the bartender for a cognac-and-vermouth.

Cognac-and-vermouth. That was the wild mixture we drank during the war because when it was mixed in the proper proportions it began to taste, after the third round, something like American whisky.

And there was only one place in Palermo which we thought handled it right, the bartender measuring the magic potion as if he were a pharmacist. The Flower Bar. That wasn't the name on the sign—I could still visualize its gold lettering—but we always called it that.

I didn't repeat my request for a second drink, not now. I had a flash thought that the place to find out about Franca was at this Flower Bar, where we had sat for many hours in the late Saturday afternoons. The bar was an inspired place beyond imitation: a flower shop in front, with all the fresh flowers and shrubs from the countryside lined up in many-colored urns—heather and thyme, rockroses and fronds of lavender—and behind it, in a hidden room partly forming

7

an outdoor garden, a dozen tables spaced privately. Half flower shop, half bar, and with the beauty and the perfume of the cut flowers somehow mingling softly with the wines. Franca knew it as she knew all the corners of her city, but I always seemed to come upon it as if by accident. It was hidden in a complex of streets somewhere near the Massimo opera house. And the knowing bartender who spoke little but knew us all by heart or instinct surely would be able to give me a lead.

I turned toward the opera square. In a moment I lost my self-assurance because the streets here were unfamiliar, the new chrome fronts unrecognizable. In the maze of twisting blocks I found myself turned around and meeting myself. I kept asking people on the street for the location of the bar selling flowers out front, but even the policemen shrugged.

Yet I felt the Flower Bar could be the link to the present. I looked at my watch. It was time to eat, but I hungered more for information. I turned back to the Via della Libertà, and it led this way to the Company's villa. There was an all-purpose man there nicknamed Subito because he always answered, *subito-subito*, indicating that he would do what was requested right away, and he seemed to know everything.

"Subito," I asked him, "did you ever hear of a place they call the Flower Bar?"

"Costanza?" he said.

Yes, that was the name on the sign outside.

"What street is it on behind the opera house?"

"No," he said, "its location was behind the Massimo when it was there but I do not think it is there any more."

"Is it anywhere?" I asked, exasperated.

"I heard that a few years ago this bar moved because the rents were increased in that section, but where they went to I myself don't know."

"Is there someone who does?"

"Of course," he replied. "A cousin of mine sells them flowers."

8

"Then surely you can find out from him," I said anxiously.

Subito said that his cousin lived in one of the hill towns behind Palermo and that he would be glad to call. I said it was all right to use the Company phone. In a few moments he returned with a piece of paper and one word written upon it: Mondello.

That was the beach town where Franca and I had spent quiet hours. I thanked Subito, who had come through nobly, and gave him a handful of paper lire. My hopes were lit again. At lunch, I sat with the two young geologists at the Company dining table and they asked me how I had enjoyed my walk and if I had run into any beautiful women. I said that I would keep them in mind in case I did. I felt elated.

In the afternoon, the fine rain stopped. I borrowed one of the Company's cars and drove down Libertà, parallel to Twentieth of September Street, past the incongruous Chinese-style mansion, and out along the wooded lands toward Mondello Lido. It was still possible to speed here for stretches, and I opened it up, slowing down along the waterfront. Inward from the bay I saw a few sailboats belonging to teams of fishermen gliding lightly into the brittle surf over broken shell and withered kelp. The water was undisturbed by wind. In front of my automobile children scampered across ropes and netting that waited for drying sunlight, and farther up the hill I saw some women stringing wash like wet sails. Sitting in their places were old men regenerating their tired bodies for the cool overnight. Except for a plush place I passed called the New Royal Mondello, with borrowed oriental décor and tiles of pastel hues, the unchanged ways of man and nature still dominated this cove.

At the tip of Mondello was a series of shops. I saw it: Costanza. Our bar's gold sign had moved, too. The place was framed by a gently banking promontory. I pulled up in front of the bar and caught my breath. There were dazzling flowers in jars and pitchers, outside the shop, and behind the glass more flowers. Only a few people lingered in the shop when

9

I entered, and for the first time all day I felt at home. They had transplanted not only the fixtures but the atmosphere of the old place. I moved familiarly to the door, past cases of flowers leading to the bar. There were a dozen tables here, but only a few were occupied. I sat down and tried to think of the name of the bartender because, looking as disarming as always, there he was—the first person I saw from those times. I wondered if he recognized me. He appeared forlorn; the years that suddenly bend a man from middle into old age had wrenched his shoulders and neckline. But he couldn't have remembered me; that would have been expecting too much. Certainly I too had grown older; but he seldom acknowledged patrons even then.

I sat down and when a waitress asked me what I would like, of course I asked for a cognac-and-vermouth. When she looked at me quizzically, I said the bartender would understand. The order aroused him. He straightened up and squinted toward me. I left my table and walked up to him at the bar. He smiled, and we shook hands. He apologized for not remembering my name, but I said, how could he, I was out of uniform.

"Cognac-and-vermouth," he said, nodding. "I haven't heard that one for a long time. Only the Americans could dream that up. I wish I could remember which one you were."

"Every Saturday afternoon for six months," I said. "It's like yesterday talking to you. I'm glad to see you again."

"Here, I've got the regular stuff now," he said. "Scotch whisky, rye whisky. All imported. What will it be?"

Half joking, I asked him, "Have you got bourbon?"

"No," he said, puzzled.

"Let it be cognac-and-vermouth then."

"You can get sick drinking that stuff," he said, shaking his head.

"Can I now?" I said. "One for old time's sake."

He poured one, and said it was on his account, and it tasted something like bourbon if you closed your eyes.

10

"It's nice seeing someone from those days," he said. "I've forgotten all the American Army slang. Plenty of excitement in the old Flower Bar then. The whole wild Allied Force stood up at this old bar, yelling and drinking. No one gets drunk here any more except the lady tourists. And the Germans, with their own bottled beer, and their knapsack lunches. Cheap bastards. I hated to serve them then and I feel the same way now."

"A lot of German travelers coming through here?" I asked him.

"With their families now," he said. "Boasting and pointing out where their old regiments were stationed. As if they weren't kicked out of Sicily!"

"Isn't that all past? All that feeling against them?"

"Not for some of us. We're too old to start to learn how to forget."

For a while, standing there at the small bar with this old bartender, I didn't say anything, and we didn't know each other's names, but we were from the same period. He poured himself a small cognac and toasted one to those times and he swished it around his teeth as if it were a mouth wash before swallowing.

The place began to empty out. The first shadows crept up the dog-shaped hill across the Mondello cove. When no one was left at the Flower Bar but the two of us, I remembered why I was here.

"Maybe you'll recognize me better now," I said. "In this light. Usually it was this time of day I'd come into the bar."

He didn't say anything. For an instant I wondered if here, too, I was about to encounter some sort of Old World code of silence. But I had to follow through.

"Her name was Franca Florio," I said. "I came to the Flower Bar because I had a notion that she might come in here now and then." I drained my glass. "That she might even be here today."

"That is impossible," he said, smiling. "That would mean

11

that she would have to be here at the exact time and day and year that you turned up accidentally."

"Not accidentally," I said. "Don't you remember her at all?"

"In connection with yourself?"

"Myself, herself. I am only trying to find out where she is now."

"Florio, eh?" he repeated aloud. "It is not an uncommon name. It depends on which Florio you mean. I don't remember a particular Franca Florio. I'm not good on Christian names—but where did they live?"

I told him they were near the railway station, near the Course of the Thousand.

"The father was the mountain guide?"

I said I didn't know exactly where her father had worked.

"He was a widower?" asked the bartender.

"Yes," I said. "Even then the mother was dead."

"Two or three daughters, that Florio?" he asked, and, eagerly, I replied, "That must be the same family."

"I thought so," said the bartender. "My head doesn't always work well but the old things I sometimes remember."

"Are the Florios still in Palermo?" I asked, leaning toward him.

"A long time ago. Maybe," he said. "The father I don't hear of. He used to do some guide work for tourists on the mountains around here, but I personally haven't seen him for a long time. Wait a minute. I think there is a daughter still here. A botanist? My own daughter knows her because of the flowers in our shop. She goes to the Botanical Garden once in a while to see the flowers, and I think she sees the Florio girl there."

"Yes," I said, grasping at the first real clue. "Her older sister was studying that work. She must be Dorotea. Has your daughter seen her recently?"

"Not more than a few weeks ago."

"Where is this Botanical Garden?"

12

"You, an American, should know that," said the bartender. "It's on the Via Lincoln."

"Lee cone?" I asked, puzzled at the word.

"That's right," he said. "Lincoln. Your President and our Garibaldi had much admiration for each other. We also have a street for Franklin Roosevelt in Sicily."

I placed some lire on the bar, but he refused to take any payment. He said he was happy to welcome back a drinker of cognac-and-vermouth—instead of Bavarian beer—in the Flower Bar. I promised him that he would see me again.

If I rushed back to town I might still get to the Botanical Garden in time to question Dorotea. I climbed into the car and took the winding road along the beach of Mondello and then past the hills and along the waterfront of Palermo. The Via Lincoln was dark by the time I arrived and the gates of the Botanical Garden were closing. Some people came out, but I couldn't tell if they were employees or visitors. By now dusk had fenced in the floral wonders for the night.

Slowly, then, thinking of what to say to Dorotea, I drove back toward the Company's villa. I checked in the keys with Subito and went up to my room to change for dinner. The other geologists were downstairs playing cards. In my high-ceilinged room, I stretched out on the bed and looked up toward the faded chandelier. The room was twice my height and then some. I didn't know why but whenever I was in some strange quarters, I liked to have a lot of air space and breathing room overhead. It spelled a personal freedom not to have a ceiling pressing down too closely. Such places were becoming harder to find any longer in the States.

Anyway, smoking a cigarette in the dark, in this peaceful Palermo, here in this room with its vast area of private silences, the present and the purpose of our Company's mission began to fade and the memories of what had happened here once swirled around in my mind.

The next morning, I arose early to go to the Botanical

Garden in search of Franca's sister. Dorotea and I had always been friends. I suspected that she knew everything that went on between us from the first days. Very little could be kept from the two sisters; and they had a loyalty and understanding which someone outside the family sensed immediately. She was older than Franca, darker and more seductive as I remembered her. At the time she was having a clandestine affair of her own with a former acquaintance from her university days who had returned to Palermo on foot after escaping and walking hundreds of miles south from a German prisoner of war camp. She dominated him, he accepted her charms gratefully, and from this pleasing state one could imagine only marriage resulting. Toward the end of my stay in Palermo, Franca hinted or said outright (by this time I could not recall which) that Dorotea was pregnant. Then, as with so many other matters, I heard no more.

The Botanical Garden on the Via Lincoln seemed an anomalous place to seek Dorotea. I pulled up before a building entrance suitably ornate to contain subtropical vegetation. The dry heat fleshed the buds of countless rows of small plants in glass-lined hothouses. I moved from one room of the cavernous building to another, but I saw only venerable attendants in faded French-blue coveralls puttering around with watering cans and stacks of clay pots. I asked one of them where the office was, and he pointed skyward to the second floor where a staircase led, winding above the glass roof. Nobody was up there. I came down quickly, my shoes sounding heavy on the stairboards, and I felt the eeriness of this strange setting. Tropical birds, horrible parrot-beaked creatures, screeched in cages in an adjoining room. I went outside.

Paths of oleander-fringed brick led past palm trees and cacti. I walked past a sign pointing out the experimental station, and quickened my step. It was a glassed building. Through the windows I could see a desk on one side and rows of pots with labels. A woman in a well-cut tight smock

14

emerged from behind boxed foliage and sat at the desk. She was making notes rapidly and she did not look up when I entered.

"Please, miss," I asked, "can you direct me?"

"The exhibits are outside," she said, without glancing up.

"I am looking for a botanist who works here," I said. "Her name was Florio."

She suddenly looked at me closely, and in her eyes I instantly recognized that this was the woman I once knew.

"Dorotea?"

"Wait a moment," she said, smiling slightly. "Yes, I am Dorotea, but I have seen you somewhere—your face is very recognizable—but I cannot think of your name or where I know you from."

I returned her smile as if this were a good joke on her. She kept scrutinizing me intently. I would not have recognized her—she was as plump as a Neapolitan housewife—were it not for her dark eyes, which still flashed excitement.

"Wait a moment," she said, making it a game of wits. "You are a foreigner, that much I can tell from your accent. What puzzles me is that you know some Sicilian phrases. You're not English—your suit fits too loosely and also you're not that polite. That leaves American. You are an American, aren't you?"

"So far, so good," I said. "But I *am* polite."

"One more sentence and I'll know," she said playfully. "Not one of the botanical schoolteachers who came through here last year—"

She stopped suddenly. Her voice froze. The lightness in her manner disappeared. She glared at me darkly, then looked back to the work on her desk. I didn't know what had come over her; but it must have been a case of mistaken identity; surely she didn't mean me.

"Dorotea," I said, "don't you recognize an old friend of the family? One more chance only and I'll—"

She eyed me coldly and said, "I know you only too well. Do you have business here? If not—"

"No," I said. "I'm Joseph Borken. You remember now? The sergeant of the Engineers? Next to the Berlitz School? I was a friend of Franca's."

"Look, American," she said. "I know who you are and what you are."

I was puzzled and shocked. She was mad; and yet she knew me. I stood there while she busied herself with the papers on her desk. She got up and walked around the hothouse, putting labels on containers, and avoiding coming near me or even looking at me. Moments passed, uncomfortably.

"Dorotea," I said. "Look here, I don't get it. You have something against me that I don't know about. I haven't seen you all this time and you won't say hello. You won't even show that politeness you said I didn't have."

I wondered if she was all right and what scars from those times were imbedded in her. She wore a wedding band and I assumed that all had gone well: with her, her pregnancies, babies following babies, and her former paramour. I didn't much care at this moment because I was only interested in finding out where Franca was.

"What do you want here?" she asked finally.

I told her I happened to be in Sicily on business and that while in Palermo I thought I would look up some old friends.

"You consider the members of the Florio family such friends?" she asked.

"Why not?"

"You should know, you're a grown man now, Joseph," she said, unwittingly allowing my name to slip out.

"But I didn't know that I did something wrong," I said, moving nearer to her desk.

Looking at me squarely, she said, "You came here to ask about Franca, didn't you?"

"Yes, of course."

"What Franca does with her life is her business," Dorotea said.

"Is she all right?" I said, adding, "Is she here in Palermo?"

"You ask about her health? Yes, Franca is well. But what concern is it of an American businessman? That is what you are, isn't it? You are here to make business?"

"I'm here as a friend," I said. "You know that. What's this nonsense about business? I wish you'd talk to me, please, not to your image of me."

"But you are a big American now, aren't you?" she said. "You come back without your uniform and you're still acting like a big shot."

"Dorotea," I said, hurt by her remarks, "we were once friends. Did I ever behave badly?"

"Not toward me," she said.

"Not toward any of the Florios," I corrected her. "I don't know what's bothering you. If it's something political, that's something else again. I came here to ask you where Franca is. I want to see her. Will you tell me where?"

"My family isn't in Palermo," she said evasively.

"I know your father isn't here. The bartender at the Flower Bar told me."

"That's how you found me, the old man told you."

"That's right—he said your father used to do some guide work around the mountains behind Mondello but he doesn't see him now."

"You speak of my father but you don't know him," she said. "How could you? You never came through the front door of our home."

"What does that mean?"

She said, "Oh, nothing."

But I knew what she meant and I said, "Those were other times, Dorotea. I am not ashamed."

This was a blank wall—and yet Dorotea was the only possible way to Franca. She hadn't said anything about her except that she was well. That was something. And that she wasn't in Palermo. But that could mean anywhere at all.

Dorotea looked at me as if her end of our conversation were over. She stopped puttering around the papers on her desk and brushed past me. She headed down a path and toward a prize olive grove, and I followed her as quickly as I could. As I went around a clump of bushes, I tripped and fell sprawling. Boxes of plants dislodged and my sleeves were full of humus and watery mud. I picked myself up, and Dorotea stood over me.

"You run too quickly," I said.

"Are you hurt?" she asked, laughing at me severely.

"No, just humiliated. I seldom run around gardens after married women, especially this early in the morning. Is there any water here without mud?"

She pointed toward a low faucet, and I took off my jacket and wiped it clean. Then I stooped low and sipped. She was still standing there, so I decided to take a fresh approach.

"Your father, I hear, was an excellent guide."

She looked puzzled, but said, "He still is one of the best on the island."

I said, "There is a good chance that my Company will need a good mountain guide in the next few days. Is he working for someone?"

"He works for different people," she replied. "Hunters, tourists."

"He must be very busy," I said, "being one of the best."

"That depends on the season," she said.

"And this, I suppose, is the busy season around here?"

"He can sometimes find time—if it is worth his while." Somehow I detected a note of resignation in her voice. I pressed my advantage.

"The Company I work for could pay him very well—if he could really be of service."

"What kind of work would your Company require?"

"From your father? Guide work," I said, wondering what she meant.

She asked me how much they could pay, and I mentioned a figure which I thought fair, but she said it was not enough and I went higher, figuring that if necessary I would pay the difference out of my own pocket. She asked if it was sure and I reassured her that I would try to help him and that it would not be for less than the figure I mentioned.

"Well, then, I hope he can benefit from any arrangement," I said. "Where does your father live?"

She hesitated for a moment, then looked at me sadly.

"I suppose you think you deceived me?" she said. "I knew what you were doing."

"Dorotea, believe me."

"If my father did not need the work—"

"I am without guile. But I do want to know about Franca. I must."

"If you see my father, you will probably see my sister, too."

I took out one of the Company's latest mechanical souvenir pencils—it was a crazy kind with liquid lead that needed occasional replacement—and handed it to Dorotea. She held it for an instant and returned it to me.

"Write the address yourself," she said, as if to expiate herself.

So I did: Nicolosi Florio, Brucia.

She said it was a small town near Mount Etna, and that it would be no trouble to reach him there through the Guides' Union.

I said, "Thank you, Dorotea," but she was running again, somewhere in the maze of flowers and subtropical plants in this Mediterranean botanical garden, and this time I did not follow her.

Later, with the smell of the flowers still clinging sweetly, I remembered that I had forgotten to ask if Franca had ever married.

But I had what I wanted: her address. And a week to pursue a dream.

CHAPTER TWO

THAT EVENING Tabbert said, "Let's look at this business realistically."

One thing I learned quickly about Tabbert: he was a very realistic man himself. As I looked at him now in the dining room of the villa, he had the manner of a fighting cock, spurs up, his iron-gray crew cut a bristling coxcomb.

I had heard a lot about him in the home office in New York from returning geologists. There weren't many people with his crisp style working in our line for the big respectable corporations. He gave the Mediterranean American Development Company something better than nine-to-five loyalty; he gave them genuine hard work. It would be easy to say he did so just for the money. Of course he must have been well paid as head of all field teams around this part of the Mediterranean. But I could not help feeling, after but a few days, that other things as well spurred him. He had not been back in the States for years.

"This isn't the kind of operation you broadcast over the Voice of America, if you get what I mean," Tabbert continued. "Let's face it—we're here to do a job. Some of you have worked with me before. Well and good. Some of you I requested because your records seemed to say that you were my kind of guy. And maybe you came out here on your own— you wangled your way or you're being palmed off on me. All right. We're all starting off on the same foot. Remember that. There are bonuses to keep you hopping, and I'm all for them. With my field teams there is no pooling of bonuses—I won't allow it. What you discover on your own shows up in your pay check. Nobody's initiative is killed that way, nobody gets a free ride on someone else's back. I got my own philosophy about business. Maybe you heard. If you work for yourself, you're working for the Company's sake. Remember that: you're not giving your all for the Company, you're doing it for yourself. I recognize and encourage that with the people under me. If that shocks some of you who've been reading all that teamwork crap in the Company's own magazine, forget it. They need us because they know the field offices produce. I produce. That's all I expect from you."

We were sitting around after dinner, getting our bearings before heading out into the field. Counting myself, there were five of us, screened from branch offices in the States and overseas. Two were older men who had served the Company for a long time in the Oklahoma branch offices, where Mediterranean American had begun at the turn of the century as a small operation. After fifty years of automobiles and wars, the centers of oil and exploration had changed—and so had the name of the Company. The other two men, Harris and Hill, were in their late twenties. They had come to Sicily from Arabia after serving as advisers to one of the Arab potentates in an oil kingdom on the Gulf of Aden. The story I had heard in New York was that they had requested transfers after six months out there because the monarch they dealt with had shown signs of an unnatural affection for them; demanded, we had heard on the Company grapevine, that the young technicians accommodate him in his perversions. I meant to ask them.

The big villa on the Via della Libertà had a forty-foot living room. It was furnished extravagantly in Milan modern, and somehow I thought we looked incongruous here. Subito slipped into the room quietly and took orders for drinks. In a whisper he asked me if everything had gone all right at the Flower Bar in Mondello, and I nodded. Somehow, he sensed this was private—the kind of intimate confidence a European can detect instantly.

From the way Tabbert spoke, it sounded as if the rumors about his bluntness were true. After all the walking on eggshells and doubletalk of interoffice communication in New York, it was already refreshing to be away here. If everything meshed as I hoped, this could be a week to cherish: it would guide me in more ways than one.

"Now we can get down to cases," Tabbert said, as Subito placed drinks in our hands. "You all know what the mission is about here so I'm not going to bother with unnecessary details. Sicily is crawling with sulphur. This island has supplied the powder for cannons for more wars than you have teeth in your head. Sulphur stinks, and I'm not a sulphur man myself. Like most of you, I've lived with crude oil and gas. But where there's sulphur, chances are good that the formation of the land and rock below encouraged other minerals. Maybe the one we're after. We've got only so much time to explore the possibilities here before moving on. Speed is necessary for reasons I can't go into—"

"I hear that the other side is hot after the stuff, too," Harris interrupted. "That they put some feelers out in this area."

"What's your name?" Tabbert asked, glaring at the young man.

Young Harris told him; but of course Tabbert knew.

"Let me straighten you out right now," Tabbert said, pointing his finger. "If you happen to have any information you've picked up in your world-wide travels, put it down on a piece

22

of paper and send it by air mail to the home office." Harris smiled weakly. "If you happen to have any knowledge of why we have to work fast in Sicily, and you're busting to tell the world, let me give you some advice. Write it in your diary. Don't tell us." The young geologist twirled his whisky glass nervously and mumbled something, but his apology was ignored.

"I'm dividing the island into five parts," Tabbert continued. "One for each man. The equipment you'll use is basic and uncomplicated. Everyone begins on the same starting line. It won't matter too much which area you go to. The stuff is either there or it isn't. It could be on the plains or in the mountains. Luck will be with you or against you. That's why I'm going to do the assignments fairly—with these."

He took a pair of dice from his pocket and began to match them. Then he cushioned the dice in his palms and clicked them affectionately, slowly. It looked as if his hands had cradled them before.

"The areas will cover the main parts of the island. You operate out of a point within your area, working your way inland. The five places are Trapani on the west, Agrigento in the south, Caltanisetta in the middle, and Mount Etna on the east coast. Someone will work out of Palermo, too. What we require now is the initial exploration. We're not definitive— all we're after is a good possibility before Company leasing commitments are made. Others will follow our exploratory team."

Tabbert and I were the only ones who had been in Sicily before, and some of the others asked where these places were and what they were like and if there was anything to do there in the evening. I wanted to say something about where I wished to go—where I had to go—but stopped myself. I was in Sicily, first of all, to do a job. The other thing was not their concern.

Tabbert laid out a cloth map of the island and tossed the dice on it.

"High number takes his pick?" he asked.

"Let's shoot regular craps while we're at it," Hill said. "Whoever gets seven in fewer throws—or craps out."

Tabbert said, "No, we'll do it my way—it's simpler."

I had a sinking feeling that either way wouldn't help because I never had had any luck with Army dice. And it seemed too uncertain a gamble to reach Franca's door.

"All right, who wants to throw first?" Tabbert asked.

They examined the cloth map, trying to determine where the exploratory areas were located, and which terrain would yield what we were looking for. The right place could bring a man thousands of dollars in bonuses and mark him as someone esteemed by the Company.

"I'll show you how it's done," Tabbert said, grinning. He rattled the dice and rolled. They tumbled on the cloth map of Sicily, two sixes, but at the last instant one six fell over and showed a four. "I'm not going anywhere—but beat ten," he said.

The first older man grabbed the dice, blew on them, and threw a three and two. "I'll take Trapani," he said. The other man from Oklahoma shot next. He rolled quickly, and two fives came up. "I'll take Caltanisetta," he said unhesitatingly. The dice lay on the map—right over the Mount Etna region. Nobody touched them. Three of us were left—Harris and Hill, the two boys from the Arabian office, and myself.

Hill took the dice, held them a foot off the map with his fingertips, and carelessly let go. A pair of threes. Harris picked up the dice and turned them over to me. I couldn't hand them back. I rolled them carefully and for luck threw them in the direction where I wanted to land myself on the map of Sicily. The number showed two fours.

"Where do you want to go, Borken?" Tabbert asked.

Before I could reply, Harris cuffed the dice and threw a nine, beating me by a point. He asked what was left.

"I'll take the Mount Etna area," he said. "That's near that fancy Taormina resort."

24

My heart fell.

Tabbert told Harris, "I should have mentioned a report that the mountain has been rumbling." He enjoyed the surprised look on Harris' face, and then said, "That's something you'll have to watch for. You'll be able to get a fuller report from the Volcanic Institute at Catania. May be nothing at that, but check there."

Tabbert turned to me.

I told him that I'd try it here, in the Palermo area. One way or another, I had to get to Brucia, which the map showed in the shadow of Etna. In the meantime I thought Palermo could be traded off most easily for where I really wanted to be.

Tabbert said, "Everybody happy?"

I kept still. But I knew that before the evening was over I would have to be alone with Harris. I might even have to tell him the truth, that there was a personal reason why I wanted to go to Etna that had nothing to do with the Company's search. Harris struck me as reasonable—and still young enough to honor sentiment.

"Well, that's settled," Tabbert said. "Let's fill you in on the situation. Here are local maps." He passed around large-scale maps of the different areas. "And here are the names of our consular and other contacts in the areas—they're confidential, of course." The maps had a faded familiarity from the invasion days here. On the edges I saw the words *Corps of Engineers* overprinted with *Property of Mediterranean American Development Company.*

Subito came in for another round of drinks. Tabbert waited until he had filled the glasses and left the room before he continued talking, more secretively. Subito's footsteps faded down the hallway.

"A final word of caution," Tabbert said, leaning forward in his chair. "We're here to do a job. All of us are Americans. None of the nationals from other countries are working with us on this one—not even any of our so-called allies. What

25

we're doing is perfectly legitimate and businesslike. That's the point. All of you have to keep your eye on the target, move in, make your investigation quietly, move out, report back to me, here. Just like that. Now someone brought up earlier the talk of the other side. Cut it. We're working for Mediterranean American Development, not the United States Government. You're not a spokesman for anyone. If you run into local officials, keep your nose clean and your mouth shut. There's a lot of trouble brewing on the island—land seizures by peasants, and so on. The ethics and the larger issues are not my concern and they shouldn't be yours. We're just private operators, we're not policymakers. My tip to you is: Don't get involved. If you keep that in mind, you'll be happier and you'll do a better job for our Mediterranean operation."

Tabbert motioned that he was finished for the evening and that the men were free until tomorrow morning, when the serious work we were here for began. The "scientists" (as they liked to call us in the magazines and newspapers, even though we considered ourselves geologists or plain researchers) began to leave the room. I hurried over to Harris and said that there was something I wanted to speak to him about. He said that he and his pal Hill would be around all evening unless they began to feel horny and wanted to prowl for women. I was about to ask him if he wanted to stay on in Palermo, in exchange for his Mount Etna area, when I felt a tap on my elbow, lightly.

It was Tabbert. I held back while the others left the dining room. French doors led out to the garden behind the villa. Tabbert whispered, "Get yourself a sweater and meet me outside in five minutes."

I did as he told me, still wondering about this man's thoughts. From the half shadows of the walks and shrubbery behind the villa, he emerged. He was wearing one of those British desert coats with wooden pegs for buttons, and I came up to him and said that I used to see a lot of those in

Africa during the war. He lighted his pipe. There was a stone bench near where he stood in darkness and he motioned me to sit down.

"Borken," he said, "you're still hot."

Of course, I knew it would be that. In the last few months it always was: the man inside the anonymous Company man showed through.

"I've been scanning your personnel file. A solid record—up to a point. The early stuff is clear enough. It's the last months that are troublesome."

"Why do you say that?"

"Troublesome may be the wrong word," he said, backing off. "I meant that the record isn't clear to someone reading it cold-assed without knowing you."

"I didn't know they sent out reports on people. I thought all they had were the usual employment files. You know, name, rank and serial number and that nonsense."

"If you thought just that, Borken, you don't know much about the company you're working for."

"Maybe I don't. But if you haven't been back in the States lately, how do you know so much?"

There it was, returning again, my new break-out of resentment against authority.

"Take it easy, Borken," Tabbert said. "I'm not knocking you down. But I'll say this—I know how the Company thinks. The flesh-and-blood mind of the corporate entity, it's like a giant human being. Memos with saved carbons and records are the skin and corpuscles of the Mediterranean American Development Company. Maybe other companies, too. I worked the New York office once, but I couldn't stand the gaff. I got out into the field and I've been a loner ever since. Here I'm considered a character. In the home office I was a nonconformist, and that's a dirty word."

"What's this got to do with me?"

"In my book, you strike me as a pro. I like a man who knows his trade—who respects his racket for his own self-

27

respect. The rest is gravy. But there are blanks in the file. I need a fill-in."

"That all?"

"No, it isn't all," he said. "I can level with you. I've got to make a written report. The usual performance chart on each man. They want more than that on you after your first field jaunt in Sicily. They're watching you."

"As your pro?"

"By their standards, yes. Not mine. They're looking for a clear sign showing more respect for the corporation. They don't like to have to prove good intent to their own employees. As far as I'm concerned, all they'll get is a signal saying I want you to stay on—or that you'd like to move on to some other branch. I won't sink so low as to file a snooping report on you or any other man. Never have, even if I have to say the records got lost in transit. I can get away with it as long as I'm producing for them. But I've got to have the real story. Not for them, for me. You can believe that or not. If you don't, we can go in now, have a drink, and forget that I ever asked."

I looked at him puffing his pipe in the darkened garden and thought of how this one thing, my one stroke of boldness against the Company, had pursued me this far, so distant from my life in recent years and so much a part of this re-created life on an old battlefield. So it was all black-marked against me in the files, but it could not have been inscribed there the way it had really happened, a record could not reflect an evolving era, could not reveal hidden thoughts that were still taking shape, like hot forged metal, in my mind. . . .

The change came about [I told Tabbert confidently, here in this warm Sicilian atmosphere] when Kurt Von Loesch reported to the main office of the Company in New York. (He knew, of course, that Von Loesch was now one of the executives in the Company? Oh, yes, he had seen pictures of him in the Mediterranean American *Pipeline*—the slick little magazine put out every month for the Company's employees, stockholders and assorted influential friends. But of course he had heard of him long before then.) It had been rumored around the office that Von Loesch was coming for weeks before his arrival—rumors which proved to be true—and there was great curiosity about him. But there was no articulated resentment. If anything, the atmosphere was receptive: to see how much he knew and how methodically his mind worked.

For myself, I enjoyed being in the New York office. After postwar studies at the Colorado School of Mines, I had landed a place with the Company which was pleasantly secure. The work was respectable, the pay fairly good, and it gave me a chance to do the work I liked professionally and experimentally. My racket—we called it that cavalierly to show that we were not just laboratory drudges but a part of everyday life—was geological testing. There were higher levels of activity I knew (and know) little about at Mediterranean American, but on the technical level, the people I worked with were serious, sometimes downright scholarly about the research we were engaged in, and congenial. Some kept studying toward higher degrees at night, myself included, though with me it was simply a case of nibbling at education, a little at a time, because I liked to be around a campus. If I looked closely, maybe I was after something—searching for it beyond the glassed-in partitions of the Company life. But I seldom looked.

Anyway, excitement and uneasiness turned up in the person of Von Loesch. He arrived one day escorted by none other than Mr. Paley himself, the executive vice-president of Mediterranean American and operating boss of the Company. It was the first time Paley had been inside my section since the previous Christmas; once a year he came around to wish everyone the season's greetings with a handshake that lasted for the next twelvemonth.

"This is Mr. Von Loesch," Paley said. "He's familiarizing himself with the different sections."

He was short, fleshy in the face, with dirty-blond hair parted dead center, and with a tough muscularity bulging out of his tight suit.

"Geological section, Borken in charge, correct?" Von Loesch said, checking off my name in a notebook he took out from inside his jacket. He also carried a leather briefcase.

I nodded in surprise, wondering if his notebook contained any other comments about me.

Paley said, "Mr. Von Loesch claims he's a little rusty on some of the basic testing methods for minerals. I personally," he said, winking for both our sakes, "don't believe him."

Von Loesch held up both his hands. "I assure you," he said deprecatingly, "that I will be asking very many foolish questions."

His English, though guttural, had a slight Oxonian accent.

"He'll be with your section for two weeks, beginning today," Paley said. "After that, he'll move ahead to Liquid Oxygen, and so on. Before he can settle down to any one phase of our operation, I want him to see all the procedures in all the laboratories."

"Once I have the over-all picture," Von Loesch said, using that familiar military phrase, "I won't bother you."

"We want to use his full creative powers," Paley said. "Isn't that right, Kurt? The whole purpose is to enable him to think on a larger scale," Paley said, turning to me, "In fact, I want everyone to think bigger now, beyond his own section. You might keep that in mind, Borken, and convey the thought to your people. I may set that down in a memorandum for all hands." Paley had been in the Navy during the war and occasionally lapsed into that lingo. "And now we've all got our own work to do, so carry on. I'll see you at lunch, Kurt."

Paley waved to the secretary in my section and turned to go. I followed him out to the door and asked quietly, "Excuse me, is Mr. Von Loesch cleared for everything?"

There were a few files in our section concerning Government work, and I was not supposed to show these to outsiders. Nothing secret, but there was some contractual agreement about having all people cleared for the Government stuff.

Paley turned on me. "Not only cleared," he said in a voice loud enough for Von Loesch to hear, "but highly recommended by the brass in Washington. Anything he wants to see is open to him."

After Paley left, I introduced Von Loesch to the others in my section; but he did not have their names in his small notebook.

I showed Von Loesch around the laboratory. He knew about our basic instruments—scintillation counters, spectrometers, magnetometers, thermocouple gauges—but some of our methods seemed unfamiliar to him. At least he said they were; it was hard at first to tell what was modesty and what politeness. He took it all in, occasionally making notes for himself in a second, larger notebook with handruled lines in it, which he kept in his briefcase. When lunchtime came, he received an alert from Paley's secretary and went apologetically to the Company's executive staff dining room.

After he had gone, Danny Horan and I walked down toward First Avenue to lunch in our favorite shamrocked bar. Horan was my assistant in the section, and a very solid citizen—he lived in the wilds of Queens, and most of his free time was taken up with his large family and the Veterans of Foreign Wars. He was a careful and clean operator around the laboratory, and I trusted his judgment.

"What do you think?" I asked, after downing a dark beer.

"A tricky one," he said. "He's too damn polite—makes me crawl."

31

"Don't hold that against him. He's trying to show us he's one of the boys."

"That's a laugh," Horan said. "Whose boys? Two to one he was once one of Hitler's bright young men."

"Von Loesch?" I said. "He doesn't look a day over forty-five—he would have to have been a kid during the war. Well, the hell with all that. He'll be with our section for two weeks, Paley said, and then he moves up and out. Maybe we can gain something from him before he goes—he may know a lot that we should."

We left it at that.

The next morning when I arrived Von Loesch was already there.

"I'm sorry if I've kept you waiting long," I found myself apologizing. "We usually get here around half past eight or a quarter to nine."

"Don't think twice about it, Mr. Borken," he said, with a reassuring smile. "I've been here only since eight but I managed to occupy myself. I went over my notes. Every day I like to learn something new. I've taken the liberty of studying this machine." He ran his stubby fingers over the electrometer, which we were adapting before sending it out to a field team in the Gulf of Aden. "It's a fine instrument," he said. "American made?"

"That one I believe is Swiss," I said. I was surprised that he did not admit noticing it because the manufacturer's name and *Berne* were imprinted on the metal.

"The watchmakers," he said, sneering. "They're very precise on the small procedures there. But the Swiss haven't the larger view like the Germans and Americans. Cuckoo, cuckoo clocks—those things aren't important in the world today. I'm talking about real hardware. You have an alert staff here?"

"Oh, yes. They're all interested in this testing. We experiment quite a bit when we're not just overwhelmed with maintenance. Hundreds of counters and all sorts of machines out in the field are freighted back here for repairs. Testing is just one part of the work."

"When do your workers arrive?" he asked.

"They should be here any moment," I said uncomfortably. I didn't consider Horan and the others my workers. At a quarter to nine, they stumbled in, carrying containers of coffee, including one for me. I offered it to Von Loesch, but he said that he never ate between meals, and the coffee remained untouched.

We repaired a dozen Geiger counters which had come in battered from teams on the Colorado plateau, replacing parts and testing efficiency. I invited Von Loesch to ask questions; he observed and took notes busily.

Toward the end of the morning, he closed his notebook dramatically and announced, "So—now I know this procedure. I would like to put it into practical application."

I said, "How's that?"

He said, "To jump in myself and get my feet wet, you know?"

"Oh, of course. Here," I said, turning to Horan, "why don't you let Mr. Von Loesch try his hand on that counter. You can get started on classifying the Rockland materials."

Horan passed him the tools, and Von Loesch thanked him elaborately.

"I enjoy working with my hands," Von Loesch announced.

At noon, the phone call came down again from Paley's office, and Von Loesch excused himself and went to the executive dining room. He seemed almost innocuous.

One day a week I would head across the Hudson River to the Company's raw materials division in Rockland County. Actual rock samples shipped in from all over the world (the Company's exploratory world, that is) were reduced to pebble here by steam-pressure force. I would co-ordinate the intake and develop patterns of geological structure for the foreign teams based on this information. The day trip was a pleasant change from the ritual of main-office routine.

After that first full day Von Loesch arrived at a quarter to nine; this time the others were there fifteen minutes earlier. On the day I went to Rockland I came in still earlier to make a bus. I looked forward to the privacy of the day.

I went to the office first to pick up some test samples. Again Von Loesch was there ahead of me, briefcase in hand.

"Today is the morning you visit Rockland?"

"I usually do go on Fridays."

"I think Mr. Paley would be interested that I should see it."

"Come along," I said, though I preferred to be alone. I still hoped to learn from him.

We traveled on the bus across the George Washington Bridge into New Jersey, where a Company limousine met us. We crossed the unseen line into New York again on the other side of the Hudson and drove up to the Rockland office. The manager there took us both around the plant. He fawned all over Von Loesch, running ahead of him a few paces. The manager, a beer-filled man in his sixties, ordered a huge lunch brought in from one of the simulated-oak taverns which dotted the countryside around here.

As I recall it, the manager said, "I know of some of your very fine plastics work, Mr. Von Loesch. Didn't you develop a process for plastics that can be subjected to high speeds without burning up?"

"Yes, I have some patents in my name," Von Loesch said. "How did you know?"

"I keep up. Wartime and later West German patents—"

"You are mistaken," Von Loesch corrected him quickly. "My patents were taken out in Buenos Aires only two years ago."

"Oh. I thought you had developed them during the war—"

"Wrong," Von Loesch said angrily. "Your memory is wrong."

The rotund manager was startled at the sudden outburst and wrung his hands apologetically.

Von Loesch recovered his composure. He turned to me and looked at his watch, one of those monstrous split-sec-

34

ond triple-dialed gadgets, and asked if it was time to leave.

I picked up my pebbles—wondering about what had upset Von Loesch—and we climbed into the Company limousine again. We rode in chauffeured silence for a few minutes.

"Peculiar man, that manager," Von Loesch said. "Inquisitive."

Actually, I didn't appreciate the toadying manager myself; but he had touched a sensitive nerve in Von Loesch.

Then, suddenly, Von Loesch brightened and turned to me.

"Do you mind if I call you by your first name?" he asked. "It's one American custom I like. You call me Kurt."

I should have been flattered; he was a man with an international reputation. Still I myself wondered now about his patents and skills—and his past.

"That insulation process you were talking about sounds interesting," I said.

"An ordinary application," he said. "We perfected it while working with scientists in Argentina. A wonderful group of men—I worked there for nearly seven years after the war. Many friends from Germany found the atmosphere excellent for experimentation—we lived like kings. What a change from that damn war."

"What did you do during the war?" I asked him, taking a chance.

He hardened his jaw for an instant.

"Oh, you know," he said, waving his hand deprecatingly, "the usual paper work. We little people were unimportant. We stumbled along, did what they told us to do, and kept our mouths shut. None of us believed in that regime, naturally. We sabotaged it as much as we could, especially the scientists."

"I was under the impression that most of the scientists in high positions played ball with the Nazis."

"Propaganda, Joseph," he said softly.

I said nothing, and he added, "A few scientists, maybe yes, forced into party membership, but they could not do

35

anything; they were obeying orders. But the rest of us, no. In fact," he added, "I helped two Jews who desired to quit the university."

I nodded.

He went on, his voice rising, droning an old tune which sounded so familiar it was almost unreal. "But that's all ancient history, that war is something from the past," Von Loesch said. He reached out and grabbed my hand firmly. "Joseph, we have to forget all that—even change its history. I give you advice—you're too simple. You must be a publicist and a scientist at the same time. We have a bigger job now, so let bygones be bygones and work together for the winning side. For new and greater causes."

I made no comment then.

The limousine halted in front of the stop near the Washington Bridge, and we caught our bus and returned to the middle of Manhattan. Von Loesch invited me to dine with him, but I refused politely, telling him I had a date that night.

Actually, I did. It was a sort of half date. If free, once a month I helped Peggy Grolier, an assistant to the personnel director for Mediterranean American, put out *Pipeline* before it went to press. Peggy was in her dwindling thirties, a big girl whose facial features might have been considered virile in a man. "My trouble," she had once confided to me, late at night after too many Scotches, "is that men consider me one of the boys," and I had consoled her and told her she was a good sport whom everyone liked, and she had cried and said, "That's the trouble." She recovered, but there was always a feeling present that she had reached the office age where career had overtaken, and surpassed, the woman.

At dinner we caught up on office gossip; there were always staff shifts from one section to another and temporary assignments abroad.

"Why haven't you tried to land one of those juicy junkets?" she demanded.

"I did get to northern Canada when the Company leased up there. That was fun for two weeks. I had a chance to make it all the way to Saudi Arabia last summer, but it didn't appeal to me. All that sand—"

"And Cadillacs with air conditioning, refrigerators filled with goodies, swimming pools lined with dancing girls."

"I wouldn't mind the dancing girls if they didn't come in the same package with the pashas out there. But nobody ever offered me an assignment to the eastern Mediterranean. I'd jump at a chance to go."

"You were there during the war?"

"Somewhat."

"Why not try South America? Where your boy, Von Loesch, came from. I hear he's taken quite a shine to you."

"I don't know where you could have heard that. Well, he'll be with my section through next week and then he graduates to Liquid Oxygen."

"No, he really did tell one of the vice-presidents, who told my boss, that he respects you for your ability. That would be a hot one—Von Loesch putting you across after—how many?—eight, ten years?"

"I'm happy in my own little world. A promotion and I'd be in trouble. Come on, Peggy, stop trying to drive me out of the country. I like it here in New York."

The waiter came around with the menus again for dessert. We ordered, and Peggy rolled out her dummies for the next issue.

"It's pretty much written except for the headlines, captions and a few last-minute holes. There's one I want you to fill."

"A story?" I said. "You know I'm a production man, you handle the stories."

"No, Joe, this one's up your alley. It's a must piece for me, anyway. Paley wants a little article on Von Loesch in the next issue of *Pipeline*. The usual—the dossier, plus some of his happy talk about the Company. I've already got a statement from him telling how glad he is to be among us, amen. And

I've got another from the president saying how happy Mediterranean American is to have so distinguished a scientist on the team, et cetera. Hasn't he talked about himself? He's been with your section so you probably know more than anyone."

"Actually I know very little about him. He's been in Buenos Aires. He was working, I believe, on that abortive atomic operation down there with some other Germans. But he clams up when you ask him about his past."

She looked at her watch.

"Tell you what. The public library is open for another hour and a half. I'm sure we can get some more facts from the old German science yearbooks there and the foreign *Who's Whos*. We can also look up the microfilm editions of *The Times*. I got some dates from their index which tell when his name appeared in the papers."

We paid our separate checks and walked over to the library.

They had a little room on the third floor with a row of microfilm machines. A librarian brought us our cardboard boxes of film quickly.

Peggy and I sat together in the half light, straining to see the magnified news columns, under the cone of light falling on the pages. She read aloud, quietly and slowly, while I made notes, and as I heard the words I felt my chest tightening.

It was all there, chronologically, in the published reports from the newspaper: 1933—At age of eighteen, Kurt Von Loesch (and three others) selected for science-exchange studies, under sponsorship of the Anglo-American Friends of New Germany Fund, at Wadham, Oxford. 1938—Von Loesch designated aide-de-camp to Colonel General Christian Kammler, chief SS works department, WVHA (Wirtschafts- und Verwaltungs-hauptamt), economic and administrative headquarters. 1945—Nuremberg Trials. Von Loesch witness at trial (*in absentia;* defendant's whereabouts unknown) of Colonel General Kammler. Von Loesch, a lieutenant colonel, served as chief of staff to Kammler all during war. Kammler built gas chambers at Auschwitz. At same time, in charge of guided missiles program. Witness Von Loesch claims he was merely technician-administration at Peenemunde rocket range, Baltic coast, says never heard of concentration camps. Kammler sentenced life imprisonment *in absentia*. 1946—U.S. Army Operation Replate scoops up two hundred scientists (Von Loesch prominent among them) for transfer States; counterpart to Russian recruitment, Soviet Zone, Germany. 1947—Von Loesch and other German scientists reported to be working for Peron Government, B.A. The final story was datelined only a few months before, and noted that Von Loesch had been hired by the Mediterranean American Development Company, which had been using his patents for some time.

"Let's get out of here," Peggy said. We skipped down the lion steps and across Fifth Avenue and hurried back to the building. A few lights twinkled down the hall in Sales. We went into her room and she pointed to the typewriter.

"Go at it, boy," she said, raising a skeptical eyebrow.

"So Danny Horan was right," I muttered. "He guessed the Nazi background." I kept shaking my head in disbelief. "Call me Kurt. . . . Call me a goddamn liar."

"I had heard half of it," Peggy said. "It was around in the trade, but I never realized how deeply Von Loesch was involved. Well," she continued, "that is neither here nor there for the moment. You, my friend, have a story to do for me. The problem now is how to word it gently."

I nodded. I sat for ten minutes, not typing a word, weighing the notes, the Company speech of welcome and acceptance. Then I started to put the sentences together, cautiously. I never liked to write, not even letters, but I was stuck. After a while, I took the two pages about Von Loesch and handed them to her.

She studied the story line for line, changing a word here

and there, with professional skill, while I looked over her shoulder.

"I think that does it," she said. "It's just about right. It doesn't conceal too much and it doesn't reveal too much— the perfect house organ personality piece."

"I'd be less than honest with myself if I left out that he was chief of staff to Kammler and that Kammler was sentenced for SS activity. It's the only war stuff in it, besides Peenemunde —but that, I'm sure, he's proud of."

"Don't worry," she said, "I'm not complaining. It quotes *The Times*—we're hanging it on a printed publication. Anybody can go to the library and look it up."

"I hope they do," I said. "That's why I included the date of the Nuremberg Trials story from the paper. When does *Pipeline* go to press?"

"Wednesday night. We'll know what your pal Herr Von Loesch thinks of it soon enough. Who knows? He may be proud of his past affiliations and thank you for the build-up."

We laughed, tentatively. Then we put the lights out in the office and I took her home in a cab because it was late. At the door she invited me in. There was the uncomfortable moment of hesitation between us. I knew if I stepped over the threshold for the nightcap it would be more than that; I had long since learned the wisdom of non-involvement with women from the office. Casual outsiders made life a lot simpler. She sensed my feelings, looked wistfully with her too-big eyes, and extended her hand. I took it and hastily brushed my lips across her cheek, the informal kiss, and went downstairs and back to my place. I thought, Such a good sport.

Monday morning all was quiet in my small office world. I liked it this way—eating breakfast out of a bag, catching up on week-end gossip, yet managing to get my work done. Von Loesch himself was not in our section that day; the bulletin board said he was scheduled to speak for Mediterranean American at an all-day seminar of advertising copywriters and public-relations men on "The Uses of Science for Product Identification."

40

At eleven my serene world caved in. I was handed a yellow-green envelope, identifying it as from Mr. Paley's office, with my name typed in impressive italics by a special electric typewriter. The note said simply that I should be in his office at exactly eleven-thirty.

When I entered the sanctum, four people were there: Paley, the personnel director, Peggy, and someone introduced as the Company's attorney. Peggy gave me a quick sidelong glance, hardly one of warm recognition, which put me on guard by its very blankness. The three executives were arranged behind the protective armor of Paley's desk, covering each other's flanks. Peggy and I sat exposed before them.

Paley stared at the others, then at me. He reached across his desk and picked up some loose page proofs. He tapped the pages on his desk noisily and suddenly tossed them at my feet. I looked down and saw the rich colors of the next cover of *Pipeline*—the only part of the house organ that had already been printed. The picture on the cover showed the magazine's usual theme of Company progress and happiness: an endless pipe, stretching into desert infinity, with a smiling turbaned Arab workman holding a wrench in his hand and a lone stage-prop camel, yawning. The rough, as yet unprinted, pages scattered at my feet included my story on Von Loesch.

The pages lay there; but I would not stoop to pick them up. I sat still, playing my timid role in this office charade.

"I would like to clear up one point," the Company attorney said to the personnel director. "Why did this man write the Von Loesch article in the first place? That is not part of his job."

"As I mentioned to Mr. Paley before you arrived," the personnel director said, "we use various employees to write for *Pipeline* about people they work with. Peggy asked Borken to do the little Von Loesch article because he's been in Borken's section all week." He paused. "As an economy measure Borken and a few others help Peggy out on some of the production details of the magazine. It's a very low-budget operation, you know, but vital."

Paley cut in. "Margaret is not at fault here." He looked toward Peggy benevolently. "I told Margaret it was an error of judgment not to remove these unwholesome facts at once, but thank heavens she checked the proofs with us before this foolish and fantastic article got printed. What I want to know from you, Mr. Borken, is why you wrote this dirt."

It was my neck, I gathered, that was on the block. Peggy looked at me helplessly.

"I obtained my facts, sir, from published reports at the library."

I was conscious of hearing myself talk, of selecting my words still more carefully. I hadn't sirred anyone, in or out of the corporation, since the war days, but it came out with caution (rather, instinctive fear) now. I hated myself for it because in the sirring I could hear the voices of office sycophants.

"No, that's not my point, you're evading the issue," Paley insisted. "You were given the biographical facts from our personnel files, but something made you do this hostile act— to rehash all this old propaganda in our Company magazine."

"I didn't consider what I wrote propaganda, sir. It's all documented. Including more—that he was chief of staff to the Auschwitz oven-builder."

"You're still not with it, Borken," he said, banging his fist into his palm. "That's almost as shocking to me as what you almost permitted to appear under your name. Don't you understand *Pipeline* circulates beyond this building, that it goes to stockholders and distributors and all sorts of people we do business with? Can you give me one good reason why you think so-called facts such as these about Von Loesch should come out now?"

"I put those facts in because they're part of Von Loesch's record, past and present, and it would be untruthful to conceal the little I did hint at."

It wasn't the full reason; but it was enough.

Paley looked at the others and shook his head, as if to indicate that I was hopeless.

His personnel director tried to explain.

"What you did, Mr. Paley means, was basically anti-Company," he said. "Von Loesch informed us last year that all those rumors and reports are inaccurate. Be that as it may—"

"Let's not go over that again," Paley said. "This is the nineteen fifties, but obviously Mr. Borken has not joined this decade yet."

I started to answer angrily, but out of the corner of my eye I saw Peggy signal me to keep my mouth shut.

Paley turned to Peggy. "There's no chance that anyone other than ourselves saw these proofs, is there?"

"This is the only set right here," she said.

"Because if this ever got out to Von Loesch we'd be extremely embarrassed," Paley said. "Besides, we need his patents and his good will with the people in Washington."

"Don't worry on that score in any event," the attorney said. "We've got him tied up in firm commitments."

"You can rest assured, Mr. Paley," the personnel director said, "that these proofs will be destroyed." He turned to Peggy. "Tell you what. We'll run a nice couple of pages of pictures on him—no words, just photographs. Von Loesch at home and on the job—you know, the typical-American-family treatment. See what I mean?"

Peggy nodded.

"What I can't understand," Paley said, facing me, "is why you should take such a chance to harm your status here. You have a clean record. Senior in charge of a section. Periodic increases, participant in Company activity, building up to a position of full trust in the Mediterranean American family. Then this thing comes along—and, frankly, it makes us all wonder."

I listened to this enumeration of virtues before my downfall, and somehow it all seemed fantastic. Paley got up and went over to a telephone in the corner of his room and asked for a number. He faced me, with the receiver in his hand, and casually asked if I had anything more to say. I said no. He turned his back rudely and took his call. All of us walked out of his office. It was almost funny: I had never been in Paley's office before. I had made it at last.

The personnel director and attorney walked away, and Peggy followed me to the elevator and my floor.

"I'm sorry," she said. "I goofed. I should have known better and cut out that Nazi connection. You helped me, and you're the scapegoat. I feel awful about this. I tried to tell them, but now they've got a fix."

"I'm not unhappy—just shocked," I said. "But I feel all right inside. There's been too much concealment about Von Loesch. When it comes to things like that, Paley may be right—maybe I am still living in the forties."

"I'm sorry," Peggy said, at the door to my laboratory.

"Forget it."

The people in my section knew something was up, and they asked me how it had gone, and I said all right. Danny Horan put his big freckled fist around my hand, after the others had returned to their places.

"I'm on your side," he said.

"Thanks," I said. "Hurrah for the enlisted men."

"What's going to be? Seriously, are you okay here?"

"I don't know for sure," I said.

"A long memory doesn't help around here," he said.

I did not see Von Loesch again—except in two pages of photographs that week in *Pipeline*. That was the last of the incident—until, one day several months later, after Von Loesch had been appointed development chief under Mr. Paley, the personnel director came up to me and asked if I wouldn't like to try the field for a while. Any place I wanted outside the United States, he said cordially. I jumped at the chance—or was it?—and picked Sicily. . . .

"So that's it," Tabbert said thoughtfully.

"Yes," I said. "I guess that's why I'm still unclean in the Company."

Tabbert sat there in the formal garden behind the villa,

quietly, and the only sign of his presence during my recital of the events leading to my return to Sicily was a struck match flaring up briefly in front of his face as he lighted his pipe. I caught its glow and warmth. He said nothing, and I took this unkindly, thinking that I had spoken without caution, that he had drawn me out with his rough masculine charm.

But he put my mind at ease.

"Borken," he said, "maybe you've got more guts than sense. I don't know you yet from this. You didn't play the game according to the rules, but you didn't grandstand either. All right, you gave me the fill-in I asked for. I needed that for myself. I'll say this—nothing that you told me, nothing you confided, will find its way into my report. *If* I file one on you."

"That's your business," I said.

"That's right, it is. I'll do what I want. But while you were talking, I wondered if the same thing might not have happened to me. I don't know, I haven't been back in the States so long that I don't know how I'd react on a daily routine with Von Loesch looking over my shoulder. I wouldn't go to bat on the same point you did—I keep my opinions to myself as a matter of privacy. I don't allow the Company or anyone else to look inside my head. But I'd blow my top some other way if I were in New York. That's one reason I'm not back. For all I know, that's why they like me better out here. Maybe I'm not fooling them, they're fooling me."

He knocked out his pipe, and we began to walk through the garden back to the big living room in the villa. Subito eased in and slipped two glasses into our hands. We drank seriously for ten minutes. Then suddenly Tabbert looked at his watch and said it was ten o'clock and he liked to arise early.

Before he went upstairs, he said, "You were in Sicily before, weren't you?" and I nodded, and he said, "Don't worry about me—you have some fun."

45

After he left, I knew I had to work fast. I could hear the others in the next room, playing poker with a deck out of a box holding the dice that Tabbert had used to pick our places in Sicily. Hill and Harris and the two older men were battling verbally; it was the kind of unfriendly poker where the losers were mad at the winners for not dealing fast enough.

I watched young Harris closely, waiting for an opening. He had the Etna region and somehow I had to get there. Since Tabbert had made us gamble for the places, he could not object to our own exchanges.

The chance came sooner than I thought. Luck was sitting with Harris, and on one large pot, which became a test of prestige, he cleaned out the angry older men. When only Harris and Hill were left, they started to shoot craps against each other at a hundred dollars a pot. They were nerveless with money. After a dozen rolls, they kept winning from each other and found themselves even—and bored.

Harris turned to me and said, "Borken, where are the dancing girls in this town?"

Hill said, "Yes, friend, we're up to here in that Arabian figi-figi. The lousiest lays around the Mediterranean. They just lay there—no action."

"What about our esteemed Arabian partners on the Gulf of Aden?" I asked. "Didn't they keep you boys in action?"

"Tried to," Hill said, "but we told them to do it to themselves, and you know something? One old bastard asked us if there was a way to!"

They broke out in winy laughter and said that it was really true.

"Come on, give out," said Hill. "You must have a pocketful of old addresses. You can't handle them all yourself."

"We'll treat you to a round," said Harris. He took out his roll of poker winnings and waved it in my face. "Here, have one on us."

"I'll buy you a piece," said Hill.

It was time to make my move.

"There's a place I heard about only yesterday," I said. "I ran into the madam and she was really something. She gave me her card." I patted my pocket. "From what she told me, her place is the greatest, and all her girls are royal and beautiful and panting."

Hill said eagerly, "Friend, be a friend. Let's saddle up one of the cars and go, go, go."

Harris said, "I'm getting horny listening to you."

"All embassy stuff there. Recommended by the U.S. consulate for visiting Congressmen and other dignitaries. They love Americans."

"That's us. Red-blooded American boys," said Hill. "We've got a reputation to uphold and let's do it. Let's go, friend."

"Wait a minute, fellows," I said. "I'm tired as hell myself. I want to get a good early start tomorrow and I'm not as chipper as you boys. You can stay up all night and be fresh in the morning. But I don't want to hold up your fun."

They both protested that they wanted me to come along with them, but I said I couldn't this night. I took the madam's card from my pocket and held it in my hand—without passing it over to either of them.

"Here's the place," I said. "It's all yours. And, by the way, one of you boys could do me a little favor, too."

"Anything you say," said Hill, reaching for the card.

"One of you boys is going to the Etna region tomorrow, right?"

"I am," said Harris.

I placed the card in his hand.

"Well, I'm anxious to look up someone from the war days who lives in that neighborhood. This week may be the last chance. I'm booked for the Palermo area myself, and I hate to give it up—the big city and all that."

"I'll change places," said Harris. "No sweat."

"Would you?" I asked, elated at having what I wanted almost within my grasp.

"Sure thing," he said. "It's a gamble, anyway. I did want to see Taormina. But I'll make it another time. You go there and I'll stay around here." He waved the card in his hand, grinning. "With all this Palermo figi-figi."

"I'll leave a note for Tabbert saying we've changed," I said, "if I don't see him and tell him in the morning."

Hill took the card from Harris' hand and looked at the number.

Then they yelled for Subito, who came running in, half dressed, saying, *Subito-subito,* and they asked him to get one of the Company cars ready.

I went up to my room. Looking out the window, I saw the headlights of the limousine flash on.

And I heard them asking Subito, faintly, "How the hell do you get to 72, Corso dei Mille?"

CHAPTER THREE

T HE TOWN OF BRUCIA, in the province of Catania, on the
eastern coast of the island of Sicily, rambles from rocky
heights toward the blue-green waters of the Ionian Sea.
Here the wind blows up from the desert of Africa, hugging
the coves across the Mediterranean, and the mistral sweeps
down over Corsica and Sardinia, collecting in the sails of ships
and stunning the stranger on the shore.

And behind Brucia, like an armed giant, looms Mount
Etna, the most terrifying volcano in all Europe, threatening
the people below.

I arrived unceremoniously on the rapid train to Catania
from Palermo, and immediately took the spur line north to
Brucia. I was on my own; there were no representatives of
the Mediterranean American Development Company to greet
me here. A few functionaries in blue uniforms, meticulously
piped with gold scrawls, loitered inside the arcaded sidewalk in front of the railway station. I took a relic of a taxicab, an old high-backed Lancia, to the Trinacria, the town's
main hotel, passing a waterfront where red- and green-sailed

fishing boats, with gashed automobile tires for prows, creaked on the sand. At the tillers sloped leather-faced men in battered fedoras. Along the curving sea line, low rows of nets with salt-bleached white corks hung loosely, and between the strands young children played quietly.

Franca was here. This little town could be the place of dreams long contained.

I walked out upon the balustrade and surveyed a bird's-nest of houses on the streets below the hotel's eaves. People strolled by, ingathering the end of the afternoon, and I withdrew deeper into the room where I could not be seen. Now that I was here, I did not want to meet her—to have her see me—accidentally. I wanted to look upon her, perhaps unfairly, first. I wondered what my face revealed, how I would appear to someone who had not seen me all this time.

It occurred to me that I thought indulgently only of how I would appear, not she to me. Because she had never changed in my mind; all the aging of face and body had not entered my vision of her.

I plunged into a bath and shaved freshly. I thought of the flaws and the years that had hardened the lines in my skin without toughening my mind. I said aloud, "Anyway, I'm clean, Franca." And hearing her name spoken, I glanced around the room, embarrassed.

I rang down to the desk clerk and asked him if there was a Brucia telephone directory, but there was none. The fair thing to do was to call Franca. And, as I had promised Dorotea, to call her father and make arrangements for my trip around Mount Etna. The clerk sent up the Catania book which did have Brucia numbers. I checked the name and address against the one Dorotea had given me. It was there, all right. I asked for the number, my face flushing at the thought that she might answer, say hello to me, that the voice would be hers. It dawned on me that I had not rehearsed my words, that I would become tongue-tied. I wanted to be casual and private: part of my nurtured illusion.

But there was no answer. I held the phone, almost with relief, as it rang. This was the only Florio, Nicolosi, in the Catania Province directory. I turned open the book again to see if Franca herself was listed separately. Dorotea had not told me if Franca lived with her father, only that she was here, somewhere. What was the exact language Dorotea had used in that fleeting remark in the Botanical Garden of Palermo? No clue about Franca's being married; or unmarried.

I walked downstairs to the lobby and asked the clerk where the Guides' Union was located.

It was only a few blocks from the hotel. Everything, he said, was only a few blocks from the Trinacria.

I started to go there when someone in the lobby, half hidden behind the gossipy English-language tabloid, *Rome Daily American,* confronted me.

"Hi there! You're from the States."

I turned toward the voice, annoyed.

A young man with blond hair brushed carefully forward and then swirled over his brow, the part on the wrong side, emerged from behind the newspaper. He was short and well built, wore a Madras polo shirt with a bow tie, dungarees and loafers. He searched me through heavy dark French tortoise-shell glasses which magnified his owl-like eyes. He continued to stare and opened his eyes wider, flickering them. Finally he smiled.

"Tony Whiteside," he said casually, extending his hand.

I mentioned my name.

"Do you expect to stay here long? No, don't answer that," he said rapidly. "I know all about the hold of this place. But if I were you I'd check out of here—I hope that man hasn't heard me—and come up to Taormina. I do love the idea of coming down here now and then and watching the native fishermen pick up their little nets. And their Easter festivals —so pagan. They're colorful people, don't you think? I'm sorry to go on this way, but you're the first American I've seen

51

here all day and I'm just dying to get back to Taormina and the crowd over there. Love them—that's civilization. Real living, fella. You ought to try it. I could bring you up there and introduce you around as my very own catch. We've got a wonderful, intimate little group."

He spoke more quickly, as if he thought I was about to run away.

"I'm in one of those really old homes, but old. Not garish, a little place with a few servants, lovely. Hand and foot service. Gosh, I love it here. And what a place to work. I don't see how anyone gets anything written or painted or designed in the States—the atmosphere is so cold. So a-cultural. I came here months ago to pick up some ideas for fashions. That's my game. You know, some men are in women's things but I'm in men's. Designing from the old Greek and Roman motifs, but honestly, I've hardly done a stitch of work."

I said that I had an appointment to keep on the other side of town.

"I'm soaking it all up. It'll all come out later because I'm really feeling. Just love looking at the people. Their bodies really shine in the sun. Do you think they oil themselves or is there something in their skins which brings out those olive pigments? That tawny bronze is a color I'd truly like to capture on cloth. Wonderful in shorts, trunks, even shirts. But you know those New England mills, terrible on the real subtleties. Gosh, it's fulfilling here. How long do you expect to stay? Oh, I haven't given you a chance."

I mumbled that it all depended, I wasn't sure of my exact plans, but probably not too long.

"You're absolutely right, absolutely. No use squandering your time on thinking of time. I hate arrivals and departures. I like that philosophy. Just live for the moment. It's the way I've always tried to conduct myself and I've found it a happy arrangement. I've worked it out beautifully with friends. The nice boys here on the fellowship gravy train. The old man-yana for mine every time. Sometimes it drives the people around you absolutely frantic, but frantic, but it keeps you free as a bird. How *do* you say bird in Italian? My house-keeper says that she never knows if I'm staying for dinner or bringing over a flock of friends. She's a darling old biddy, but real Italian. She's truly wonderful about it all. Are you free for dinner tonight?"

I said that I was sorry.

"She cooks magnificently. Tomorrow?"

I said probably not, that it depended on my work schedule. He asked what I did.

I told him, vaguely.

"How frightfully dull and impressive," the young man said.

"You know," he said slyly, "I knew you were here. You couldn't escape me even if you wanted to. I have friends here who tell me when any likely young Americans arrive. Well, I'm off for the villina. Here's my card if you change your mind and really want to go places with our own colony."

He touched my hand. On the small finger of his left hand he wore a large silver ring engraved with a crest of some kind.

Then, in a plaintive voice, he said, "Do make time, fella. It does get lonely."

He picked up a beach bag and tossed it over his shoulder, hobo-style, skipped out of the lobby, and drove off in his spidery German Volkswagen.

I looked toward the desk clerk who had been watching us, and he winked at me and said, "*Americani.*"

Outside, the street in front of the Trinacria was sliced with the last reflecting streaks of sun. I followed the directions toward the Guides' Union. It was located in a store along the waterfront. A few of the men, with the word *Guide* scrawled in metal letters on their caps, loitered in front; inside a half dozen more played cards, or dozed in soft chairs reserved for tourists. But business clearly was not thriving. The faces of the guides looked somber by contrast beneath the gay posters announcing this as Sicily, the Isle of Eternal Spring.

"Nicolosi Florio?"

One of the faces dozing in a chair arose quickly and saluted. So this was Franca's father, the man I had avoided during the war.

He was middle-aged, slight in build, with thin features. But he had the same gray eyes. He made a graceful ballet gesture in front of me, and I wondered why. I heard one of the others mutter something about his being a clown, cajoling for business.

"You know my name," he said, loud enough for his compatriots to hear.

"Yes. You were recommended."

"Recommended by some of my American friends, eh? The family from Rome who were here last week?"

"No, your daughter suggested that you might be free."

His friends laughed, saying he surely did have time on his hands and that the only one who would recommend him was his daughter.

He walked outside, beyond the ears of his friends.

"You met Franca?"

I hesitated, and then realized he meant had I met her recently.

"No. Dorotea. I was in Palermo earlier this week."

"Excellent, excellent. I have not seen her for a few months. She is all right? Her family?"

"I saw her only briefly at the Botanical Garden. She seemed all right."

"Good. Thank you. Tell me, what can I do for you? Will you be around here long?"

"It depends."

He said that most of the tourists had come and gone but they expected more to arrive soon, that this was a slow week, and that there was so much to see around of the ancient cultures, the monuments and the stones of antiquity.

I said that this job I had for him to do was more in the way of a special project, and he asked for how long, and I said for about five days. We found ourselves walking along the waterfront, watching the fishing boats come in. I kept looking into his eyes.

"This is the greatest sight we have to offer," he said. "The men coming with their catch, as if they had just defeated the United States Sixth Fleet instead of only a few hundred pounds of fish."

"That's a curious analogy," I said.

He glanced at me quickly, and said, "Well, you know, where there are fish there are fleets."

I looked at him, wondering what he meant, if this was some sort of elaborate Sicilian proverb I could not catch, and at his knowledge of modern history.

"Vacation?" he asked.

When I hesitated, he added that he did not mean to be personal.

"That's all right," I said. "A little business, a little work."

"Work's always good if you can find it. Then you take a vacation with your earned money and feel good. But in Brucia most of us vacation for more weeks a year than we work. It's no joke. Indeed, I can't laugh as hard as I should about it."

I offered him an old soldier's calling card, a cigarette, and he took it, and offered me one of his. I wondered how to bring the conversation around to Franca gracefully.

"You won't have any problem leaving your family for several days?" I asked.

"I'd better leave them if they want to eat," he said. "Where did you say you were going? Any place in particular or all around?"

"Up Etna," I said.

"Beh. Our mountain?"

"That's right, your mountain."

"Would you require transportation—an automobile, perhaps?"

"No," I said, "by heel and toe."

I felt that going up a mountain by car was like shooting

lions on safari from a moving vehicle—somehow not playing the game. Besides, the Colorado prospectors always said that a car became a burden and restricted your movement to the beaten path.

He nodded his head, pleased.

"Can you hear it?" he asked.

I listened but replied that I heard nothing.

"Our mountain is firing up. Several of the smaller craters are smoking. It's not the best moment to attempt a trip up for pleasure."

"There's no danger of an eruption, is there?"

He shrugged. "It's been dangerous to live under Etna for two thousand years, but people still do. No, I don't know if the danger is greater than it was last week or it will be next. It's something people who exist on the slopes sense in their bones and nostrils. Some of the old boys say they can hear it rumbling at night, when all Brucia is asleep and it's quiet outside."

"There's a Volcanic Institute in Catania, isn't there?" Tabbert had said it would be wise to check there for local conditions.

"Yes, the Guides' Union receives its report every day. But I'm talking about what the people who actually work on the mountain regularly feel."

"That's not very scientific, is it? I'll stick with the official reports."

He took my measure slowly with his cool eyes. I imagined my appearance in Brucia seemed strange at a time when most American tourists were in Taormina. Getting the once-over, I wondered how deeply he could see: if he had any suspicions about my work—or myself.

"You know Sicily?"

"Only a little."

"But you have been here before—or is this a first visit?"

"During the war, but briefly."

He nodded but didn't pursue the questioning. I changed

my line, still uncertain how to introduce Franca's name without revealing our old relationship; wondering if he suspected that there was an American once.

I talked business; that, after all, was what Tabbert had said I should do. I explained that what I wanted was a guide and possibly a porter for a somewhat unorthodox trip up one particular area of Etna, not the ordinary bus excursion, but going around the western end partially by foot and taking a few days in order to do it right, then calling for transportation down.

"The authorities demand a permit on the upper slope beyond the Osservatorio because of the danger to strangers unfamiliar with the terrain. Would you go that high?"

"That would depend on what I saw until I got to that point. What I learned on the way up."

He was silent for a moment.

"Are you a poet—the view, perhaps?"

I shook my head, allowing my first relaxed laughter to come out. (No, I wasn't here to write about a mountain, about the snow and sky. No, Mr. Florio, I am here because I want to see your daughter, to possess her again.)

So I said, "I want to study the rocks."

"There's no end of them you can see up there," he said, laughing. "You've certainly come to the right place."

I liked him; he was Franca's father.

"For the permit you can put down 'Geologic reasons' if you wish," I said.

But he seemed puzzled. Tabbert had not covered all contingencies.

"Yes," I continued, "the different rocks below the volcanic ash." I paused. "Can you handle the permits?"

"There won't be any trouble. I know all this territory. I come from around here originally—I was brought up as a boy below Etna."

He pulled out his card from the Guides' Union. It had a crest, and House of Savoy seal, and his name elaborately scrawled on it. Some of the royal marks, like some of the Fascist commemorative street names and slogans, still lingered on as reminders of the minor accretions, in spite of changing governments, in the Mediterranean world.

It was nearly dark now and the streets were almost deserted.

"Well, that is done, Mr. Florio. We can start up the mountain tomorrow." I hesitated before saying casually, "Does my guide know where I can get a good dinner hereabouts?"

"You're at the Trinacria?"

I said that I was, but I wondered if there was some place outside a hotel where I might taste the real vines of the country with the local crayfish.

"A good fisherman's restaurant? There's one around the corner which would have the service you desire."

"No, nothing that formal. I want to get something of a genuine atmosphere, if possible. Could you dine with me? That way, too," I added innocently, "we can get a head start talking about the trip tomorrow."

"I much appreciate your invitation," he said, "but I am obliged to go home to my family. To my daughter and the old folks. They expect me."

"I understand perfectly. I would not want to interfere with your family meal."

Suddenly he awoke.

"Wait a moment," he said. "Would you care to join my family at dinner?"

I protested mildly, and he made apologies for what they would have, but I confessed this was exactly what I desired, a chance to sit down with a family in Sicily rather than in a cold restaurant or hotel.

He said it was done then, and all he would have to do was call his home and tell them to put on an extra plate. I invited him back to my hotel, and it was from my room that I heard him ask for Franca. Someone else got on and then I heard the father utter his daughter's name—her name, her voice. I tried

58

to look away as he spoke, but I overheard him say: You will make room at the table for an American who is dining with us . . . a very gentle one . . . sent by Dorotea . . . work for a week . . . scamper and scrounge around for the best.

Then, smiling, he turned to me.

"We'll enjoy having someone from some place other than Brucia in our house. It is good for my family to meet the outside world. There has been so little of that for us. During the war, yes. For myself, especially. Besides, I can tell you my stories around the table. So you're really doing me a favor."

"If you insist," I said, elated.

I went to the window and through a corner watched him emerge from the entrance and move away in the darkness. I looked at my watch; in an hour I would be dining at her table.

I shut the balcony window and placed a chair against it. The Company equipment in the room could be attractive to prowlers. There seemed to be no reason to suspect anyone in the hotel, but Tabbert had instilled a caution in me about our work. The testing equipment itself was not the prize, after all, but what it revealed below the surface. The ore I sought could be discovered with these instruments, a pickax and luck.

I cleaned up, changed my clothes, and let my mind take wing. So much depended on Franca.

Downstairs, I gave the clerk the Florio number and address in case Tabbert or one of the Company contacts he had mentioned wanted to reach me. The clerk came out from behind his desk, walked to the doorway, and motioned the way to the street where Florio lived.

I went out into the cool night air, quickening my step, hearing the sound of my heels magnified.

Her house stood on a pale street cobblestoned up to the building front, a little above and north of the town, facing the volcanic mountain. Across the street was a row of newly built apartments made of tufa stone. Not far away, the spire of Brucia's marbled cathedral interrupted the stars. I thought there would be some difficulty picking out the house from the others because each stood regimented in its ancient place. But the pattern was familiar: tall flat gate of wood, smaller door within a portal, courtyard of rubbed, glistening stone. I hesitated; almost by chance I noticed a young boy at my elbow, guiding me quietly. He had been designated as a lookout and I was his conspicuous foreign prey. Even under the dim street light, the Florio house appeared to be sealed by the aged, claylike surface that weathers the architecture of the Mediterranean. The shutters repelled all but the tiniest leaking pinpoints of light from within. At the doorway, the young boy lifted the knocker twice. It made a frighteningly loud, hollow noise. Then he disappeared in the complex of alleyways.

And I stood there alone, waiting for someone to open the door.

I heard footsteps tapping down a stone hallway inside, coming nearer. Then, the unlocking of the latch, the unhinging of the doorway, the flesh-pale streak of light glancing faintly over the threshold.

Franca faced my face. . . .

Her eyes widened, almost in fright, and she gasped.

I stared at her breathlessly, unable to say a word.

We did not speak, could not, but continued to look into each other's eyes, for a long moment.

Then she looked at me, perplexed.

"Joseph?" she whispered, low in her throat.

"Franca," I said. "Franca, Franca."

"*You* are the American?"

"Yes."

"Does my father know?"

"About us? Before? No."

"Is it some kind of trick that brought you here?"

"No," I whispered, shaking my head. "Don't think that."

From the large room beyond the dim hallway I heard the voices of other people.

Her father called out, "Is he there? Welcome him, Franca; bring in our guest."

Franca turned and began to move down the hallway toward the lighted room. I reached out quickly for her hand. Our fingertips touched; I was aware that my hands were cold. And she pulled hers away. She turned in surprise, fearful.

We entered the family room together, and I tried to calm the rising color on my face.

"Family," said Mr. Florio formally, "this is my friend Mr. Borken. My father, my mother-in-law, my daughter Franca."

I nodded to all of them, my face a mask of innocence. Franca looked up at me, and then lowered her eyes.

I glanced at her fingers: they were ringless.

The room felt dark green and faded carmine. It was strewn with the accumulation of several generations: shawls, bits of mahogany, carved cut glass, tinted wedding photographs of mustached ancestors, all so Old World. In the center, around a grand oval table, the family were seated, Sicilian Gothics, all except Franca.

So I saw her in the light, after these vague and fleeting years, for the first time: she still had the softness in her skin, the flowing almond-brown hair, the slender grace of form. Her youthful freshness had changed into mature womanhood, and there was a thoughtfulness around her eyes which seemed, now, still deeper in her face, gull gray and somehow sad.

(I wondered, How do I appear to you, Franca?)

Mr. Florio poured wine for all of us and passed around a bowl of nuts. After drinking two glasses of nameless brown wine quickly, he told me that it was easier to drop the mister, that all the guides were called by their Christian names. Awkwardly, I looked at Franca, but she made no sign of approval.

"Where's Edoardo, Franca?" asked Nicolosi. "Didn't you tell him to be here the right time?"

"He'll come later, Papa," she said. "After we eat."

61

"He should have come. There's always plenty for everyone at my table."

"He's studying, Papa. But I am sure he wants to meet the gentleman."

"What's he studying? A correspondence course from Catania is not college to me. It didn't bring this family wealth, all that education. What good is that training going to do him in Brucia? Please, I like Edoardo, that's the only reason I say this. Why shouldn't he study what will be of use around here? Let him learn to fake passports! The last one he writes can be in his own name. That's the thing to do for any smart Sicilian! Scratch out a living here? Eating herb roots? If I were younger I'd pack up the family and move out. We would start answering to ourselves. We'd go to Venezuela, to Brazil, even to Tunisia—"

"Not Tunis again, Papa," Franca said. "We've heard all the stories."

"I said Tunis," Nicolosi insisted. I was amused by the parental annoyance. "And compared to here it was a paradise." He turned to me. "Franca says I can't forget my war. Who can? I remember my leave from Ethiopia in Tunis. It's true, it was an unusual time. I happened to work it then so I was assigned permanently there for a half year and never had to get back to my regiment in the desert. The city was full of Italians even though it was half run by the French. The city Arabs have it now. And good Italians they were at that time. In solid with the people who counted, a minority everyone wanted to please. A nice buffer between the Bey of Tunis and his natives and the French colonial administration. The education in politics one can get there!"

The two older people sat silently, drinking and eating the nuts, and Franca said, "It is getting late, Papa."

Franca finished the settings and called out to someone in the kitchen to bring in the food. I had not noticed anyone else there, but apparently there was a servant girl. She came out of the kitchen carrying a huge mound of pasta and tomato sauce. There was a hurried conversation among themselves at the table to the effect that this servant girl, a lovely eighteen-year-old cousin from the interior of the island, should not eat at the table with us because I might object.

Franca said, somewhat impatiently, that the girl should be allowed to sit down regardless of who was in the house.

I interrupted to say that I hoped they would allow the girl to join us.

"Spoken like a true Peasants party member!" said the old grandfather, aroused for the first time. "No lack of equality because of age or station. Democracy for the young and the middle-aged. I congratulate you on your comradely feelings."

"Me?" I said. I was startled and yet pleased by his outburst.

"What did you say your name was? Here—" He raised himself, walked over and extended his hand. Then he turned to his son, Nicolosi. "The girl eats with us, you heard what the comrade said."

Nicolosi protested that he only meant that there might not be enough room, and then shrugged and invited the girl to sit with us.

Franca said, "Grandpa means well. He's probably trying to convert you—he fancies himself a radical. But Americans are not politically minded, are they, Mr. Borken?"

In all the time before, Franca and I had never talked of politics, and this hint of sarcasm was something new. I looked at her, wondering what changes time had inscribed in her nature.

"I don't fancy myself," the grandfather said. "I am. I have as much vigor at seventy-seven as any of the young members in our party. My value is as a theoretician. I bring a past and a dignity to those young radicals. And I don't miss a meeting. I'm a real believer. I'm against the government in Brucia, I'm against the government of the province of Catania, I'm against the legislators of Palermo, and I despise the government in Rome. What have any of them done for us? And in this gentleman, I see a kindred spirit."

He turned to Nicolosi.

"Have you told him about the seizures?" The old man's eyes shone. "If all goes as planned, we march to possess the land of the estateholders this week. Down with the absentee landlords! Those who till, reap. Correct?"

I regarded the old man with amusement and, looking straight at Franca, said, "That seems to be a good goal. Why not?"

Nicolosi seemed astonished. Franca said nothing.

I said, "I'm afraid I touched off a political discussion when all I wanted to say was that it's okay with me for anyone at all to eat with us. I appreciate your invitation."

Nicolosi's old mother-in-law, who had been concentrating on her food and wine, muttered loudly, "Such an old fool!" She looked at the old man distastefully. Then, lowering her head, she prayed, "Father, forgive him, for he knows not what he does. Because by Thy Holy Cross Thou hast redeemed the world. Glory be to the Father . . ."

The old man pointed at her. "You're only an old lady controlled by the mumblings of the priests," he shouted. "Please. Keep your mouth shut and don't ask the Lord to save me so damn much. Speak to Him for yourself if you want to but keep your prayers off me. Whose side do you think He's on, anyway?"

"Come, you two, stop battling!" Nicolosi said. "You'll give the wrong impression of the kind of people we are. What are you trying to do? I promised to tell Joseph one or two stories and offer him a pleasant meal. He told me he didn't want to eat at the Trinacria or in a restaurant, that he wanted to eat with us and meet all of you. Shame."

Franca glanced at me, recognizing that I had wormed this invitation from her father. For the first time I detected the beginnings of a smile in the corners of her mouth.

The old people eyed each other. The old lady dipped her bread in the wine and sucked it between her gums. Then she fingered her rosaries, praying and rocking, and seemed to immerse herself and forget the rancor against the old man.

Franca and the cousin emerged from the closet of a kitchen with a swirl of steaming food heaped on family-sized earthenware platters. A hill of beans floated on an island of peppers and some sort of greens, and the smell of the spices tingled my nostrils. A giant loaf of brown, almost black, bread was brought out, still hot and retaining the look of the wheatfield instead of the chemist's pantry. I asked where this beautiful bread came from, and they admitted it was a product of the bake shop at my hotel. It did not occur to me until later that the whole meal consisted of bread and wine and pasta and beans, and there was no meat. I complimented the teen-age cousin on the food, and she blushed. Nicolosi added that the beans too were "imported" because they were brought down from the interior of the island and hauled into markets by commission middlemen and resold several times before coming to rest on his table. He called them landowner's beans.

I wondered how much of a strain on the family resources a meal of this sort represented. Apparently Nicolosi had ordered it to be rolled out and they all had exerted their talents and funds. I suspected that the Florios were not a poor family at all—at least Franca and Dorotea had both been able to attend college—and that they belonged to the middle classes here. That meant they were well off, for Sicily.

The knocker from the front portal resounded in the family room.

"It's Edoardo," Nicolosi said. "About time he showed up. That young man of yours isn't very prompt."

I exchanged a quick look with Franca. She said nothing but got up to answer the door. I waited and watched uneasily for Franca and this stranger to come down the hallway.

He was strong-looking, with an overly serious expression, a few years younger than myself, with a sullen handsomeness. Nicolosi introduced us and Edoardo glowered. My chair faced Franca's. Had she whispered something to him in the hallway before they entered about having known me before?

I looked at them, trying to imagine how close they were. And I felt uneasy for the first time, coming here to break the inexorable strides of life—Franca's and my own.

"How did you make out?" Nicolosi asked.

"Nothing, still no word," Edoardo replied. "If I don't hear from one of the countries soon I'm going to tell them to forget it. Maybe one of those busybody clerks has something on me, I don't know. Maybe they don't like my face." Suddenly he turned to me. "Did you ever try to get an entry permit to an American country, Mr. Borken?" I made no answer. "Don't try," he continued bitterly, "or you're liable to find yourself stuck in Sicily for the rest of your life. You wouldn't want that to happen to you, would you, Mr. Borken?"

"Wait a moment," I said. "I don't know what is troubling you, but don't blame me. I don't work in anybody's consulate."

"It's your consulate, not mine," he said angrily.

"Edoardo!" It was Franca. "This is our guest. Papa is his guide."

I looked at her gratefully.

"Excuse me," he continued. "I was talking generally and not at any person. When a clerk in a consulate tells me there's nothing to be done here or to file still another paper, then I blow up. I know it's not your fault. I'm sorry."

Nicolosi turned toward me, his palms open in despair.

"They tell us in the *News of Catania* that the only solution to what they call the Sicilian Problem is mass migration. That the land can't support the people, that the young ones must move to parts of the world where youth and skill can be useful. Edoardo and my Franca should get that kind of fresh start—you can't blame them, can you?"

So it was Edoardo and Franca.

Edoardo said to me, "You get your passport from here all right, as long as you pay out enough. Then you sit and wait for a visa. This country has its quota filled, that country requires security, the next country wants you to guarantee that you won't be a public case. They don't want to take chances on people any more."

The old grandfather interrupted. "Our party would fix those visa people properly. We're not afraid to be angry. People have forgotten that it's good to be mad sometimes. They just take it from where it comes, they listen to governments too much. Nobody is speaking up."

"Beh," said Nicolosi, "you can talk the teeth right out of your head and a lot of good it will do you. I have a different attitude. I say that North and South America should be hoped for—keep alive the dream. But, meanwhile, ways must be found right here in Brucia and all over Sicily to survive. The whole place has to be organized and changed from top to bottom, starting with the large estates. You can't keep running around to consulates day after day. If they really wanted you to come to their country they'd find a way. All offices have papers, but there are really only two kinds: Yes papers and No papers. Regardless of governments—we've all types here in this century. The right push from the top moves everything below like a rock slide down Etna. It's when you're pushing from the bottom up that you need extra strength. And there's nobody who needs it more than someone from Sicily."

"Why bother Mr. Borken with these family matters?" Franca said. "Let's talk about more pleasant things. Maybe he can tell us about himself."

I did not want to now in front of all of them.

The outspoken grandfather broke in again. "I can't always understand young people today who want to go, just to pick up and leave all their troubles behind on the island, leave the mountain and the sea and run away. You can work in the quarries here, you can build industries, whatever an engineer does in Naples or Rome or Brazil, he can do in Brucia. Don't we need sewers here and a hundred other things? Engineers like Edoardo should make things run with buttons and handles, like in a Milan factory. Even if you could build a good sewage system here, they'd take down the statue of Saint Agatha and put yours up."

Edoardo finished his meal and made motions to leave.

"If I'm ever going to be an engineer, I'd better get back to my studies," he said.

Nicolosi said to me, "I wanted you to meet Edoardo because he will help carry our equipment." He smiled. "We can keep the income within the family."

I turned toward Nicolosi, trapped by this sudden plan. I had not expected that Franca's friend, of all people, would accompany me. Still, I said it would be all right to have him come along. It did not dawn on me till later that Edoardo with his engineering knowledge would be able to deduce what the Company was after.

Edoardo asked Nicolosi when he would be needed for the trip; he did not ask me directly.

I said we should get started early, and Nicolosi said, "By the time the sun is high we should be well along inside the pine forests."

"You're the leader," I told him.

Edoardo got up and said good night and Franca walked him to the door.

When she returned, the electricity in the room blinked and dimmed. It signaled that this was enough for one day in Brucia.

The older people were asleep in the room, and the servant cousin was cleaning up in the kitchen. I said that it was time to get back to my hotel for a night's rest before we set out tomorrow. Nicolosi asked me if I could find the Trinacria all right, and I said I thought so.

Franca suddenly said, "Why don't I show him the way back to his hotel?"

"If you don't mind," Nicolosi said. "It'll give you a chance to speak some English. We've all been talking so much that you haven't had a chance to." He turned to me and said, "Franca speaks English well, doesn't she?"

I nodded. "Like an American," I said.

She looked at me, her eyes twinkling.

"Do you mind?" he asked her again. "It's late and I want to rest."

"Not at all, Papa," she said; but he missed her nuance.

I rose to go and she put on a light jacket. Nicolosi told me to be up bright and early, that he would pick me up at the Trinacria at daybreak. I said I'd be waiting for him—and, oddly, Edoardo, for whom I had not bargained.

We went down the corridor and she opened the latch and at last, for the first time, alone in the street, we were together. For a block we walked in silence, hearing our heels. I kept looking at her and marveling that this actually was happening, this dream realized after the years of drifting. I wanted to reach for her hand; but there was Edoardo to think about. That meant that we were only—how I disliked the word now —friends. Friendship could be cruel with love intended.

Beyond her street, I asked, "Franca, you're not angry with me?"

She said, "No, Joseph."

"Then what is it?"

"I am shocked. You surprised me. I open the door of my own home and an American comes in, an impersonal person with whom my father has business. How would you feel?"

"It was a rotten thing to do. I should have warned you in some way first. I did try to call late in the afternoon but there was no answer."

"You did?"

"Of course, I didn't mean to embarrass you. I wouldn't do such a thing to you, darling."

The endearing word slipped out and she stopped and faced me. She seemed about to say something, but then did not.

"Yes," I continued, as we walked on, "I was surprised when no one answered after seeing the whole family."

"They all were out at that hour. Grandpa with his politicians. Grandma at the Cathedral. I was at school. I teach English to the upper-grade students in Brucia."

"That is marvelous—you did not forget your Berlitz courses."

"We used to speak French, didn't we? Anglo-French-Italian, rather. It was a language all our own."

"If we got stuck in one language, we'd use another. You wanted to speak English and I wanted to speak Italian and we'd lapse into our school French."

"Joseph, it seems so long ago, not five years or ten years but part of another era actually, more like someone else's life than mine. The war didn't just end the war, it ended one life. Another began. I think I have had one or two different lives since then."

"Who has not? Yes, I've felt the same way. But I'm glad that you're not offended. I find it hard even now speaking this formally to you. There's so much to say, so much I'd like to hear."

We walked slowly and now we were on the principal street leading to the waterfront where the Trinacria faced the cool Ionian Sea. There was warmth in her manner after the shock and the quiet of our encounter.

"I could talk to you for hours," I said.

"There it is," she said, pointing out the dark outlines of the hotel.

She stopped and looked at me, smiling beautifully, and I looked at her with a joy I had not felt for so long. She stood there, slender and more graceful than I remembered from the grasped six months of our life together.

She extended her hand, as if she were ready to leave.

"Please don't go yet, Franca. I'd like to be with you for a little while longer."

I reached out for her hand, stroking it gently, feeling the vibrations of her self and my self, and I asked, "Are you cold?"

And she said, "Only a little, not my hands."

I asked, "Is there some place where we can go to sit down for a drink?"

She said, "I think it would be best not out in the open."

We walked, then, along the waterfront, and I followed her as she led us to a quiet place facing the Ionian, a low dock where the fleet of Brucia's fishermen was anchored. The sea was calm and lapped against the moorings, and we sat down on some piles of cork and netting. It was absolutely still and we could look out to the end of the world where the horizon met the sea, and it was as if we were back again, in the years at the beginning of youth.

I said, "This is how I visualized it, the two of us here."

She said, "My God, I can't believe it yet. Just like that—a life comes back from the past, breathing new life."

"Franca, it's me."

"But how, from where?"

"From a little place behind the opera house in Palermo called—"

"The Flower Bar," she said quickly. "That was our rendez-vous. But it's not there any longer."

"The bartender at Mondello." I laughed. "I asked him for cognac-and-vermouth."

"I never liked that. So you found our bar at Mondello and he passed you on to Dorotea."

"But I had not meant to shock you in your own house. I wanted it to be sweet and private. All the way across Sicily, on the train, I visualized how it would be. I would come upon you working perhaps in the local museum—I don't even know if there is one here—and I would say, I'll buy reproductions of this Grecian urn and that Etruscan horse. But wait: Signorina . . . Miss . . . Mademoiselle, don't I know you from somewhere?"

I saw that she was smiling now.

"Oh, I had another vision, too. The game in which I was heralded with fanfare, the conquering hero returning to claim his prize of war, dramatic long-distance phone calls, flowers wired ahead to you, a low open car arriving with horn honking at your doorstep, and you waiting breathlessly."

She was laughing now, listening to my nonsense, and peering into the corners of my face as I had examined her, unbelieving, when she stood at the threshold of her home only hours ago.

"Maybe it's better this way, now," Franca said softly.

I leaned forward to encircle her waist, but she caught my hand, squeezing warmly before releasing her fingers. I reached quickly for her hand and lowered my head into her palm and kissed it. Her fingers felt my lips and it all came surging back, all the tenderness and warmth that preceded our love-making. Her hand felt for the features of my face, touching my brow and running along my cheek. I moved my face closer to hers, peering into the depth of her dark-rimmed glowing eyes, and we looked through each other as intimately as if locked in embrace. The rhythms of memory stroked in our minds. I leaned toward her mouth but she turned her face slightly, delicately pleading in anticipation and fear.

"It's so late, Joseph," she whispered.

"It's us, Franca," I said quietly.

She looked at me and said, "You're shivering," and I said it was not from the cold. In love, desire appeared first as a chill; and she remembered.

Franca reached for my hands, and, holding them, said, "What happened?"

I cradled her hands in mine, feeling the warmth returning, lingering over the thought of reunion.

"Do you remember my last words," she said, "before you went on to Italy and then home?"

"I've always remembered—more than words of love, they carried me back here. *Do not forget me, Joseph.* Why did you say that?"

"Because I knew when you left we would never see each other again. No, don't apologize, I'm not asking you to give me reasons."

"But you were right. How could you tell? I had intended to return here on the way home, but everything happened at once, the war ending and a chance to fly home from Naples, and a terribly strong desire to see my country again."

"Yes, you wrote that to me. Your letters were strange, very formal and cold. They said the words but they weren't you. From the first letters, I knew it was over for us. You have a tenderness, Joseph, but you wrote schoolbook phrases—your heart is not attached to your pen."

"I sensed that myself. I disliked writing letters or anything else. I could never get across what I really meant."

"But, Joseph, it was more than the letters. If I thought that was the only problem, maybe I could have bent more toward you in my own. But I felt we had reached the end, that we were destined only for those wild months during the war. Everything seemed to be one episode then—our meeting, love and separation. They all run together in my mind without a beginning or ending."

"I thought it would work out for us, Franca. We did write for a long time."

"Only two years. And then only the most vapid things. How are you, how are you, take care of yourself, do you need anything? You sent packages—that was generous but not enough. The packages without letters I resented—as if you were making amends."

She turned her head shyly and looked away from me toward the water and the docked fishing fleet.

"I wish I could tell you what it was," I said. "The years drifted away, and I with them. I had ambitions to progress quickly, establish myself, and return for you or send for you. I went to school to learn about geology, which had always interested me. I became preoccupied with my work. Then, too, there was the ordinary, everyday job of living somewhere and eating and laundry—and the months and years ran away. After time passed I didn't have the courage to come back. I wonder how many other Americans left their courage on your hillsides?"

"You were never married?" she asked quickly.

I said there was never one girl I had thought about that seriously; perhaps it was part of that same courage.

"Once I was married," she said.

I glanced at her, puzzled.

"Six years ago," she said. "Long after our letters and it was all over. There was a boy I had known from the university. He had contracted malaria in Libya when his regiment was forced to serve under the Afrika Korps. Later he was in a British prisoner-of-war camp and exchanged. Half the time we were married he was in a hospital. Eight months after our marriage, he was dead."

All I could think of saying was "Did you love him very much?"

"He was my husband. He was kind. We were happy and young and ready to build a life and family. Then it was all over so fast, and I was a widow."

"I never thought of you unhappy. I don't know why."

"The years pass, things happen to people slowly," she said.

We heard footsteps along the cobbled street near the dock. It was one of the fishermen making a check of the mooring on his boat. Franca whispered to me to keep still, and she changed her position so that she was not in the line of vision from the waterfront. The fisherman peered in our direction and then walked down the street and out of sight.

Franca said, "People talk. It would not be good to have it all over town that I was here alone with an American. Not that I care what they think—I'm no child—but it is gossip which might disturb my family."

I said, "Unfortunately, we are not doing anything."

She raised her eyebrows and then we both laughed, sitting close together on this bed of netting and cork.

I asked, "Why was your sister angry with me? Dorotea and I were always friends."

74

"Oh, she probably thinks you might harm my chances of remarrying by showing up here. There's a provincial attitude in this country about women seen with outsiders."

"It's your friend Edoardo, isn't it? Dorotea knows him?"

"Yes, Edoardo and I have kept company for two years."

"He must be a happy man."

"You'll get to know him. I think you'll like him."

I wondered how I could, knowing that he stood between us.

Franca rose and said that she had to return home quickly. I helped her up, putting my hand around her waist, saying, "You're still so slender."

She smiled and said, "You look unchanged in my eyes, but more serious, as if disturbed."

I told her nothing about the business with the Company.

"Sometimes I wish I were not so thin," she said, looking down at herself. "I envy the plump women who are fat as pregnant cats, and I dislike my barren body—it is still like a girl's."

We came down the dock and I gripped her hand. There were no lights showing except far at the end of the street where a bar restrained the town's midnight people and tourists. Franca told me to stand here in shadow until she passed by alone through the streets.

Her face came close to my face and I drew her near, kissing her full on the lips, touching her body to mine and saying, "I love you, Franca." She responded for a moment with the full strength of her mouth. Then she quickly pulled away, as if awaking from a shocking dream.

I waited for Franca to say something, to bring it all rushing back. But she only stared at me wistfully, containing her emotions. "Joseph, Joseph," she whispered. Then she turned and strode away deliberately, breaking into a run until she disappeared in the shadowed streets.

I touched my hand and brushed my fingers over my lips, and then I searched for her in the reflections of the water below the dock. It was cold: I had not realized that. I strolled down the street toward the strange bar and looked through the window. A row of men and women stood loosely at the rail, draining from their glasses the dregs of forced laughter. I turned away and walked back to my hotel room.

I opened the windowed doors, and the night air came in, arousing me gently with its sweetness; the coastal breakers rolling into Brucia carried their own salty perfume. There was hardly a sound from the streets below. The town slumbered beneath its mountain.

I checked under the bed to see that my equipment and luggage were intact. The water in the washbasin sounded as if drawn from kettledrums clanked by ghostly irons from somewhere deep in the cellars of the Trinacria. It began to drizzle outside, and I got out of bed to see that nothing trickled into the room through a missing pane on one of the window doors.

The newspaper I had bought that morning made a good stuffing across the glass opening. I reread the screaming headline across the front page of the Paris *Herald* and the story predicting that certain small war rumblings were serious and therefore might lead to more trouble. The headline said: PEACE THREATENED. The headlines in the papers never seemed to change in the years since the end of our war.

I reached for a cigarette. Now I knew this: Franca still excited me as did no other woman in my life. I tossed the glowing butt on the glistening wetness of the balustrade and watched the faint drops pelt out the light.

Part Two

CHAPTER FOUR

SOMEWHERE IN THE STREET BELOW a child's shrill voice pleaded a song for a few lire, accompanied by a piano mounted on a wagon—Verdi at sunrise—and a peddler on a decorated cart sang the praises of his lemons and tangerines. These were the first dim sounds floating up to my room. I couldn't tell the time in the half darkness and I was too drugged with sleep, after a night's implausible dreams, to shake daylight into my head.

Like a distant campanile on a medieval hillside in Tuscany, I heard an insistent whispering: "Six o'clock, six o'clock, six o'clock."

Moments later I recognized the voice of Nicolosi Florio.

I opened the door and let him in, self-consciously; I wore only shorts. He was alone. A pile of equipment lay at his feet.

"Where's Edoardo?"

"It's all right, then, if he accompanies us? I was not sure."

"It's up to you. You're the guide—you wanted him."

"He can really help us, Joseph, otherwise I would not have suggested him. But we do need another man for the amount

77

of walking you want to do. I have him marketing along the waterfront now for fresh food. I've got the ropes and tarpaulin. You have spiked shoes for the climb?"

"Only these old high ones. The Army uses them. These boots have been on the mountains of Sicily before, they'll hold up."

I began to dress quickly as the morning light glanced through the windows of my room. It seemed like a good day to explore—neither cold nor oppressively sticky—though I knew that the weather on the Mediterranean island could be full of deceptively vagrant winds.

"What's the report from the mountain?" I asked him.

"Unchanged since yesterday. The guides are still taking out automobile tours, but no one is going beyond the Osservatorio."

I reached for the telephone and dialed the number of the Volcanic Institute in Catania. I asked the voice on the other end to give me the daily mountain report; it was almost like getting a weather bulletin. I repeated to Nicolosi exactly what I heard: north side widening an old fissure; some tremors; no unnecessary trips.

"You could have saved the telephone call," he said. "I checked with the institute a half hour ago."

"I'm sorry," I said. "I should have asked you first."

"I don't rely solely on the instincts of the old-timers," he said, "but I don't ignore them either."

"Well, then, what do you think?" I asked, hoping I had not offended him.

"There's a risk, no denying it. But we can keep near the main roadway in case of an emergency. There's usually enough of a warning period."

"Let's get started," I said resolutely.

I was anxious to see what the mountain was like geologically—it was a challenging place to one long confined in a laboratory—and I wanted to test my own instincts as a professional in search of the world's new lodestones.

78

Nicolosi went to the window and looked at the telltale fishing fleet. Nearly all the ships were out—a good portent, he said, that it would be clear.

While he was on the balustrade I seized the opportunity to open my small bag, which held various mineral samples. They were arranged neatly by shades, with a line describing whether they were shale, surface or sub-surface. All came from European and Mediterranean areas. The samples had been collected shortly after the second big war by the Company, which had moved in as the new Occupation, so to speak, when the fighting soldiers moved out. All this fine-tooth combing of the scarred earth was by no means one-sided; the journals reported that the other side had been busy charting and ravishing the mineral lands of its satellites.

Etna was special: it could be the tip-off for the Company on what minerals the island hid deep beneath its charred surface, besides containing its own strips of wealth. Centuries of lava had encrusted the mountain walls with layers of rock, dirt and fibrous vegetation—it was a geologist's dream. Eruption had been piled on denudations and regrowth for thousands of years; at least eighty recorded times the mountain had blown its top. Richer layers of land were reborn from catastrophe; natural and man-made scratches gave each generation new fears, yet a fresh chance. It could be my chance, too—an opportunity for a comeback with the Company.

Nicolosi turned away from the window and I closed the straps on the bag. What was inside wasn't his business. He probably could not guess even if he saw the samples; but Edoardo might. Tabbert had said to play it cool. All right: if anyone asked I was comparing ancient geological periods and their effects on the history of rocks, or some such nonsense. One could cloak a lot behind the mask of scholarship.

Downstairs, I asked Nicolosi if there was some place we could be reached on the mountain. He said he had designated way points that would not restrict our movements. We could check in, if necessary, by going to one of the houses listed on his charts with phone lines running down to Brucia.

"All set," Nicolosi said. "If Edoardo's back holds up we're off."

Edoardo was outside. He looked tough and ruggedly virile. He was dressed like a working alpine skier, the kind imitated gaudily by the crowd that came down from the toy hotels in Taormina for a day on the slopes. Edoardo, her friend . . .

"Good morning, Mr. Borken," he said. "Do you still plan to go up our mountain?"

"Morning. Do you know of any reason why I should not?"

"I suppose you've heard the volcanic report for today."

"Yes, what about it?"

He hesitated for a moment and then said, "Well, it's your trip."

Nicolosi interrupted. "We've talked it over already and Joseph is determined. Come on, let's get the load on you."

"I've got a strong back," Edoardo said.

"And a big stomach," Nicolosi added.

"This big pack is going to be eaten as we go along and I promise to do my share to lighten its load," Edoardo said, laughing.

He had a sense of humor, anyway, to temper his sarcasm. But I would not admit what I felt would please him: my concern about the warnings from the mountain.

Nicolosi and Edoardo began to divide the provisions more evenly. Both were loaded down heavily and I could see it really was a three-man job. I made them break down the load into three piles, though Nicolosi protested, and I insisted upon pulling my weight.

While we were rearranging the packs, I saw her. She walked quickly; rather, she skipped along, dancing between the drying lines of nets along the waterfront. She came up to us, smiling coyly.

"Franca," her father asked, "what are you doing here this early?"

"I've packed some sandwiches for your trip," she said.

"Sandwiches?" said Edoardo. "What for? We're loaded."

"I thought Mr. Borken might want something American style. You can eat them, too, Edoardo—there's nothing inside that'll harm you."

"If Franca made them they must be good," Nicolosi said, as if to convince me. "We'll all be hungry after a couple of hours of climbing. We won't have to open the provisions. The sandwiches will come in handy."

She gave her father the package and he sniffed the sandwiches inside before passing them to me.

Edoardo scowled, and Franca came to his side and patted his cheek.

"You don't have to climb the mountain holding the sandwiches that way in your hand," she said, teasing me.

I said, "Would you please unfasten the straps on my bag and put the sandwiches inside?"

She did so, coming around behind me. We were so casual.

"Thank you very much, Franca," I said quietly.

"You're welcome, Mr. Borken," she replied, laughing.

"You seem in very good spirits at the crack of dawn," Edoardo said. "I never knew you to be up this early before."

Franca said, "Don't you care to see me?"

Edoardo grabbed for her hand playfully.

"Let's get going," Nicolosi said. "Franca, you'd better catch an hour's sleep before your classes begin or you'll doze in front of your students."

"All right, Papa," she said. "Have a good trip. Home safe."

She ran into his arms, and father and daughter kissed tenderly.

She patted Edoardo on his cheek.

She held out her hand to me, looking deeply into my eyes for the first time this morning.

"Good trip," she said softly.

"Thank you for the American-style sandwiches," I said, pressing her hand.

She turned and waved as we walked away. I only glanced over my shoulder once.

So we started to climb the ten-thousand-foot mountain. Not alone at first, for now the sun was up and some of Brucia's children were underfoot, moving half-clothed through the square and trailing after us as we made haste. They had an objective; they eyed not us but our pockets and packs. They begged for nothing out of the ordinary: Food-food, they exclaimed, touching their tight small fists to their mouths—no different now than in wartime. One bold youngster made a joke of lunging at his own empty shoulders, as if he held a fat pack, too, unloading the contents his fingers found there in the nothingness, eating the thin air, and grinning bonily. It was a sickening performance for food-food by an undernourished boy-clown.

It took no more than a half hour to get to the edge of Brucia. The day was breaking beautifully. Edoardo's sullenness began to vanish under the weight of his pack. Nicolosi's hop as he walked seemed reassuring; here Franca got her litheness. Near the low rise where the town's cathedral stood the mountain seemed imposing. If it had been rumbling during the week, nothing disturbed the air now. The straps were beginning to mark our shoulders and we dropped the packs to the ground next to the cathedral, unlimbering like boxers. From here at the edge of town the roadways began to grade upward and rise in the distance by horizontal carvings along the mountain.

"It looks taller as we get closer," I said to Nicolosi.

"Wait till you get above the forest land," he said. "You'll think you're walking an inch below the clouds."

We rested. I thought of the coppery hills of the Rockies where I had taken wartime training in an Army Corps of Engineers school; how we had retreated to the mountains after examinations to celebrate our freedom from studies on dates with the local week-end girls. The hills were different then: ours were filled with hope, new and unscarred, somehow still a frontier; and these, old and traditional, tangled with disputed vines and despair. And the times were different: in the nineteen fifties, recalling the nineteen forties, there was a lack of idealism and conscience, the news of the moment threatened instead of succored us; being an American abroad meant something else now. I wondered what would happen when my companions discovered what I was really looking for here on their mountain for the Mediterranean American Development Company.

"Anyone coming inside with me? Edoardo?"

Nicolosi brushed himself off, straightened his collar, and polished the toecaps of his shoes against the back of his cuffs. He started toward the cathedral, glancing over his shoulder to see if we followed.

The cathedral was indistinguishable from dozens of similar churches in Sicily and Italy, except for its own markings—two rows of white Carrara and green Serpentine marble placed like stacks of dominoes all around the foundation. No movement came from inside the church; it was a time of quiet reverence between masses. An old man in the shadows near the entrance neither prayed nor begged but simply stood there resignedly, as much a part of the façade as the main doors; the town's ransom could be bought with these carved bronze doors.

Nicolosi turned on Edoardo.

"A little precaution," he said. "You know, Saint Agatha might be very helpful in case our mountain starts acting up."

"And so would Saint Rosalia and Saint Christopher and Saint Anthony's pig!" Edoardo muttered. "What's the point? You go ahead and fix it up right for all of us."

"A little respect, Edoardo. I'm not an old lady. The Lord knows I've knocked around in my time. But I'm not doing this for myself. Personally I'm a fatalist. Eruptions, wars, deaths, all the same thing. They come or they don't. But as long as I'm serving as guide for this precious cargo—" he smiled and pointed at me—"then I'll take every precaution, including prayer, to protect the man who's going to pay us for this trip. Here. I put it up to the American gentleman: isn't that good business?"

"It has nothing to do with my being an American," I said, "but if I'm cargo, that's okay with me—it's your business. I'm for returning in one piece. If that's what you want to pray for, go right ahead. Only I think you ought to get it over with so we can get as high as possible before nightfall."

I felt funny speaking this rigidly to Nicolosi, but there was a job to do.

"My regards to Agatha," Edoardo mocked.

Nicolosi turned on his heel and entered the church.

The easy relationship between the young man and the older man slated to be his father-in-law was surprising. Maybe something of the old family relationships was breaking down in Sicily, as elsewhere in Europe. Franca, too, had acted with an openness toward her father that I had not anticipated, but then Franca was always straightforward in her manner; even before.

When we were alone, Edoardo turned toward me.

"You knew her before, didn't you?" he said.

I glanced anxiously toward the door of the church, hoping that her father would not emerge now. I looked at him quizzically, not saying anything, trying to recall if some chance remark—some intimate sign of recognition that time could not efface—had passed between Franca and myself when she had brought us the sandwiches. I pretended that I didn't understand.

"Yes," Edoardo repeated, "I think it is obvious that you knew her before."

I wondered what he was aiming at. He didn't sound angry. Maybe this was only a shot in the dark. Still, the more I remained silent, the more he would assume that his guess was correct. How did he know? Had she told him herself? Franca was so playful earlier in the morning, almost childlike in her happiness. Her father and friend could notice those changes.

Edoardo persisted, in his own bold way.

"Mr. Borken, did I hear you say you were in Sicily during the war?"

For the first time since he had brought up the matter, I answered, but matter-of-factly.

"I was on the island for a while. Also, on two or three other islands around the Mediterranean."

Having my response, he pursued the advantage.

"You were around Palermo," he said.

And I replied, "Yes, with a hundred thousand other Americans."

"So was the Florio family. Did you know that?"

"I heard they were here now from a daughter in Palermo," I said evasively.

"You've met Dorotea before?"

"My company has an office in Palermo," I told him, trying to use the Company as a shield. "We were looking for good guides in various parts of Sicily. Nicolosi was recommended by his daughter in Palermo."

"Then you knew the family?" Edoardo said.

I saw no harm in admitting something; he was tenacious, and the best way to shake him was to take the angry bit out of his mouth.

"Casually," I replied. "There were all sorts of civilians around. I believe the Florios were not too distant from where my outfit was living."

"Nicolosi doesn't know," he said.

"Doesn't know what?" I replied. "That I had met his daughters? Perhaps he doesn't. What of it?"

"Why doesn't he know—"

"Look here. I don't know what you're driving at. You've been hired to do a job. I don't mind being courteous, but you seem to be trying to imply something wrong from all this. Forget it."

"I could tell the moment I saw her come running to you this morning," he said. "She has never behaved that way before.

It even surprised her father. And when she came up with the sandwiches, I knew that it was you."

"What do you mean—me?"

"She admitted there was once an American. During the war. Now you've come back. You know she was married once, that she's a widow?"

"I heard. But why tell me these things? You're engaged to her, aren't you?"

"Mr. Borken, I'm not like a lot of other men here. I've knocked around. Franca is a different kind of girl—I recognize that. I'm trying to build a life for myself, and then my future will include Franca. Understand?"

There was the sullen tone again. But I didn't have to answer him: Who the hell did he think he was?

We were still fuming when Nicolosi emerged from the church. This could get complicated. In the back of my mind was Tabbert's advice to steer clear of personal or political complications with the local people. I was plunging into a situation, alone on the mountain with these two Sicilians, that began to forebode trouble.

When Nicolosi joined us on the grass in front of the church, Edoardo said, "Did you speak to your saintly saint?"

"Agatha is supposed to be the saint who wards off Etna's eruptive force," Nicolosi said. "She isn't our town's saint. We never could afford to have one just for this town. Brucia is too poor. She belongs to Catania."

"Besides, she had her breasts cut off, poor girl, thousands of years ago," said Edoardo, speaking aloud to no one in particular, "and I can't work up any interest in worshiping a girl that way. Excuse the blasphemy," he added, turning to Nicolosi, "but they'll get me inside one of these churches only for a wedding—and then not my own. You wouldn't want to marry a girl in one of our churches, would you, Mr. Borken? No, you, I expect, would not. Churches are places for priests and women. They only confuse me. There's no saint to pray to who'll get me a visa to go to South America with Franca.

What Sicily needs is a modern saint—the guardian angel of the forged passport."

"I hear this all the time," said Nicolosi. "What makes you think that all your problems will be solved in another part of the world? Other places have their difficulties, too."

"Only intellectual ones," said Edoardo. "Academic problems to keep legislatures busy debating. Those aren't real problems. When you haven't enough skin to go all the way around your bones, when it rains in on your head, then everything else becomes a luxury."

We shifted into our packs once more at Nicolosi's urging. We looked up at the mountain and moved toward the roadway again.

"No place is free of disturbance," I said. "When you've got an extra skin, a luxury skin, there are other problems which are more wearing—at least, for civilized persons—than your mere physical ones. I'm not underestimating those. Most people worry only about the survival skin. But there's the inside skin. It's the more sensitive one below the surface—the one that itches the mind and causes all the headaches."

Edoardo was listening to me now, as we walked, and I still couldn't tell if he was angry. ("I think you'll like him"—so Franca said. And if she liked him, he was bound to have saving graces.)

"I just want to taste my share of luxury for once," he said. "I'm liable to be redrafted into the army—and the Sicilians don't get the fairest shake. I know if I'm around I'll be in."

I said to him, "They can't take you twice, can they? You seem too young to have been through it all once."

"Since sixteen," he snapped at me. "Three years. I was taking my training just outside Catania in a big camp when the British came fighting through here. See that valley to the left?" His arm swept in a semicircle. "That's where the bloody Germans had us plant mines with their guns in our backs. We retreated across Messina with them, doing their dirty work. I was finally captured by the French up around the Apennines. From them I learned that all armies are the same. Their soldiers didn't have a picnic either."

"It wasn't a picnic for the strangers who came here," I told him.

"But you had your pleasurable moments, didn't you, Mr. Borken?" he said, turning on me. "It wasn't that hard for some of you in Palermo, for instance?"

Nicolosi broke in. "All army nonsense," he said. "They're all no good."

"I'll say this," Edoardo continued. "It's never the hardships alone. I've heard and read all that stuff about how the Italians are terrible soldiers, that we'd rather sing than fight. But I knew some buggers in the British and French armies—I won't mention the American—who didn't know which end of their rifle to fire, who never knew how to fix a bayonet and then use it. No, it depends what fighting you're talking about. Our regulars won't admit it, but the partisans fought bravely north of Florence. They had self-respect. Anyone can fight well if his head is high. No, I'm talking about the routine of military life—the assault on self-respect. I could do it only once in my life—nobody should serve in two wars unless he's a general."

"Don't worry, you won't have to go again," Nicolosi said, as we moved on. "They're taking volunteers these days. You'll be in South America by the time it's your turn. Anyway, they've got Germans in the European army now. They'll fill it up, they thrive on the dull routine we all despise."

"They can have it," Edoardo said.

I called a halt to get my bearings. So far I had not shared my information or objectives with my companions. I didn't intend to. But now I took out the Corps of Engineers map and spread it on the ground. A red streak was marked by Tabbert which pretty much followed the main roadway to the Osservatorio, but with several exploratory inroads along the edges and side roads to get a picture of typical rock samples along the whole stretch. I pointed out the paths to be covered without telling them precisely what I was after.

" 'Property of Mediterranean American Development Company,' " Nicolosi said, reading the words surprinted on the former military map covering his mountain.

I nodded, looking sidelong at Edoardo, but neither said anything further.

The goal I set the first day was the marked area halfway to the Osservatorio, the main building near the top of the mountain, only about an hour from the huge crater. On the slopes below the volcanic observatory the rock was accessible; here the nature of the mountain's geology could be determined. Beyond the Osservatorio lay a vast bleakness—an ancient forge where mythical gods still stirred thunderbolts.

As we walked in this lower region of the mountain, above the spires of Brucia's cathedral, the land looked reassuring. Groves of pink-red oranges hung thickly from dwarf trees arranged in patterns of long rectangles. Vines broke the regular sequence of the fruit trees. This was part of the blood and salt of Sicily; and tension and profits to the estate holders who dominated the island. We stuck to the roadway, sucking in the clean air. I thought of the time once on the hills when to walk along the soft shoulders of a road could mean death unless we engineers had swept it first and marked the safe zones; it had taken me a long time afterward to lose the fear of mines lurking beneath the soil, even in a peaceful, grassy city park.

We walked in file. Occasionally a small truck propelled by a motorcycle motor forced us over into the brush. Nicolosi knew every inch of this countryside. We began to head east toward the Valle del Bove, passing rows of farmhouses. The land here was lush, and I wondered how there could be any trouble in such a luxuriant atmosphere, why seizures and strikes and antagonisms were happening regularly. From a small elevation the fields took on every imaginable shade of green, from the deep tones of the citrons to the silvery hues of the olives. The sharp tang of the lemon groves tickled the nostrils. Once, through a break in the mountain valley, the

Ionian Sea came into view, cobalt and patched with luminous blue reflections.

My muscles began to ache and my back curled; office life in New York hardly prepared the body for an ascent of Mount Etna. I called a halt and we undid our packs. It was time to get down to business. I had reached the first point where I wanted to take a rock sample. I ordered them to wait here by the side of the road and I went on alone, unguided, two hundred feet along a twisting side road, until a hillock of fibrous brush concealed me from their view.

With my pickax, I chipped off a piece of rock. It was part of a ribbon of gray I noticed wedged along a wall of lava stone. It clicked under instrumentation. I marked the height and location with a crayon pencil and tossed the sample into my bag. Then I chipped away again until I had extracted a second rock sample a half foot beneath the surface. I examined it hastily for yellowish streaks, looking for the oxidized markings. It was fissile rock, finely stratified, and appeared rich with minerals. The exploratory paths marked by Tabbert on the map had been compiled from old Italian geological reports; I was not merely operating in the dark. This stuff could be reduced easily into a concentrate at the Company's Rockland plant. I compared it to some of the assayed ore samples I carried. It looked better than a lot of the low-grade shale deposits I had seen turned into yellowcake. This could be fun poking around in the field.

I packed the samples, put them out of sight, and returned to the roadway.

"Find what you're after?" Nicolosi asked. "Any interesting rocks?"

I wondered what had passed between them while I was gone for ten minutes.

"A question of luck," I said casually.

Nicolosi's hand brushed up a piece of lava which was shot through with white marbleized streaks like chips of broken mosaic.

90

"How is this for a nice one?" he asked.

I looked at the ground from which he had picked it and said, "Looks like a lava specimen."

Edoardo spoke up. "Is that what you're looking for?"

I said, "It may be. I cannot tell exactly."

"An expensive hobby," Edoardo said.

Nicolosi turned on him sharply. "What business is it of yours, anyway? You're getting paid to walk, you're a muscle, not a rock specialist. Joseph will tell us when we're on the right track. Relax, and don't lose anything."

Edoardo shrugged. But I thought he needed some casual explanation of what I was after—enough for him to be helpful in the search, yet not enough to know precisely what Mediterranean American really sought. In his foul mood, he might take it the wrong way. Maybe he wouldn't appreciate the idea of a development company combing the soil of his country for a critical material. Still, I had to tell him something; to fall back on scholarliness.

"I think the true minerals in Etna's soil exist somewhere on the upper level. Not exactly the stones washed by lava but those which have had time to set for ages. Streaks probably run vertically, but there are more accretions on this lower level which are confusing. I think we'll get a better idea when we're up a little higher."

Edoardo nodded, but he didn't say anything. I was sure that he had (as did I) more than geological formations on his mind. Still, here we were, walking together—working together, almost.

I began to get hungry and thought of the sandwiches Franca had packed for us. I had a wild thought: Maybe there was a note inside one for me.

I said to them, "Right now I'm ready to trade some of the space in the packs with the food for some of the space in my stomach. What do you say we eat before the sun gets any higher and hotter?"

"All right," Nicolosi said, "but let's put a few more milestones behind us. There's a farmer, a distant cousin of mine, up another thousand feet, around the curve in that ridge. We can rest in his orchard and drink some of his good Etna wine. Edoardo, have you ever met my cousin Vittorio?"

"I think Grandpa mentioned him. One of his pals, isn't he?"

"That's right. They belong to the Peasant party—he's one of the few Grandpa respects. Even for a tenant farmer he's a tough one. If you want to get in good with him, just call him Garibaldi. He fancies himself a great leader. But then, every one of the Peasant party members nowadays considers himself a little Garibaldi."

"Any difference between the Peasant party and the Communists?" I asked. I didn't know the nomenclature here; sometimes party names meant something else.

"Definitely," Nicolosi said. "Right now the Peasant party has occasional Communist help. But the Peasants are a legitimate party who have a good local cause. The Communists support them but they don't support the Communists—it's politics. The Peasants talk through their hats or through the Jesuits on the big world issues but they're very popular on land reform, especially among the peasants who haven't any."

As we walked, I kept my eyes peeled for possible surface mineral outcroppings. And I sniffed the air for an unfamiliar smell; volcanic fissures.

"Vittorio is leading the next seizure," Edoardo said. "That's the story in Brucia."

"He sounds like a gramophone record to me, but the peasants are impressed with him," Nicolosi said. "He's a tenant, like the others, but not for long if you listen to him. I hear that over in Calabria last month some peasants seized land they tilled and got away with it. Whoever comes across the straits from Italy talks big, especially the Calabrese, but they're very provincial people—I wouldn't live on the mainland if they gave me my own house. Especially in the South— it's dull, no new faces. But they did get away with the land. I'll give them credit for that."

A few minutes later we came to a farmhouse made of stone, corrugated metal and wooden board. It was cut into a ridge halfway between an overhanging ledge of rock and a fertile field. Nicolosi went up to the door and whistled for someone to open. Vittorio's wife emerged.

She was short and plain-faced, but there was a flashing around her eyes, as if she had put feminine modesty aside and now boldly regarded men only for their masculine potential.

"Vittorio's at a meeting," she said huskily. "I could use him here and off he goes with the other men. Always he says he has to organize, organize, but maybe they drink a little too. *Beh,* Vittorio leaves and three men come to replace him." She laughed. "He understands?" she asked, and Nicolosi said she had better watch out because I knew what she was saying. She shook her shoulders. "Well, Vittorio is my leader, too," she said proudly.

Nicolosi said, "All I hear from Grandpa is about what a fine fellow your husband is. Old Grandpa is one of his comrades."

"How about you?" she asked Nicolosi.

"Me? Nobody ever asked me to join. Anyway, I belong to nothing. I'm a porter and a guide and an ex-circus performer. The only party I belong to is the tired-back party. A big organization. I'm not fighting anyone."

"You're not the only member of the tired-back party," she said. "Are women eligible to join? If you're married to a man like Vittorio—" She broke out into laughter again. "You always were an individualist, Nicolosi, you're not one for organizations."

"I'm just a little weary," he said. "I've seen too much to believe in parties any more, to tell the truth. But I do admire Vittorio for his enthusiasm."

Then she switched into dialect and I missed what she said.

I hoped to see this Vittorio; he sounded like a vital man. And with the countryside alive with land seizures, it would be interesting to hear what he had to say about this old battlefield, Sicily. While they talked I thought of the difference that time had wrought here in this matter of seizures—once, when we had come here in uniform, the objective was always to seize the high ground; now, it was the tilled ground.

We sat and munched grapes that she brought from a vine that ran above the doorway, and she gave us a bottle of Etna wine. I insisted that she take one of our tins of food. And then I brought out the sandwiches.

The package was wrapped carefully, almost prettily, and inside were two sandwiches for each of us, cheese that I had never tasted before and crushed olives. Of course, no notes inside: the sandwiches themselves were messages.

"The woman's touch," said Vittorio's wife, as I unwrapped the package.

"They're from Franca," her father said proudly. "She gave them to us for lunch—crazy girl got up at the crack of dawn and made them. Still can't understand why."

"Young men to impress, why not?" Vittorio's wife explained. "I'd do the same thing if I had a couple of handsome bucks around." She looked at Edoardo hungrily and then turned her eyes on me. I grinned back when she raised her eyebrows, but Edoardo didn't seem to see the earthy humor flowing beneath the exterior of this woman.

I passed a sandwich to Nicolosi and handed one to Edoardo, but he said, "I don't want sandwiches."

All of us, I knew, were hungry after a half-day's walking, and I couldn't understand what he meant. I extended my hand with the sandwiches again, and Edoardo stood up and walked a few feet away, anger boiling up.

I turned to Nicolosi, puzzled. He approached Edoardo.

"What the hell's the matter with you?" he asked. Edoardo stood silent. "Don't you feel well? The trip tire out your stomach as well as your feet? Speak!"

Edoardo whirled on both of us.

"I don't like sandwiches," he muttered.

"What do you mean don't like these sandwiches?" Nicolosi

said, agitated. He grabbed the sandwiches from me and forced them into Edoardo's hands, but Edoardo dropped his hands quickly to his sides. The sandwiches fell open, spilling over the floor. Edoardo's face reddened.

"There!" said Nicolosi, looking at the mess. "There are your sandwiches! Made by my daughter for you—that's your appreciation."

"For me?" Edoardo said, too calmly. "She didn't make them for me."

"What do you mean didn't make them for you? There are two sandwiches for each of us—and there are yours. Pick them up."

Edoardo didn't move, and I stooped to gather the pieces of bread together, and Vittorio's wife came along with a spoon and began to scoop the cheese and olives from the floor. But Nicolosi now was blowing angrily.

"Help them," he ordered Edoardo. Edoardo hesitated, but then joined us on the floor.

Nicolosi and I ate the sandwiches in silence, washing them down with the wine. Edoardo drank with us, and Vittorio's wife cut up some of her cheese and put it on the table in front of him. He gobbled it hungrily.

"It's the same damn cheese," Nicolosi said, taunting Edoardo.

"I don't like eating it in an American-style sandwich," Edoardo said, looking squarely at me.

Nicolosi said, "The bread is from Brucia, the cheese and olives are from Brucia, so where's the American sandwich? You're insulting."

"Franca's sandwiches are excellent," I said. I wasn't going to let him get away with it. "I never knew sandwiches had a nationality before."

"You know why I'm not eating those sandwiches," he said to me bitterly.

I thought he was going to blurt out what he suspected about Franca and myself. I didn't want Nicolosi to know—

not accidentally this way—unless his own daughter told him. It was queer enough right now, having her father as a guide and her friend as porter. But the whole trip could fly apart if Nicolosi found out; a personal element would be introduced which would harm the smoothness of my field trip. It wouldn't advance the job at hand.

Around the bend leading to the farmhouse came the *put-put* of a two-cylinder motor scooter. The noise of the motor interrupted the last of our midday meal, and we followed Vittorio's eager wife as she ran out to greet her husband. He was a big man, big head of hair, big nose, big voice, and confident manner. He displayed no surprise that three people were in his home, and before I could be introduced to him he ordered his wife, with brusque affection, to bring out more wine. He wasn't mad at all when Nicolosi told him I was an American.

"I've just come from a meeting," Vittorio informed us. "We're finally going to pull off a land seizure in Brucia. The vote was taken, democratically, and we become a pitchfork army in a matter of days—the right moment."

Edoardo shook his head in my direction to caution the Peasant party leader against speaking in front of me.

"Don't tell me what I can say and where," Vittorio exclaimed. "I'm in my house—my home." He addressed himself to Edoardo. "I'm not afraid of this gentleman—why the hell would he want to be against us? Do you think he's going to go running to the authorities to tell them we're going to strike out? He's in my house, he's a guest. He's a man, he can see conditions for himself. And furthermore, he's an American. We want to own the land we till. That's an American idea—it's not European, I can tell you that." He turned his back on Edoardo and faced me. "Mr. Borken, are you for us? For the ideals of my party?"

I said, "If you're asking me personally am I for the peasants owning their own land, sure, why not? But I don't know anything about your party. Besides, all your political parties confuse me. I speak only for myself."

"Good enough for me," Vittorio said. "That's a straight answer."

He turned upon Edoardo and said, "What did I tell you? You're too damn anti-American. Like those party intellectuals in Palermo, you talk too much. Even if it's unpopular here now, I like Americans. They've never done any harm on this island. They're the only ones of all the foreigners who occupied Sicily who left more than they took. People forget that. I don't know what their high government policies are in Washington, or even in Rome. All I know is that the Americans I've met here are not against us."

Edoardo shrugged, and mumbled something about the need for security in carrying out a land strike.

I said to Vittorio that his was the only pro-American statement I had heard since I had arrived again in Sicily—and I thanked him. The moment I did so I felt a twinge of regret. This was exactly what Tabbert had warned me and the others in the Company against—being a spokesman for the United States instead of for Mediterranean American. Well, my thoughts could hardly get back to Palermo from here.

It was late in the afternoon. We eased into our packs. Vittorio and his wife forced a bottle on us, and I left some of our tins of food for them. I wished him and his peasants luck.

I remembered that I had not yet taken a rock sample along this level, excused myself, and chipped off a piece of rock and marked it. Vittorio and Nicolosi stood and put their heads together, as if to explain this queer American rock collector's behavior. Then my companions joined me on the roadway.

We climbed slowly along the still-green terraces of the mountain. An occasional private automobile passed us and small produce trucks continued to make their trips up and down in spite of the Volcanic Institute's cautioning. Nicolosi sniffed professionally, and I asked him if he smelled trouble;

the incandescent magma on the walls of an eruptive funnel usually sent forth heralds of sulphurous acids. If he did, he did not say so but advanced confidently.

Now the land began to change in appearance. We were leaving behind the tall pines and woods and farmhouses, and the region became rockier. I stopped more frequently to examine formations of rock outcroppings. It was infectious. Nicolosi, too, observing me, trying to determine why I passed over some and stopped for other rocks, picked with his own handax. He wanted to be helpful. I tried to remain polite when he said wasn't this one beautiful and that one valuable, but I did not put their loose stone in my growing pack of mountain specimens.

It was essential to keep the exact nature of the search to myself—especially with Edoardo's steaming manner. And yet they both joined in now, and I called on my knowledge of the rock formations to identify them. The mountain contained a wealth of conglomerates whose names they did not know. I knew the names in English only. It became a little game among us, I mentioning the igneous, sedimentary and metamorphic classifications and they trying to translate them. But Edoardo kept prying around the edges of my real objective.

I looked for help from Nicolosi, waiting to be rescued from Edoardo's annoying questions. For a moment I considered showing these men, still strangers, the samples in my pack. But who were they anyway? What would Tabbert think if he knew I was allowing private interests to interfere with the work? Work for yourself; therefore you work for the Company. He put it a strange way. If I didn't straighten myself out first with the Company, anyway, there wouldn't be a chance to clear my head about Franca. My loyalties became sharply etched.

"*Beh*," Nicolosi muttered, relying on the all-purpose Sicilian word, "we've got a long way to go yet. There's a whole mountain of rocks and stones and pebbles to choose from. Who cares if it's square or circular or a red or black one? Who wants to argue about a few rotten rocks?"

Saying so, he picked a stone off the ground, shined smoothly by the rough aeons of time, and skimmed it toward a naked cedar. The stone circled and rose and dropped weakly to the ground. Edoardo also stooped for a stone and threw it at the tree, and both now did so, again and again, and I joined them in this act of release, striking at the tree, like boys skipping rocks.

That was the way the climb began the first day, here on the lower levels of Etna. We called a halt when the sun went down and Nicolosi found one of the open Alpine huts used by skiers in wintertime. We bedded down for the night, my muscles stretched as if I had been climbing for days.

I thought of Franca and my chances, her impulsive act of delivering the sandwiches at daybreak, and the wild hope that she had done so because the fires were lighting for both of us again. And I wondered if, as in the armed combat I had once seen on this remembered island, things became better in a human way as one moved closer to the field of danger.

CHAPTER FIVE

BY THE CROWN of the next afternoon, a drizzle that was
intermittent thickened into rain. Winds trapped in the
valleys of the mountain swirled the water around our bodies
and trickled it down our collars and lashed us across the face.
The mountain here began to be its more awesome self; the
land was wilder and the delicately shaped flowers of the
slopes below became sturdy rib-stemmed brush closely anchored to the coarse terrain. My feet held the ground, muscles
long dormant stretched forward as I experienced a second
wind. I felt strong.

The earth grew soggy. Nicolosi walking ahead motioned
us off the shoulders and back toward the roadway. Few vehicles passed us now. Only when we walked in a file on the
high center of the road could we keep ourselves out of the
path of the streams of sliding water. The tarmac road was
reassuring, a man-made slit curling around the mountainside.
No shelter that I could see beckoned in any direction. I looked
back toward Edoardo. He walked with his face down so the
drops pelted him on the forehead instead of across the mouth.

His grimace angered the lines around his temples, but it might have been only a tight look against the weather. I waited until he caught up. Then I shook my fist at the rain, mocking the sky.

"Can we dig out the tarpaulins?" I asked. "Who's got them?"

Edoardo said, "They're in here." He had them on his back.

Nicolosi turned to us. "No sense opening up anything now. Follow me—I've been through dozens of these showers on the mountains."

"How long is this liable to last?"

"It may be over in a couple of hours or less. It's been heading this way for days and now it's finally breaking."

"Where were we supposed to be by nightfall?"

"Where did you want to be—for your work?"

I had not set a time limit. The samples I had picked up beyond the roadway bore the signs of high mineral content. I spaced my sampling according to designated marks on the exploratory map. The counter had registered positively; I had managed to conceal the instrument from them so far. My work was going along on schedule, and it made no sense being uncomfortable.

"Any place out of the rain," I said. "Let's get Edoardo dry. He looks like he could use fins."

"Don't worry about me," he said. "This is your game."

It was damn wet, but I felt exhilarated up here.

I turned to Nicolosi. "You're the leader. Where do you suggest we go?"

"One of the skiing refuges. We've been making good time. It's only a few hundred meters up those rocks and around to the western side. We'll get there if we keep at it for an hour."

"We'll all be fish if we don't reach cover before then. Isn't there any place at all where we can stop for a while till this blows over? If not, let's get out the tarps right here."

Nicolosi leaned his pack against a road sign telling the distance to the Osservatorio. Above the drumming of the rain, he shouted, "There's a place up ahead but it's usually shut tight. It's private property. Let's keep going because it's not far from the refuge. We'll stop soon for the night even if the sky clears."

I looked around for a rock ledge or tree, but the land was barren of natural protection.

And then, a moment later, as we started to walk again, I thought I heard an alien sound—the hollow barking of animals faintly ahead. I strained forward, listening. Looking up, I saw a strange sight. Bounding toward us came three dogs, tumbling and sniffing through the brush, and their shrill howls were fierce. One was a massive animal and I thought it was coming directly at me. The beast snarled and started to yap around my shanks and I crouched in self-protection, ready to try and catch his throat.

The long one-note of a police whistle tore sharply through the air. The dogs turned around as quickly as they had arrived and bounded toward the mechanical command. I could see nothing through the slanting rain as they raced out of sight beyond a knoll. In the distance I heard a shotgun blast.

I ducked to the ground instinctively (away from the mined shoulders of the road . . . the unswept iron traps . . . the enemy one hill ahead in Sicily). Sweat and cold rain mingled on my brow, the years floating back across memory to other gunfire, and I crouched rigidly.

A hunter emerged, and then behind him a second. The dogs slobbered insanely over the rugged ground looking for the bird. I saw the hunter put the whistle to his mouth and signal again. The forlorn dogs tracked back to their master. The hunter walked directly to a bush and reached down. His hand pulled out a limp dove, still breathing, but its peace about to come forever. With a casual motion he placed the bird inside a stuffed bag hanging across his shoulder. The second hunter trailed him.

I looked toward Nicolosi and Edoardo, puzzled. They whispered together in what seemed like fear.

"Who's that? Do you know him?" I asked.

"It's the Baron," Nicolosi said, as if I should know.

He emerged from within the dense film of rain. The first part of him I saw was the glistening front sight of his shotgun, pointing safely to the ground, and behind the gun, the man. He was dressed in a special many-pocketed outer garment of rainproof khaki cloth, and I recognized it as a model that had been issued to selected mountain troops of ours who had fought in the Apennines and, for all I knew, were still stationed somewhere up there with postwar forces. He wore high leather boots—paratrooper boots. At second glance, his clothing was sturdier than himself. A face with delicate features peered from inside the parka, and his lines marked him as a well-kept man in his fifties. I nodded in recognition. He glanced away, ignoring me. In the local dialect which I could not make out, he asked Nicolosi who I was. His voice was strangely high-pitched.

Nicolosi explained that I was an American he was guiding up the mountain.

I said to the Baron, "I hope we're not interfering with your hunting."

He looked me over, studying my clothing and trying to see through our packs and equipment.

"Nothing interferes with my hunting," he said.

"I thought we would be the only ones caught in the rain. I was surprised to hear your dogs."

"I'm not caught in the rain, sir," he corrected me. "I anticipated this weather and came fully prepared for it."

For the moment his face seemed animated instead of suspicious. "No, my dear sir, on the contrary. Are you a hunter? Too bad. This is the best weather for shooting birds. I never fail to bring back a nice bagful when it rains. I am old-fashioned. Isn't that right, Nicolosi? I believe that when you go hunting you are not out for the exercise—you pit yourself against a wild creature that can fly. You cannot fly. Somehow you must make the match even. It's a matter of personal satisfaction, do you understand?"

I looked at him, without knowing what he was driving at, but kept still. His eyes burned darkly.

"Very fundamental. In the sun the bird can see you and move quickly to cover. From the hunter's viewpoint, it is perhaps more convenient on a clear day, but this is marred by the fact that the reflections off your shotgun give you away and the bright light may cause you to lose sight of the bird. When it's raining I find that the drops of water beating down on the bird's wings slow its flight. Ah, but the shot from my gun is just as rapid in clear or rainy weather. When the dogs flush out the bird he cannot fly as quickly weighted down with water. The bird is confused. Now the bird must look out for both weather and hunter." The Baron smiled. "Oh, yes, I get a little wet," he said. "But I kill my doves."

I had never hunted in my life. But I had eaten game and, logically, I could not be squeamish. Yet, I sensed something unsporting, if not immoral, about this method of hunting. I looked at Nicolosi and Edoardo for a sign of the revulsion I felt. But their faces were immobile, frozen into silence. I was about to say something and then decided that this was not the moment.

I turned to the second hunter, who stood behind the Baron, and asked him, "Is there anywhere we can find a place out of this rain? We've been walking all day—nothing would look better than the dry insides of a room."

"I don't know," the second hunter said. "I am not from here."

He had an accent that I could not make out.

The Baron said, "Come, all of you. I've had a good afternoon in the field and my day is over anyway. Come to my place."

Nicolosi and Edoardo scraped thankfully, and we followed the Baron and the second hunter. We walked around a curve in the roadway and came upon the Baron's hunting lodge.

The windows were barred and a printed notice tacked on the door said this was private and not part of the provincial land. Inside the spacious room a caretaker heated a kettle of soup over a fireplace primitively. I was ready to flop on the rug near the fire when I noticed that my companions had not followed me into the lodge. I asked them if they preferred to remain wet, but the Baron saw no humor in this. He gave them permission to come inside. Nicolosi knew Bardi, the caretaker, and they began to speak the dialect of the interior, which was filled with ancient *thous* and *thees*, an apologetic tongue.

The Baron stretched out on a couch, after carefully hanging his U.S. parka to dry near the fire. He stepped out of his hunting boots and changed into a pair of waterproof British oxfords. We edged closer to the fire and took off our shoes, too. The dogs lay at the Baron's feet, yawning.

Nobody said anything, but I sensed the hostility in the air.

I looked at the second hunter. He was dressed rather cheaply in an ill-fitting, coarse wool plaid suit. He was fair, wore a little mustache, and was a few inches shorter than myself. He seemed uncomfortable.

I said, "My name is Borken. This is Nicolosi and Edoardo."

He said, "I'm Wernher. A tourist here."

The moment he pronounced his own name, I knew he was from Germany. The facelessness and the shotgun in his hand went together in my willing mind. I wondered if Wernher really was a tourist, and if so, why he was high up the mountain in this weather.

The Baron broke in quietly. "Now, what are you doing on my land?"

His voice cut through my reverie.

I caught Nicolosi's eye. He seemed bewildered. Edoardo kept still.

"Is this part of Etna private?" I asked.

"It's been private for more than one hundred years in my family's name," he replied. "Yes, Mr. Borken—do I pronounce your name correctly?—it's clearly marked as a hunting preserve." He smiled through his lecture. "Since I'm the owner and nobody asked me for permission, or checked with my office in Catania, I must consider you a trespasser. As for your guide, I can also bring charges against him to have his license revoked for leading you onto my land."

"Look here," I said angrily, "if there was any trespassing it wasn't Nicolosi's fault but mine. It was I who told him to come this way. We came off the highway in the rain and we can damn well go back that way. But don't talk about anyone's responsibility but mine."

I walked away from the fire and toward the packs on the floor. I didn't want to get Franca's father into trouble with the Government martinets who passed out licenses. It would be a hell of a way to introduce myself into her life again.

"Mr. Borken, I didn't say anything about responsibility. I didn't even say I was going to bring anyone to court on trespassing charges. I merely apprised you of my rights. I'm not interested in causing you inconvenience. What would I gain from it? If you left the roadway during the rain and happened to come upon my place, it was only to seek shelter, isn't that correct?"

"It's about right," I said, still angry.

"But one must be careful. You're liable to get shot otherwise. We hunt up here. It's no place for tourists unless they're my guests. Such as Wernher here. He came in an orderly way to my office, he inquired, he assured me that there was only a pleasure trip involved. Isn't that so?"

The German tourist said, "I wanted to see this part of the mountain again. A sentimental trip. I was here once."

"During the war, I suppose?" I asked him.

Wernher answered, "Yes, in a hospital below this face of the mountain. I could look up this way. Isn't it beautiful country?"

And I didn't know whether to agree, jealous that he considered these hills his sentimental property, too.

"You're both my guests now," the Baron exclaimed. "Well. We Catanians are indeed fortunate. It isn't often we get a visitor from the great United States this way. But you're not dressed like some of your countrymen and women who visit Taormina. Pardon, I hope I am not saying something out of turn—I talk too much, don't I, Nicolosi?"

Nicolosi said, "No, Baron."

He continued, "Anyway, I want to listen to what you have to say. Wernher here is a sentimental tourist. Why are you here?"

I hesitated, wondering how much he knew. His patronizing manner could not conceal that he was fencing with me.

"Nothing special," I said, playing it close. "America is full of Sicilians and Sicily is full of Americans."

"Come, come," he said, "you're not walking up Etna with a guide and porter for the exercise. And why walk when you can ride most of the way? Of course, you don't have to tell me. I'm only here myself to hunt my few birds. Nothing else. I don't want to disturb you in your work."

I said nothing, but he went on probing.

"No, not me, that wouldn't be a way to treat a guest. We all have our private adventures. I don't know what yours is, but it is possible I can be of some help. You can ask your workers about me."

Nicolosi nodded and muttered something about the Baron's importance.

"If it's business maybe my interests in Catania can be useful. We're not the biggest and don't know all the latest American ways but we can be of some help here."

I thought, You're so obvious it isn't funny. Squirm some more, and stop throwing around that poor-European-big-American line, which you don't believe anyway. You'll make me a patriot in spite of myself.

I said, "I appreciate your kind offer of assistance, Baron. It's more than generous of you. I'll certainly take you up on it in case we run into any difficulty. You've helped already by allowing us to dry our skins."

He turned to Nicolosi. "Are you registered for the trip?"

Nicolosi nodded, and I spotted his game immediately.

The Baron tried to be casual. "Let's see what forms they make you fill out these days. You know, I myself have not been all the way to the summit for years. And I keep this place almost in sight of the crater. Here." He extended his hand.

Nicolosi fumbled in his pockets nervously, waiting for a word from me. Wernher glanced at me to see what I would do. I didn't want to lose face in front of him.

I said, "Our interest here is a simple one, Baron. I'm a rock collector. All kinds of rocks interest me."

Nicolosi stopped looking for the papers.

"Ah," the Baron said triumphantly. "Do rocks have value now in America? Like canceled stamps? How much is each worth? A very interesting work. Believe me, you couldn't have picked a better place. There are plenty of rocks here." He made a little joke. "There's a good rock for your collection —the biggest volcano in Europe—ten thousand feet! A hobby? That's very, very good."

The tension in the room relaxed and everybody lay back, the strain off our shoulders. That was enough information for the Baron. Remember what Tabbert had said: A little more love of corporation. But now my own instincts were at work against this man; I was not thinking only of the Mediterranean American Development Company.

Nicolosi and the Baron's caretaker talked quietly, and Edoardo stroked one of the hunting dogs. The Baron ordered the soup kettle brought out, and Bardi dished it among us. It was burning hot, the first warming food we had had in hours.

Afterward, the Baron mused, "It seems to be a growing business, this rock-collecting hobby. Only a few months ago, my friends informed me that a group of English scientists passed through Palermo guided by the Rome Government, all loaded down with special equipment." He shrugged. "But

108

I suppose there are all kinds of collectors. Like hunters. Some are content to shoot birds in the brushland of Sicily, others aren't happy unless they shoot big animals in Africa."

He had sensitive antennae.

"You look more like a big-game rock hunter, Mr. Borken," he said, smiling.

The mild way he said it, I could not tell if he meant something specific about our Company's competitors in the search or if he was simply being sociable. He mixed information with brashness, and I kept up my guard.

I took out some of the tins from the food pack and passed them around. I wanted to repay the price exacted for the Baron's open door in the rain. Bardi collected the tins and stored them on the full shelves. We talked of the conditions on the mountain. The Baron told Nicolosi that the *News of Catania* had reported that Etna was acting up on the western side, with one of the subsidiary crevices smoking. We had not heard this the day before from the Volcanic Institute. Nicolosi and I exchanged glances. We were climbing westward.

For the first time, the Baron turned upon Edoardo and said, "And you, sir, have you succeeded in getting your passport to leave our poor land yet?"

"I'm pleased to know that the Baron takes such an interest in my personal affairs," Edoardo replied.

It surprised me to hear him snap back toughly. We had our own rivalry going over Franca—that was private—but the hostility between these two Sicilians seemed deep-grained.

"No offense," the Baron said. "I just have a good memory for names, and these things get around in a small region like ours. We all know one another's affairs, don't we? I know, for example, that Nicolosi's daughter teaches the students in Brucia. A young widow. I've always believed it's good for all of us to know one another's problems. These are unhappy times on the island—in fact, all over Europe—and it always hurts my pride a little to hear of young people quitting."

Nicolosi shifted the talk back to the volcanic conditions on the mountain. But the Baron ignored him.

"Most of us old-timers have no complaints," the Baron continued. "My caretaker, Nicolosi, and many other people here have lived good lives. We don't complain, we love our province. Sometimes we have bad seasons, but there is nothing drastic to make us want to abandon Sicily permanently."

Edoardo said boldly, "There are different levels of living on the island, Baron. We have many poor people in Brucia—"

"That's always the answer they give," the Baron said to me. "The class differences, the old class war. That's all I hear these days. Don't taxes take away our income? All that's left is our land, the tired land. You would think that the lowliest peasant would understand this, but what do they talk about at their meetings? Land seizures in Calabria. How the comrades—most of them never turned the soil—led a group of farmers in this or that village. We're blamed for everything, we're supposed to be the answer to all ills. Who took care of this land, paid the debts on it when it yielded nothing, who supported your fathers and their fathers when things were rotten? I'll tell you—the same absentee landlords they now accuse. If the peasants did in your country what these men try here, they would all be in jail."

I thought this was no time to go into the nature of the American economy. At least when he ranted this way, attention was drawn away from my mission here for the Company.

But now, for the first time, Nicolosi intervened. I was wondering what there was about Franca's father which made him this servile before the Baron.

"Pardon, Baron," he said, "but nobody is talking about the owners of small areas. It's the big fish who take no interest in the people working their land but only collect who are at fault."

"The big landowners? Those of us who have a few extra acres tilled to nothingness? It's one thing if you blame the

110

really big ones in Palermo and Naples, but you shouldn't attack your own kind."

Edoardo said sarcastically, "Yes, don't forget the Baron is just like ourselves."

He kept asking for it all the time.

"In Calabria," Nicolosi said, "even the church is helping on the seizure. Someone came over from Reggio the other day and said that a priest from the village led a group of tenant farmers onto some unoccupied land and later conducted a service right then and there and, what's more, he squatted with them for twenty-four hours. When the authorities asked him if he represented the peasants, do you know what this priest said? He who tills the land owns the land, he who works the land reaps its fruits."

"Ah," the Baron said, "but whose land was seized? Was it church property or someone else's?"

"I don't know whose. I suppose—"

"Naturally. That's all the trouble with these rumor stories. Propaganda. Would a priest dare to seize land in his own parish that belonged to the church? All you troublemaking idealists! I tell you, if Sicily truly ruled herself we wouldn't have these troubles."

To my surprise, all the men in the lodge nodded agreement. On political separatism, at least, things had not changed since the war. But, then, things changed little in Sicily, I was discovering, with politics or people.

The Baron continued. "I'm not saying a few improvements are not necessary, but slowly. It is like integration with the Negroes in the United States. Correct? Nobody is rushing that in your country. They know they cannot make Negroes white men. It's all right to talk, to make brave statements, everything is propaganda, but we have our situation and you have yours. You think we can make peasants into landowners overnight?"

"It's not the same at all," I said. "Not every American thinks

111

the way you read about it in your European doctrinaire newspapers."

I moved over toward the window to see if the rain had subsided. But it still beat down heavily on the roof of the lodge. The dogs stirred and followed me closely with their tails.

The Baron turned on Edoardo.

"You think that all the troubles would end tomorrow if the land were turned over to the peasants? Or if passports were given indiscriminately?"

"One has nothing to do with the other," Edoardo said.

"You don't know what is behind these land seizures, young man. It's a gang worse than those in Rome, more brutal than the old castor oil and the new jeep squads. They want to seize control and overturn the regime. They're all from the mainland, anyway."

"The ones I know aren't politicians, Baron," Edoardo said. "They're some of the people from Brucia."

The Baron ignored him, focusing on Nicolosi.

"All right, let us assume this all happened on my piece of land. Let us say that my man, Bardi, instead of working for me was aroused to take away my land. He is down in Catania listening to the talk of the troublemakers. They single him out, as I have seen them do with others, and call him to the platform. It happens all over, this deifying of plain people. So they invite him to come to the Peasant party meeting—you will excuse me if I call it the Communist—and after the flattery my caretaker is ready to do their bidding."

"I've never been to one of those places!" Bardi muttered.

"Please. Well, your comrades come here with their tools and sit here for a day and divide up the fields and say, Bardi, this is yours. So he takes it. Now, what do you think would happen?"

"I'm not interested in that," Bardi protested weakly. "I like working here for you. I don't want to lose my job."

"There's your answer, gentlemen," the Baron said, striking

112

his small hand in his fist. "Not from my mouth but from a worker's. My man, Bardi, does not want to take the extra burden and responsibility of taxes and employment, of risks of weather and grain, of damages to crops and losses and government inspectors. He knows that even if he did squat on the land for a week, if all the priests and bishops in the province blessed him and his land, he'd have only a new set of worries. Believe me, it's just as wrong to force a piece of land upon a man who doesn't want to be bothered with all its headaches as it is to take away the land from its lawful owner."

I reminded him that American technical missions had helped out here since the war. But the Baron twisted that, too.

"It never worked," he said. "You're not dealing with mechanics here like those who grow up with a driver's wheel in their hands in your country. Our people would break them into pieces and there wouldn't be any spare parts. You cannot put modern farm machines in the hands of peasants with little skill. That's something your technicians don't understand. We know what's good for our kind."

Edoardo sprang forward. "Don't try to give the American that noise," he said. "We learned how to handle artillery pieces and how to drive military vehicles during the war. The peasants here could just as easily learn to run their own tractors if they weren't held back deliberately."

The Baron's voice lowered. He looked at Edoardo with a malicious smile. "That is dangerous thinking, young man. You can't call me names and bring down threats. Especially not in front of Mr. Borken. I'm used to abuse. Half the peasant leaders in Brucia have made names for themselves by calling me names. But you are giving this American the wrong impression. I think you should apologize to him. Because if you don't—"

I cut in quickly. "Edoardo said nothing to offend me."

The Baron shouted at him, "I have a mind to report you to the authorities. But you're too unimportant to bother about.

Anyway, your thoughts are punishment enough since you must live with them."

He turned his back on Edoardo just as Edoardo shouted back defiantly, "Baron, I don't care who reports me for what I think, including you!"

For a moment it looked as if one or the other would strike out. They stood there, neither one moving, glowering like two gladiators. Nicolosi paled, watching them. I glanced at Werher for a reaction, but he, too, was only an outsider looking in.

Their anger finally simmered down.

"We've had enough of this," the Baron said, recovering his composure. "While anyone is under my roof I refuse to argue with him. Let's talk about more pleasant things. Nicolosi, tell me, how does your daughter find things here? Does she think much of the caliber of the students on this side of the island?"

Nicolosi, who had been shaken by the argument, replied, "You know Franca?"

The Baron said, "She has a good reputation—as a teacher."

Something about the manner in which he said the words struck me as queer. And I could see that Edoardo detected the emphasis, too.

Nicolosi said, "She likes her classroom work. She doesn't talk too much to me about it, but she has some good students, I'm sure."

"Too bad," the Baron continued, "that she cannot use her talents in a bigger school. Perhaps Catania. She studied at Palermo University, didn't she? I seem to recall that from her records when she applied for the position in the Brucia school."

"My daughter likes teaching in Brucia," Nicolosi responded quickly.

Edoardo and I exchanged glances, looking for another one of the Baron's traps.

"No offense," the Baron said. "I was only trying to explore a mutual subject between us. Anyway, I suppose your problems will be over soon with Franca—when she gets a visa to go somewhere. Where does she prefer to go?"

"Do you think you can help her?" Nicolosi asked. "What about the visas, the quotas?"

"That depends where she is going," the Baron said importantly. "If she is going alone or with someone."

Suddenly Edoardo leaped from the floor and confronted the Baron. "How Franca goes or with whom is none of your business," he snarled.

The Baron drew back and edged his hand toward his shotgun. In a second he gripped it menacingly in front of his body, but more as a club than as a gun. The two men stood their ground, fuming and snorting, neither daring to move, knowing that a misstep now and their violent insides would explode all over the lodge.

Wernher looked at me blankly; he made no move. Nicolosi stared, frightened. Then I advanced to the center of the room and stepped between the Baron's shotgun and Edoardo.

"Please, for my sake," I said. "This is no time to behave thoughtlessly. We all have work to do. Let's not fight one another. The elements are bad enough."

Slowly the two men backed away from me, and each other.

Now Nicolosi stepped toward Edoardo and with a series of silent hand motions persuaded him to restrain himself.

The Baron walked over to the window and announced that the rain was letting up. He was serving notice, in his unsubtle way, that it was time for us to move along. He said as much a second later when he asked where we were staying and regretted that there was no room, of course, at his lodge. I was not ready to beg for a position near his fireplace. The incident in the lodge could become troublesome for Mediterranean American—it was an involvement—but my relationship to Nicolosi and Edoardo meant more to me at this moment.

I suggested that we should get moving now—before we were told to go. The Baron made no sign of protest as we began to pack our stuff again, watching us with unconcealed distaste. Bardi gave Nicolosi the directions to the next skiing refuge on the higher reaches of Etna. Edoardo picked up his own pack and Nicolosi's and slung both over his shoulders, in a show of strength. Then he and Nicolosi bolted outside.

"I hope you find the rocks you're looking for," the Baron said to me. He lowered his voice. "I can be reached at my office in Catania. As I mentioned, there are others around here from other countries also looking. Nobody will get anywhere without co-operation from the right people. When are you coming down off the mountain?"

I said that it depended.

"Call me in the city as soon as you do. I think I may have some information that can be useful. By the way, forget the incident here with your men. They're just local Sicilians, I regret to say, argumentative and grasping. But between us, Mr. Borken, there can be a mutually profitable relationship. Please, take my card."

He reached into his parka and held one out. It read: Barone Vincenzo D. Magliocco. Plus a crest and address, all engraved handsomely.

"It's not necessary," I said, refusing his card. "I'll remember you."

I stared at Wernher, standing behind the Baron in the dry room, and turned my back.

Outside, the three of us stood in silence in the driving rain. There was nothing to do but walk down the pathway in front of the lighted hunting lodge. At the edge of the stone fence around the property, Nicolosi stopped.

He asked if I thought it would be all right to cut across a corner of the Baron's land in order to save about a half mile instead of returning to the roadway and then walking ahead.

I told him that as far I was concerned, I was on the mountain and not on anybody's land, that he should go the way that would get us out of the rain the fastest. The ground was mushy and I put on a pair of spikes that Nicolosi had carried along for me. I followed my companions in the trailing position.

In a half hour we came to the refuge, placed there by the alpine clubs as a rescue and resting point for skiers and hikers. It was partially on one side. We threw ourselves down on the blankets, putting the rest of our supplies in a pile in front of our feet to help cut off the wind. I placed my bag with the samples near my head. It was damn cold up there, more like a winter's night than autumn. A thousand feet higher patches of snow chalked the mountain's crevices.

Nicolosi was in charge again, here on his familiar land. He asked us to gather some brushwood. We lighted a small fire in front of the refuge. Then we crawled into our blanket sacks and smoked the last cigarette in bed, the calming one, and watched the going fire from the comforting protection of the refuge hut.

Nicolosi broke the bedtime silence.

"The Baron said some things that troubled me."

I looked toward Edoardo, but he did not turn his head. Neither of us said a word.

Nicolosi continued, "Personal family matters. They're not his business."

After a while I said, "I didn't know such nobility existed any longer—what's this 'Baron' stuff?"

Edoardo said, "Every town or region has one. A leftover from the old days. The title is unimportant. He's the power man, the one who has the strength. Brucia happens to have a primitive titled one. I was ready to cut him down."

"It must be hard for an American to understand," Nicolosi said, "but a man like the Baron can be very helpful. You cannot go around antagonizing him. He hasn't kept up his estates without talents of his own—he knows people. For someone marked as a friend, or who is recommended by a friend, he can accomplish things. So he's a Baron in a monarchy that no longer exists. Play along with him. That's the only realistic attitude that works."

"Come on, Nicolosi," I said. "What do you really think of the Baron—apart from what you must think for practical reasons?"

"It's a game of words with the Baron. I don't expect to change things singlehanded."

"You won't have to," I said, surprised to hear myself say so.

"*Beh,*" Nicolosi said, "he can't help it if his father inherited land and passed it on to him. Who knows how I'd act if I owned a few thousand acres?"

"Would you want to be in the Baron's shoes?" I asked him.

Nicolosi said, "Who's paid to think such things? I'm a guide."

"If you don't wish to speak up," I said, "that's okay. I was only asking for your honest opinion."

Edoardo said, "I'll tell you why. He's afraid to say what he really feels in front of an American." He propped himself up on his elbows and looked at me. "I'm not sure myself what your attitude is toward the Baron. That I can say for myself, even if Nicolosi is silent. You're paying us for working for you."

"I don't know what you mean," I said, although I suspected what he meant. "I work for a living, too. I work for a corporation. I have to tolerate things that I don't believe in. I know what Nicolosi means—I know about concessions to survival."

"Here's the way it is here," Edoardo said. "The Baron's a big shot. And to us an American is a big shot, too. We see the same things in the Americans that we see in our local enemies. We see the money, the rich food, the fancy clothes, the long cars. We envy that in our own kind. But then sometimes we see something else in the Americans, too—the passport and the visa dream. So we're half and half. If they recognize us, we like them still more. If they consort with our local enemies, well—"

"So that's what you're thinking," I said, turning to Nicolosi. "The big shots stick with the big shots." In the dark all I could see was the yellow-orange glow of his cigarette. "I sensed that's what it was."

We were silent. I heard only the movement of the wind against the cracks of the hut and the crackling of the burning brushwood. I listened for their regular breathing. But they were awake. Waiting. Franca's father and her friend.

"I'll tell you," I said softly, and my voice was alone and clear, as if speaking to myself. "I think we believe in many similar things. I am more than one contradiction myself, but I cannot be connected to the ideas the Baron stands for. Also, I'm not a big shot—that's the last thing I could be."

When I paused, Edoardo said, "What do *you* think of the Baron?"

"That's easy," I replied. "He's rotten inside."

"Rotten?" Nicolosi repeated. "Yes, that's exactly what he is."

"A bastard of a bastard's son," Edoardo added.

"All right," I said, laughing, "he's probably that, too."

"Now you're talking like a friend," Nicolosi said. "Joseph, I'll say this, you're a different American."

"A thing up the Baron's ass!" Edoardo shouted to the mountain.

They knew I wasn't on the Baron's side, and it made me feel a oneness with them here on the volcanic mountain's western side.

"All the way up and break it off inside!" Edoardo said furiously.

I said, "The same goes for his German friend down there."

Edoardo and Nicolosi joined me in that and also called the Baron terrible names, and they knew some beauties in Sicilian that came across just by the sounds, rich with violence.

I felt good about it all for no reason that had to do with rocks or their valuable properties because all of us felt comfortable here before the embers; and this was a beginning again for a stranger once on these shores. We were companions, and it was a stroke of luck that we had run into the rotten bastard of a Baron because in our common despise of what

119

he meant we had achieved something that pulled us the same way. I was happy that they now knew this side of me: of good intentions.

And tomorrow: I had to remember to rise early, before the others, and chip some samples of precious rock at this level, put them under the concealed instrument, work over their mountain.

CHAPTER SIX

A<small>T DAWN</small> the mountain rumbled. Below me I became aware that there was a powerful, inevitable movement; where, it was not yet possible to surmise. The wind bore an odor of smoking ashes, as if from fires lighted aeons ago and fanned into second life after long, smoldering silences. Nature's forces began to move in.

It was time to move on. I had done my early-morning work in half darkness. While my companions still dozed in their blankets, I shook the weight of sleep from my stirring mind. Lacing my shoes quickly, I slipped out of the hut. One hundred feet in from the roadway, above and out of sight, I took the instrument and brushed it back and forth over the rough land. The needle registered weakly. This surface rock had been leached out by high winds and snows since before man began to claw at the mountain; only extensive drilling hundreds of feet down would tell if anything worth exploring further lay here. I checked the height on the map and noted the samples. On the way back to the hut, I gathered some brushwood for the morning fire. Nicolosi and Edoardo were both up when I returned. I put down the brushwood of pretext near the fire Nicolosi had already begun.

We drank our coffee in silence. In the distance, on the far western side of Etna still shrouded in darkness, the sky fumed in a spreading mushroom of black smoke. I looked anxiously at Nicolosi, waiting for his experienced decision to proceed: up or down. I wondered what a wildcatter like Tabbert would do now; he, with his rationale of loyalty to oneself driving him on to greater efforts for Mediterranean American. The streak of red crayon on his marked map still ordered me to continue higher.

Now reason and with it doubt began to return. Last night I had joined the tirade against the Baron. If the Baron was a bastard, that wasn't my concern. I had not come to Brucia to reform its ways in less than a week. Especially not to take sides. The Baron was right when he hinted that nobody did business without enlisting the power men, such as himself, locally. If the time came for drilling here as a result of my preliminary exploration, it would be the Baron and other estate holders whose co-operation we would need—and who would profit.

Usually the Company managed to enter these primitive corners of the Mediterranean world unnoticed by hiring out the land for other uses to cover the real nature of a development. Sometimes individuals balked. Then it became a straight business relationship which the Company certainly could respect—the philosophy, of course, was that everyone had a price. It worked in the United States; and it worked from Gibraltar to the Red Sea. If the lawyers couldn't achieve it, the public-relations counselors could. Sometimes the landowners would hold out for what they thought were fantastic sums, but this was no obstacle. Once Mediterranean American—M.A.D. some of the cynical employees called the development company—knew the property could be measured in terms of money, it was only a matter of bargaining. A few Cadillacs, air-conditioned if necessary for the warmer climates, and quietly bullet-proofed in Detroit as a precaution against the meddlesome poor, sealed our bargains and showed our good faith.

The Company wisely preferred to deal with the large land-owners rather than with the governments; the former stayed in power, regardless. Tabbert had said that in some stubborn cases foreign governments could be prevailed upon to confiscate land, but the Company preferred not to do things that way; it wasn't businesslike and, besides, there were always closer accountings. For these reasons, it was important not to antagonize people like the Baron who could serve our ends. One couldn't be "merely a scientist"; I remembered that phrase from one of the man-to-man monthly columns by Mr. Paley which appeared in *Pipeline*. One couldn't walk through life armed only with a pickax, a Geiger counter and a microscope; he wrote that "practical factors" had to be weighed.

A volcanic thunderclap signaled far ahead, and echoed in the valleys we had come from. I put on my pack, frightened.

"Do you think we have to turn back?" I asked Nicolosi.

"Here's where we're standing," he said. "The fissure was supposed to be a little above the Valle del Bove and off to the northern slope. Nothing's doing on this side of the roadway. It sounds to me like a friendly one—you know, there must be three hundred fissures on our mountain. Some are dead, some alive, some napping and some sleeping soundly."

"I don't want to be caught near one that you think is sleeping when it's only napping," Edoardo said dryly.

"Naturally, everyone thinks it is coming toward him."

"Sometimes it does," Edoardo said.

"Save your wind for the walk," Nicolosi said.

"Are you sure we can make it safely to the Osservatorio?" I asked, wondering what drove him on. On the mountain, in command, he was more vital.

"Leave it to me," Nicolosi said confidently.

As the sun rose, we began to walk around to the west, crossing off the roadway on an angle in order to conserve our strength and cover more territory with our eyes. Before the houses on the slope had been of stone, surrounded by gardens of cacti and grape vines; later there were orange and lemon trees and fewer houses; then the trees became sturdy chestnuts and evergreens and birchwoods. The land thinned out. Dew wet our trouser cuffs. Some distance below, one house could be seen off the roadway, its corrugated metal roof returning a dazzling reflected light. It belonged to the Baron, and I imagined he and his friend Wernher had had a comfortable night's rest.

On a mountain, I thought, luckily there is always the next step: there is no standing still. We could reach the Osservatorio in two hours of walking. It was the official building maintained by the Government to determine in advance the nature and intensity of these eruptions in order to warn the villages on the slopes. The Osservatorio was the final stop made by the guides because, a thousand feet above, the main crater of Etna gaped open on the sky.

I kept looking toward the fresh wisps of smoke rising through the clouds.

"There's nothing to fear on this ridge," Nicolosi said.

"I trust your judgment," I said. "Do you think they would allow me to use their telephone?"

Edoardo said, "You want to call the gods and ask them to turn off the steam?"

"I never knew their number," I replied.

I wanted to try to speak to Franca. We had been vague. I had to see her—privately—when we came off the mountain. And—perhaps—to speak to Tabbert.

We cut over a wooded area toward the roadway again. Now we were no more than three or four thousand feet from the crater. I could feel the colder air and smell the sulphur dioxide in the wind. We angled our bodies forward under our packs. In the bending roadway, as we toed up, I could sometimes see a break through valleys clear down to the sea below. Here, snowdrifts piled in the niches of the mountain, defying the autumn sun.

Twice I stopped to chip at rock formations. Nicolosi and Edoardo halted, waiting for me to catch up. By this time, neither made an effort to pick up stones as they had done voluntarily the first morning. I avoided the rocks encrusted with an overlay of lava; a deceptive high metallic content without meaning came from the depths of extinct fissures. Nicolosi and Edoardo watched me, standing apart, saying nothing.

A mountain in Sicily again. I couldn't step off the roadway without thinking of the little tapes, our tapes, the British tapes, the enemy tapes, all delineating the impermanent, shifting borders of death. I visualized their cautioning signs— *Achtung Minen,* and ours, Beware of Soft Shoulders. This hard road was home, safe from imagined mines.

When we had walked a half hour, I heard the sound of a motor behind us, and soon a motorcycle tugging an open delivery trailer *pluck-plucked* into sight. The cyclist looked happy to meet us here and asked if we wanted a lift up to the Osservatorio. I laughed aloud; his motor looked as though it could barely pull one passenger, let alone three more. Not that it would make any difference to my work if we rode the rest of the way. There was little topographical change between here and the Osservatorio. We hopped on, the motor flourished and caught, we got off, let the motor wagon move, then got on again, running ahead and hitching one at a time.

"Have you heard any word about the eruption?" I shouted, over the noise.

"Nothing on the western side," the driver said. "First report was something doing around Fornazzo and Milo. Can't always believe the experts. Our butcher's sister lives up around there and she telephoned him. Lots of ash and smoke but nothing to worry about. Try to figure out how lava runs. *Beh.*"

The motor stalled at one point. I ran quickly to the side of the road, chipped off a piece of stone from a ledge, and jumped back on.

"Looking for gold?" the driver kidded, over his shoulder.

I laughed, but Nicolosi turned on the driver, protecting me.

"That's right, gold," Nicolosi said belligerently. "Anything wrong with gold?"

The startled driver said nothing, and for the rest of the way we bunched together, silent.

The large Osservatorio this high on Mount Etna seemed, like so many things in Sicily, grandly out of place. Yet because it was built by men and looked of the city, it gave me a sense of security. Whoever had put up the building had selected an ideal location for detecting the tremors. It was on a slight elevation, apart from the crater line. White patches of snow clung to its eaves. The view from here was beautiful; and frightening. The earth colors blended with snow turned blue by the sky's reflections.

Several men emerged from the building and greeted the driver as if he were bringing provisions to a stranded lighthouse. The vulcanologist, his assistant and a machinist helped to unload the vehicle. Then the driver took off, in low gear, down the roadway and back to Catania.

If the people here were surprised at seeing three strangers arrive, they didn't show it.

"Is anyone interested in warming up by the fireplace?" the vulcanologist asked us.

We thanked him. Our boots crunched over the snow and we stamped our feet before entering the building.

Nicolosi called the vulcanologist the "Professor." His name was Carlo Salomone. He was in his early fifties, a university man who appeared much younger than his age because of a jaunty manner. His gray hair was close-cropped; beneath his bushy brows deep brown eyes twinkled wisely. He seemed part student in spite of his age, part professorial in spite of his youthful looks.

We shed our heavy clothes without invitation. The machinist placed still-green pine branches on the fire, which flared up in smoke, smelling of the forests on the lower slopes. Nicolosi seemed at home here. The Professor did not distinguish between myself, obviously an outsider (so far nobody had failed to recognize me as an American), my guide or porter.

The uncertainty that had haunted me periodically on the mountain returned: I wondered if he suspected my real mission. I compounded the notion crazily . . . someone had been assigned to bring me up here through a series of planned coincidences . . . I was delivered by Nicolosi and Edoardo for cross-examination by an experienced scientist. . . . If I answered the questions truthfully I would be permitted to descend to Franca again . . . or I would be kept here in lofty imprisonment indefinitely away from civilization—it was all a mosaic pieced together with unmatched suppositions.

The Professor's manner was reassuring. "What have you travelers to report to us from the plains?" he asked.

Not, What are you doing on my mountain in the middle of a threatening eruption? Edoardo and Nicolosi, sensing that explanations would have to come from me, offered nothing but the pleasantries. Well, it was bound to come out.

I parried, hoping he would not withdraw the hand of friendship.

"We came up here, Professor, to inquire about the danger," I said evasively.

"Oh, yes, the eruption," he replied matter-of-factly.

"If there is any possibility of its coming down on this slope. Or toward Brucia."

The Professor said, "One must consult the machines. You wanted to know only that?"

I nodded. He did not pursue the point.

He ushered us toward the basement of the Osservatorio. A room there was filled with table cabinets, covered with glass, holding small machines. These wriggled with continuously-writing instruments like drugstore window pens which execute perfect interlocking ovals automatically.

"These are ways to detect activity," the Professor said. "But we also like to believe that up here we have a clearer use of our brains to judge what comes in through our senses."

"Do these instruments predict the direction?" I asked him. "I'm familiar with the seismograph from my own laboratory work."

"The seismograph," the Professor said. "Very simple, as any fundamental instrument must be, whether it slows down fissionable matter or registers the shocks of eruptions. Machines are very sensible in their way. For us, as you can imagine, the seismograph registers a meaning more imperative than for someone living in Rome or New York or even Catania. I myself am from Rome. In Rome, the authorities do not particularly care what happens when the lava overflows in the plains below as long as there is a good seismograph here. That completes responsibility." My companions nodded, agreeing with anyone who found fault with the authorities in Rome. "This one, gentlemen, is a good seismograph. I helped to make it after the war."

"Did the Professor really invent this machine?" Nicolosi asked, awed.

"Not invent, but I did build it. There's a company in Berlin which makes many for export. None of ours are German made. But that's another story. Anyway, the scribblings made by the stylus determine how strong a disturbance is. Now, take a close look. Wouldn't you say there is an eruption?"

Nicolosi peered over Edoardo's shoulder. He exclaimed that the lines were running up and down.

"There must be an eruption on Etna somewhere," said the Professor, smiling. I wondered if he was playing down the danger for our benefit. "But do not be alarmed because that needle has oscillated for several days that way. Etna is not the best place to look at a seismograph for the first time—too alarming. If the oscillations were this irregular on the machine in Rome, you could be sure that the central crater was blowing. But our seismograph is accurate, too, unless the mountain blows it away altogether."

We laughed with him, nervously.

I read the label on one of the instruments.

"Here's one," I said, pleased, "that was manufactured in the U.S.A."

"Yes, I don't mind using American machines," he said. "It's a seismotron. The first one of its kind—it works with this cylindrical pick-up and a pair of magnetic earphones. Like an electronic stethoscope which predicts rock falls before they occur."

As we left the roomful of instruments, I said impatiently, "I still wonder if it's dangerous for us to move around above the Osservatorio."

The Professor walked over to a large wall map.

"We're here," he said. "The fumes are coming from this lower slope. I have already warned the villages on the plain below. They are alerted for evacuation. Above that particular fissure, up here, we are out of danger."

Edoardo's finger traced a course downward on the map. Quickly, he said, "Brucia is in the line of danger."

"The ridges there are so formed that if the fissure blows, the momentum will carry it on fixed lines to the sea. Are you from Brucia?"

"Our families are there," Nicolosi said.

Nicolosi looked toward me. As my guide, he was committed to our arrangement.

I walked around the vast hallway of the Osservatorio, went to the door, and peered outside for a clue to the threatening eruption. A wind bore the rotten smell of sulphur through a crack and caught nauseatingly in my throat. Standing in the doorway, I heard bells tolling; for an instant I thought I was hearing things in this snow-capped world.

I returned to the room; the Professor was not in sight.

"He plays those bells beautifully, doesn't he?" his assistant said. "I never tire of them."

"That's his dream," Nicolosi said. "The sound carries—I hear them whenever I'm anywhere near the Osservatorio."

The Professor called down from the loggia running around the hallway. "You're right, Nicolosi, my dream." He had overheard. "Every mountain man carries a vision. Your circus, for example, which I have heard you mention."

Edoardo turned to me in an aside. "The Professor and Nicolosi—two men living in the past."

Nicolosi said, "The 'Flying Nicolosi.' You saw us perform, didn't you?"

The Professor spoke down from the upper story, "Once in Naples."

"We toured from town to town," Nicolosi said, for my benefit. "We would take turns as clowns, in tumbling acts, feats of magic, directing the trick dogs. The troupe carried my name—there were four of us—and we tried to give the impression we were brothers because that appealed to audiences. They love performing families. In the last act, a grand finale, the 'Flying Nicolosi' exploded in smoke from the mouth of a cannon! Oh, well, real families broke us up. My daughters were born, the others in the troupe got married. We see one another once in a while and magnify what we did—not boasting, but you know what sentiment does to the truth. Mind you, I'm not sorry that my children got in the way of the act. But the 'Flying Nicolosi' were fun. Someone should invent a way of making life more of a circus."

Franca's father had his unfulfilled dreams, too.

The Professor descended and joined us in the hallway. The echo of bells still sounded in my ears. I searched for the telephone, but it was not in this room.

"Yes, even vulcanologists on mountain peaks," the Professor said. "You have your circuses, Nicolosi, I have my bell ringing. That is what I would like to do: ring church bells all the day long. It is one of the most artful occupations. One needs endless time and is controlled by time, patience, virtue

130

and religion, but the only one of these virtues I have is time. Not to work but to ring a carillon all the day for a village in Tuscany. That would be most satisfying to me. I could be away from all the tragedy, not harming anyone, full of good music, bringing a classic order to life. When I was a student, many years ago, I did what I wanted, I rang the bells for a small church near Rome. I keep in practice against the time when I can be a carillonneur."

He paused, but the sequence was inevitable in this atmosphere.

"And what would you like to do later, Mr. Borken?" he asked.

I said, "I'm not ready to look that far ahead. I've got a mark to make yet."

"Oh, everyone who works deserves to think about a contemplative time."

"It depends on what kind of work you do," Nicolosi said, laughing. "I wouldn't mind being a philanthropist when I'm old."

The Professor said, "One cannot be a complete creature of municipalities or corporations—they are man-made and impermanent."

The Professor's assistant turned to me. "What is your work, Mr. Borken?"

It had come this far. I did not mind telling the vulcanologist, as another scientist, but I wondered how it would strike Nicolosi, with his instinctive human nature. Edoardo was easier to predict; his warmth was hidden beneath a tough hide.

All of them directed their eyes on me.

"I'm only a student of rocks," I said.

The Professor's assistant said, "A geologist, correct?"

"Yes."

"Are you writing a paper on volcanic rock?" the Professor asked. "They are the most interesting. Much variety here, in

131

the lower slopes, where the lava has flowed in some of the dried-up river beds. Are you studying with the Americans at Perugia?"

"Oh, no, I finished my school work after the war. It's my job."

Nicolosi and Edoardo looked up.

The Professor smiled. "But that is your bell ringing, is it not? Ideal—out of doors all the time. Well, have you found any good rocks on our mountain?"

I said, "A few . . ."

The Professor asked, "Precious ones?"

"A good joke," said Nicolosi. "Imagine finding gold and silver on Etna."

"I'm serious," the Professor said. "Mr. Borken can tell you more, I am sure. The precious metals used as currency are base metals for the first time in history compared to other metals in the world today. Even gold and silver cannot purchase these."

Edoardo said, "Such as our own sulphur quarries here? Sicily has more sulphur than any country in the world, but where has that got us?"

"Yes, sulphur is certainly important on the island," the Professor said. "But there are other minerals here—graphite, lead, zinc, iron ore. And what else in small quantities I don't know. But rock formations are not my specialty. Mr. Borken, you are more expert. Men who say little know much."

"I'm the wrong person," I said. "I'm no expert on Sicily's rocks, not in the company of people who've lived here all their lives."

Silence. They seemed to say, in their silence, that, since the Professor himself had requested it, my refusing to speak was impolite.

Desperately, I thought of Tabbert and Mediterranean American, of the Company's cause and my personal cause, of the chances of blowing the assignment, ironically, by telling the real purpose of the exploration. But these were individuals, and I felt a greater need for their friendship.

132

"It is really more complex than sulphur. I am seeking something unlike it, a metallic element. I don't know what it is called here, but in my country it is called carnotite."

The word was out, the true mission on the mountain revealed.

"Carnotite," Nicolosi said, his mouth encircling the strange word.

Edoardo met my look of uncertainty toward him.

"Is it more valuable than sulphur?" Nicolosi asked.

"Much more," said the Professor, answering for me. "But what makes you think there is any to be found around here?"

"The sulphur," I said, "occurs in large quantities in volcanic regions. It forms yellow crusty masses. Carnotite often appears in this form—we call the concentrate yellowcake. Coloring is one indication of the quality of rock. We are not sure, but the search is worth the chance. The chance is that the same aging and conditions hundreds of thousands of years ago which produced carnotite deposits in Colorado and many thousands of feet above sea level in New Mexico could produce it here."

"Colorado, cowboys, Indians!" the assistant said, shooting with his thumb and index finger.

"I see you've seen some American movies," I said. "The cowboys have probably left their ranches and are out prospecting for carnotite."

From within the mountain, we heard a deep-centered rumbling, audible for the first time since the early morning. Nicolosi walked over to the window and looked anxiously toward the summit, then strained his body to sweep the view below. He turned not to me but to the Professor.

"Brucia and the other towns would become wealthy if this was discovered on our mountain?"

Edoardo interrupted, "Who says so? The Baron would probably have his fingers in it somehow long before the Americans left the country. Sulphur or anything else, here it stays the same."

The Professor remained silent. But his assistant could not restrain himself; his face mirrored the scowl on Edoardo's face.

"Would you say what this carnotite is used for?"

I could not conceal what he could read in a modern physics textbook. He knew the answer, I was sure, but wanted me to come out and say it.

"Carnotite is a uranium source."

The word exploded like a grenade in the still air of the room. Nicolosi repeated: "Uranium." The Professor nodded slowly. Edoardo, with whom I had declared an emotional truce last night in the mountain hut, lashed out.

"Do you work for the United States Sixth Fleet?" he said bitterly.

"Of course not," I replied calmly.

"Your fleet here has atomic weapons—isn't that your business?"

"I don't know what they have. I have nothing to do with the Government."

"But uranium is for their weapons," Edoardo shouted. "What's the difference?"

"Look here," I said, "I have nothing to do with the Army or the Navy or the Government. I work for a private company. It is neither illegal nor dishonest, understand?"

"We have been helping him in this evil task—carrying his supplies," Edoardo said. "So he can discover uranium for weapons? So Sicily can be a new arsenal—another battlefield? So that—"

The Professor broke into this tirade. "What do you want from this gentleman?" he asked.

"I want nothing from him," Edoardo said coldly.

"Then will you permit me to say something?" the Professor said. "I am a man of science, too. So is Mr. Borken. Up here, I think, our view is larger. Let us show some tolerance. If he were not looking, can we not assume that someone else would,

134

from his country or another or even ours? That is a starting point of personal judgment in this case."

It was as if I were on trial before them. I found myself listening intently to his rationale.

Something of the same thinking had entered my mind occasionally in the last year of work for Mediterranean American. Yet in New York, in the momentum of a large office, with its routine, its records, and its monthly IBM paycheck, there was little time for introspection. Employees who left surreptitiously, muttering against the corporation to which we all paid homage, disappeared into a void beyond Mediterranean American; such people became untouchables, sneered at over the luncheon drinks and forgotten. I had never seriously questioned the work I was engaged in—until the incident concerning Von Loesch had marred my record.

"You must make yourself separate the moral man from the job he may be doing at the moment," the Professor said. "If you are disappointed in what our friend here is doing, be disappointed in his work rather than in him. The two, the man and his work, are separable in these times. We—at least I—do not know what sort of person Mr. Borken is, his life, whether he is single or married, but I am willing to give him the benefit of a doubt. He seems to me a most gentle American. Is there any one of you who can say I am wrong?"

I walked away, toward the window of the Osservatorio. The volcanic sounds on the mountain became audible again, but nothing ominous to the eye was visible from here. Only the blackened waste of the final rock ledge leading to the central crater loomed ahead.

The Professor understood the nature of my work. I had to swing him to my side in front of them. I did not want to irritate Nicolosi. He was Franca's father; I deferred to him. Edoardo I could handle on my own terms.

The Professor asked me what instruments I used in the search. He had willingly shown me his. I reached into my personal pack, which I had concealed so carefully from my climbing companions, and unstrapped the Geiger counter. He and his assistant examined it closely, and Nicolosi and the machinist here watched them. Edoardo refused to allow himself to look.

The vulcanologists and I talked now on scientific terms. Their interest in the geological work in their own land overcame any hostility to the search for uranium. I had had enough for a while on the subject of rocks. The passing afternoon eased the tensions in the room, and we ate quietly around the fireplace, so convenient for consuming the enflamed emotions that licked at their thoughts.

Nicolosi said resignedly, "*Beh.*"

And the Professor said softly, "So this time it's carnotite." He regarded me without animosity. "I suppose that is the way it must be in Sicily, my friends, that is the importance of the island to the Rome Government and to others who have never heard of our land. Sicily was important during the war, too, at least for a few months. It was good for military reputations. I have read some of the memoirs of your generals. Up here one has much time to read."

He looked at his watch, excused himself, went up to the roof to his carillon, and returned as quietly.

"There are all kinds of scientists, but we are human beings, too, are we not? We are products of experiences outside our specific knowledge. You have heard of the Todt labor battalions that the Germans had working for them during the war?" I said that I had, of course, and Nicolosi scowled at the mention of the name. "I was conscripted by them, with the kind help of the Fascist Government, as a labor supervisor. We worked in the sulphur mines. The sulphur—as your uranium—is used for explosives. Somewhat smaller. The forced laborers also did the dirty work, dug toilets, carried supplies, helped place the mines in the roads to blow up the Allied vehicles."

"You did that?" I said, smiling. "You kept me busy for a year. My job was to remove the mines!"

"I trust you did a more efficient job of it," the Professor said. He had, at least, calmed some nerves.

"Luckily, when I was captured, the British recognized that the Todt laborers were forced to do what they did. I was released. Then I tried to reconcile all the years of scientific study with what I had seen and heard over the long years of war and political famine. I wanted some sort of work that would give me a crust of bread without having to trouble with the major problems of the world, my country, or myself. I went underground. I avoided the dozens of amenities necessary to get ahead in overcivilized society. It was monastic thinking, and bell ringing was the symbol of my resignation. I took this assignment sitting on top of Etna. The world did not follow me up here, temporarily.

"And then I began to read in the scientific journals—none of us can really be isolated—that the search was on again for what they called the critical materials. Sicily, as usual, was mentioned as one of the potential sources of minerals. I wondered, then, how many other small and unimportant places, generally useless to governments, forgotten when it comes to improvements and reforms, would be stirred again."

Nicolosi looked puzzled for a moment. "You expected us?" he inquired.

"Not you or you," the Professor said. "No one in particular. But you could say that I expected Mr. Borken theoretically."

Nicolosi nodded.

"Sicily isn't the only place where there are scientists seeking these materials," I said. "One thing cannot be discounted. Our journals have reported mines going twenty-four hours a day in Saxony and in Czechoslovakia."

The Professor said, "But I do not, for myself, follow the behavior of people I do not respect. I have my own conscience to heed."

I said defensively, "There can be good which comes of this, too—employment and the development of peaceful enterprises that can bring well-being to the Catania plain."

"Brucia wants no part of such advantages," Edoardo muttered.

"Don't they?" Nicolosi said. "I wouldn't try to ask them." He nodded to himself. "Anyway, I can't think that this carnotite will be found here. Every inch of this soil has been dug and redug and tilled and eroded for two thousand years. Whatever good is left in the soil is the excrement that the animals have put back. All we have here is lava, which even nature rejects."

Outside, another volcanic shudder blasted the stillness of the mountain. The sound magnified upward at this height. I asked the Professor if he would show me the instruments registering. We went downstairs, alone. I took a hurried look at the seismograph registering its penmanship of catastrophe.

"Is your telephone down here?"

He pointed toward a small desk in a darkened corner.

"May I make a call? It is important."

He said apologetically that I would be required to pay for it because of regulations. He switched on a desk lamp and I reached for the telephone. He busied himself with one of the machines, out of hearing range.

I lifted the receiver and after a long minute an operator asked for the number. I whispered Franca's number, but the operator asked me to repeat it, louder, and I watched the stairway and listened for footsteps. I heard the crackle of static, as if this were a call across the Atlantic instead of only thousands of feet down the mountain from here. Two operators in Catania and Brucia argued politely.

Then I heard her voice pierce the noise on the wire and we shouted wildly at each other to make ourselves clear. She asked where I was calling from and I said from the Osservatorio and she asked how her father was and I said all right and I asked how she was and she was all right and she had heard of the possibility of an eruption on the mountain and were we careful, was I, I, Joseph, watching myself and how was Edoardo and when were we descending and I said we would be off the mountain tomorrow and that is what I was calling about (and the operators clawed each other again) because, because I must see you Franca, alone, the two of us, and she laughed in unpremeditated love and said to me, I will see you, Joseph, and I said that when we had come down Etna I would be at the hotel and she would meet me there, alone, alone, and I lowered my voice and whispered love and (the crackling of static) it was over, the telephone clicking off into a vast subterranean silence.

"Did you get your party?" the Professor asked, coming away from the seismograph, hearing that I had hung up.

"Yes, thank you." I gave him several hundred lire to cover the cost, and he returned one of the bills to me, saying the remainder would surely be enough, and I thanked him again.

Upstairs, I looked at Edoardo, wondering if he could see in my face that I had heard her voice again.

The Professor liberated long-contained thoughts. "Etna was always the place for forging the weapons of war. How ironical of history if again it is used. Virgil said that the furnaces of Vulcan fashioned implements of war for Mars beneath here. When the smoke rose from the crater it indicated to the civilizations of those times that the gods were busy making weapons, for their own good and righteous side of the war, naturally. Nobody, no country, Mr. Borken, ever suspected that the resources of a region did not exist for their purposes. So it was when the Caesars ruled Rome, and again when the new Duce came into power. And today."

"But you cannot compare all its conquerors evenly," I said. "Genuine efforts were made on the island after the fighting stopped to help the people caught between the crossfire of war and occupation."

"True, true," said Nicolosi. "There was help at the beginning. And hope."

Edoardo looked at me accusingly, and said, "Now only the smell of war brings people back here. Sicily is a war barometer. When things are hot, suddenly the admirals discover that the island is the largest in the Mediterranean. Sicily is no longer a beggar on the coattails of Italy: suddenly, we're a crossroads."

The Professor shook his head, and said, "For me the value of the lava is not in how much carnotite it covers but in its timeless story. That is the real wealth here on the mountain. It is what might be more profitably taken away by the men and companies. Just as the crater and cones erupt periodically, so the world. But this is uncontrollable and man is humiliated by it, unable to control his own explosive forces— his man-made troubles. The monoliths of the world today all have the ultimate weapons, the mushrooming bombs and missiles, and these can give the world its final warning. Sanity may arise from fear, fear may bring stalemate, stalemate can lead to ultimate sanity. Here, on Etna, the natural forces of disaster unify our thoughts. This knowledge of a greater force can resurrect us humbly. It is something to bring back to earth, together with the minute chips of rock."

The mountain outside the Osservatorio was silent, temporarily. The blue-blackness had crept up the snow line, brushing on twilight. I went to a window. It was comforting to gaze out, and my eyes moved to the summit and the sky above, now nearer and more intimate. The open slopes shone with rich pathways of light, as if illuminated by giant bulbs; but in some corners, beyond where the cool winds of night penetrated and became trapped in the snow pits, where the snow was swept aside on the steep escarpments and no patch of sward thrived, the mountain was shadowy and obscure.

I wanted to see the sun rising over the peaks of Etna. Not for the job; I had nearly all the samples that could reveal the geologic information on the mountain. The final thousand feet from the Osservatorio to the top were too remote for development even if a seam existed. Snow covered the summit most of the year. Going the distance was this challenge: to see clearly.

140

We lay down on the wooden floor, spreading packs and blankets, at the invitation of the Professor. He had had his say: exposing my mission, yet accepting me by his fireplace. I wondered if all the others in the room were as kindly disposed.

By five in the morning, I felt as if I had barely closed my eyes. I got up, looked out, and lighted a cigarette. One of the heaps on the floor stirred. I thought that instead of trying to sleep for another hour I would wait it out. Quietly, Nicolosi and Edoardo arose. They fumbled in the darkness for their clothing. It was too late to tell them to relax in sleep. Somehow in the still dark I found the bathroom. Then they washed and rolled our packs.

I whispered, "Hear anything?"

"What?" Nicolosi yawned.

"You think it's blown out?"

"Who knows?" he said quietly.

"Maybe we ought to check before going on. Those instruments are sensitive. I think I can read to see if there's any further danger."

"I would not do so," Edoardo declared. "Don't go near the Professor's instruments."

"What's the matter with eyes and ears?" Nicolosi said.

"Okay with me. You're my guide."

We had said our goodbyes last night to the Professor and his assistant and machinist. If anything serious developed, we would know soon enough.

We stepped outside on the mountain. We adjusted one another's packs, as if this was a morning a half week—weeks it seemed—ago. The cold air ripped into the openings of our faces.

Nicolosi led. We started down the flat pathway which extended for some few hundred feet against the sides of the warm building. Then at a bend we stopped. To the left one thousand feet up was the summit, with its huge central crater;

to the right, the roadway leading down toward the town of Brucia and the pine forests and the villages of the Catania plain. And Franca . . .

The choice at the fork, the very thought that it was a choice, struck me forcefully. Nicolosi hesitated, as if waiting for some supernatural guidance. I felt, in spite of my personal reason for being in Brucia, the need to continue. Etna was nothing to Nicolosi, to Edoardo, and at the same time everything, the towering mountain above their town. I wanted to go on for myself, not for Mediterranean American, but to round off a personal meaning.

I walked around Edoardo, pushing him aside accidentally, and stepped in front of Nicolosi. Edoardo was caught off-balance and spun into a pile of snow. He arose quickly and came charging toward me. I wheeled at the last moment and tripped him by throwing my pack at his feet. He rolled and jumped over it and rushed at me, knocking me to the ground. We piled and turned on each other, breathing angrily and grunting, fighting from instinct now but without any reason. Then we broke apart and began to circle.

Nicolosi stepped in between, yelling, "What the hell is this all about?"

Neither of us spoke, stoking up anger, our hands clenched.

"What's the matter with you, Edoardo? Are you starting something?"

"No."

Nicolosi turned to me, his face pained, asking, "What's wrong?"

"Nothing," I said. I would not reveal the roots of our rivalry.

"Come on, then," he said, "let's grow up."

He spoke paternally.

I picked up my pack, strapped myself in, and looked toward the summit.

"I'm going ahead," I announced.

Neither of them moved.

I started to walk, heeling sideways but unhurried, up the last stretch of mountain. The pathway narrowed from the broad flat around the Osservatorio. The blackness of the ground deepened. I did not look back, knowing that they would have to follow. In a few moments they had caught up and I could hear them breathing behind me. My excitement at reaching the summit grew. It was dangerous and assertive; it broke the normal pattern. I continued. The road became steeper. The summit seemed now only a long hand's clutch, but it was actually many hundreds of feet from where I stood. Winds, subhuman and animal-like in their shrillness, perforated the air up here, and yet there were huge silences. Ahead, the snow-crowned peak stood in cold immaculate splendor.

And then, as I took another step forward, I turned to look back at them. They trudged along, only employees of mine, subcontractors, so to speak, of Mediterranean American, under packs they found burdensome, and I realized they were being put upon by me. They did not want to continue to the top. Nicolosi, I knew, hoped to get down quickly to see that his family was safe in Brucia. Edoardo, for his own reasons, did not want to help me in my work. Each step forward they took served me, but it hurt them. I was driving them unwillingly, as the unseen Company urged me on, for another chip of rock.

I stopped short, suddenly aware that to gain their fellowship and respect formed a greater challenge to me than the vain desire to see the crater.

There were higher summits to reach for than this one.

"Where are you going?" I yelled down. They were twenty or thirty feet below.

"We will stick closer," Nicolosi said, not understanding.

"You're going the wrong way," I shouted.

They both opened their hands widely in motions of confusion.

I pointed to the crater with one hand and then, still pointing, crossed the palm of my other hand against my muscle obscenely.

"Screw the mountain!" I yelled.

"You, Joseph, what say?" Edoardo yelled back, incredulous.

"Hey, *beh!*" Nicolosi screamed.

They rushed up and I tumbled down the short distance toward them. And now no distance stood between us.

Nicolosi came up to me, laughing and smiling. "Don't you want to see the crater?"

"The hell with the crater," I said, grinning.

"It's a very impressive hole," Edoardo said, laughing.

"Sure, sometime I'll see it," I said. "Look, you've both done your work, you've helped me, you've led and followed."

"We'll be honest about it," Nicolosi said. "There may be some trouble on the plain. I feel it, no matter what the instruments show."

"Let's go, then."

Nicolosi turned on Edoardo and said, "Well, what do you say now?"

Edoardo stuck out his mittened hand. We shook, and again I felt the bond we had that night after leaving the lodge of the Baron and his German friend.

I said, "Nicolosi doesn't know the way up, anyway; he'd probably get us all lost."

From the Osservatorio, we heard the sound of bells ringing, echoing on the mountain. We checked our watches by the carillon, standing still, awed.

Then we pounded one another's packs securely, entwined if only briefly, and began the long walk down. Forgetting the consequences, doing what emotion and not cold sense dictated, this I knew now: I was involved.

CHAPTER SEVEN

Night began to fold and find common cause with morning on the mountain. Our boots crunching on the snow and rock magnified the silence. No animal life existed in the lava region; even the sparse vegetation appeared masked in grayness. The air grew lean and cool, the wind more gentle and familiar. My companions moved downward swiftly. If we kept up the pace we would be in Brucia again early in the afternoon. I knew, following the compass of human instinct, that this was my direction.

We turned on the roadway below the Osservatorio and found ourselves moving sideways along an escarpment. Now the lava grayness returned to planetoid recesses and dawn colored the sky. For the first time since going past the Baron's lands on the lower slopes we saw the whole sweep of the valleys below: the encrusted sides of the deserted regions and the pine-forested hills and, beyond, where the faintness of the new day lighted the horizon, the Monel-metal surface of the Ionian Sea flowing along the coast line of Sicily.

After walking hard for an hour, we paused hungrily on a

ledge of rock. Resting, we opened packs and stretched out, taking time to chew on some hard goat-milk cheese. From here we watched the early light creeping up the slopes, up the groves and villages perched everlastingly on these mountains, up the landscape of silvery white-green and black-green, green that was white and green that smoked blackly in the trees, smearing rose-pink light in the rising, glaring, harsh Sicilian morning.

Suddenly we saw it. The sight widened our eyes in fear. As the sun illuminated our field of vision, directly below on the eastern slope we noticed a steaming cloud forming from a fissure. Here was the cause of the squiggling alarm recorded on the seismographs. We strained forward on the ledge of rock and looked intently through the delicate morning mist. The depth of the fissure appeared bottomless. From its center small cracks radiated. A bubbling stone-gray liquid stream of lava oozed from the fissure.

Nicolosi looked concerned. He sniffed the air authoritatively.

"It smells the same as around Fornazzo," Edoardo muttered.

They had been on volunteer rescue duty there a few years before.

"The lava went into the Fontanelle River then."

I asked, "How about Brucia?"

Neither of them replied. The path of the lava was uncertain; the answers lay hidden beneath the vaults of the mountain.

Now I sniffed the finely ground powder ash, rock, scrub and burning sulphur. The whole fissure line was scorched within the abyss where the steaming hole had blown. A vaporous fumarole of gases filled the nostrils; freshets of wind moving briskly at this height fought in the air with the sulphurous smell of a hundred thousand rotten eggs.

The full morning brightness now brought out an ominous scene. The wonder of the sunrise was overwhelmed by the

146

eruption; transfixed, we watched the crawling caterpillar of hissing lava sliding down its slope, slowly, inches at a time.

It seemed hardly to move, and I asked them, "Is it going slower than usual?"

"Now very slowly," Nicolosi said, without taking his eyes off the sliding stream. "It all depends on the line, everything depends on the incline."

"Is it very big inside and below?"

"It looks like a minor one to me," Edoardo said.

"You know these things?" Nicolosi said.

"I didn't say. It may get better or worse." Edoardo appeared defensive. "Why don't you ask Joseph here? He's an expert on mountains, the properties they contain, their true worth—"

"Pipe down!" Nicolosi said tensely. Edoardo's tongue still flicked almost uncontrollably. "What's eating you, anyway? What do you want from Joseph? He's concerned for Brucia."

"All I wanted to know," I said, trying to calm them both, "is if there's any danger to the places inhabited directly below. Could it reach the Baron's place or Vittorio's?"

"That depends on the incline," Nicolosi said. "Some people have different theories, even superstitions, about the volcanic rock flowing here. I side with those who think it's the slope of the mountain that determines the lava stream." He pointed to the stream of lava and traced its course from the fissure. "Then some think that what counts is the nature of the ash and the weight it carries forward."

"The Catania vulcanologists talk two ways," Edoardo said. "I heard one last year. He said that there is something deep down inside that determines if the stuff is coming at you or fizzing out. That what counts is the nature of the rock underneath, that it has been predetermined years ago. Before all the civilizations that came and lived and got buried here, almost from the time that God created the mountains. When He rested on the seventh day, the devil in the mountain started his work deep inside the earth to protest the stresses and strains."

"That's a lot of mythical nonsense," Nicolosi said. "I lean to the incline theory." And he added, "Anyway, God is on the side of people in valleys."

The sound of their voices on the shelf of rock was interrupted by a steam blast rising from somewhere in the volcanic ash. The lava path opened up as if hollowed from a decayed tree trunk that had been smeared with layers of dripping black pitch. For moments the pit lay visibly alive and then the two sides of lava issuing from the crack in the mountain came together again, and the stream continued to crawl downward as the steam from the blast dissolved.

We watched this spectacle of violent nature from our hunched position on the escarpment. The lava mass changed constantly as it moved. It had two arms, a forestream trickling thin tentacles into the land's openings and a second, heavier stream snaking ponderously and falling deeply into the exploring stream's path. We observed with morbid fascination. The sun reached its early-morning zenith, bluing the sky, and soon it hung in front of our shelf. Clouds which had fogged the morning with a glaze of dew turned cottony.

And now the lava stream clearly began to bend in the direction of the coastal villages, away from the diverting river bed which had caught and sunk the hot ashes in the past. Along the ridges which acted as a retaining wall we saw the forestream coursing steadily.

"The wrong season," Nicolosi said, his face strained. He signaled us to get up and put on the packs again. "A few months before or after, but not now, not now. If the snow hadn't melted or if it were another time we would have had snow in the opening and that would have carried the lava over. The people down there usually pack the snow in for the summer months and use it for ice, but it's all melted or removed, and this has become a raceway instead of a barrier."

"Where does it lead?"

"To the next barrier."

"Can it hold the stream?"

"Providence forgot to provide hills in the path of these eruptions," Edoardo answered. "That the saints and our bishop couldn't allow for Brucia. The people on the other side of the mountain, yes, but not us."

Nicolosi moved quickly. And I followed his feet which now seemed to dance down the mountain, stepping in and out of rough places in the roadway and continuing a fast pace for his younger companions. We raced on, exhilarated by the height, and now there was only one thought in our minds regardless of the doubts that had developed among us when they discovered that they were helping me to locate carnotite for Mediterranean American. We wanted to reach Brucia, each for his own reason.

A few hundred yards later we came face to face with a sign announcing that all the land to the right of the highway was posted. There were irregular fences of wood and piled stone. Barbed wire interlaced the top of the stone but with many breaks where trespassers could walk through if they tried. The Baron's name was printed below; I had seen none of these warnings the night before, in the rain, but Nicolosi knew of the private hunting lands.

We stuck to the road, carefully avoiding the Baron's land. I saw the lodge. There was a small truck parked near the entrance. It was just what we needed to get to Brucia quickly. The truck was partly loaded with supplies and indefinite shapes underneath heavy tarpaulin. I could not tell whether they were preparing to go down quickly, too, ahead of the crawling stream of lava, or if this was loaded from the hunting day before when we had seen the Baron and his German friend behind their glistening shotguns. I was still trying to get the lay of the land and their situation when we heard the Baron's dogs snarling. But with the stench of the lava gases on the mountain, the animals could not smell us. They tumbled wildly in front of the stone house, playing hard or frightened.

Nicolosi stepped forward near an opening in the stone fence. I heard a grinding click. A trap shut around his foot and he fell to the ground, gritting his teeth and muttering in the back of his throat. I sprang toward his fallen body a second after Edoardo. A spring held his ankle as if he were a trapped hare. He clawed at the iron clamps in shock and pain, trying to break the grip. Cursing through clenched teeth, he rolled on the ground. But he did not cry out. Edoardo tried to separate the jaws of the trap. He pulled desperately but could not work it until we each took a side and slid out Nicolosi's foot. Blood spotted his trousers. We ripped off his shoes and stretched him on the ground. Above his ankle two slashing iron teeth marks had sunk into his flesh.

"Get the sulfa and bandages," I ordered Edoardo.

"We haven't any," he said, bewildered.

"In my pack at the bottom," I said. "A little Red Cross tin box."

He opened the straps on my pack, and his hand reached through the rock samples I had collected. Carefully, he placed the samples back in the pack.

I sprinkled the sulfa on the flesh wounds and asked Nicolosi if it hurt.

"Like knives," he said, gritting.

"This will prevent infection. I've seen it work before."

"The poor animals," he said.

"It won't hurt. It's only in the flesh, luckily."

"Very lucky," Edoardo said. "That damn Baron."

"The big hunter," I added. "With the shotguns in the rain and the dogs and traps."

Nicolosi's color began to return to his face as the initial shock wore off. It was a dreadful thing being caught without warning this way, all the more painful because of the surprise. It wasn't a bad wound; I had seen worse.

But Nicolosi couldn't walk the rest of the way, that was

certain. Now we had to get a ride down in the Baron's truck. The thought occurred to each of us at the same time.

"Don't try to stand up," I said to Nicolosi. He began to struggle on one foot. "Don't worry, we'll get you down the mountain." He pushed himself and stood on his good foot and then stepped down on both. He took a few tentative steps and announced that he was all right, but we would not allow him to put his shoe on over the bandage. I felt a responsibility for him; he was guiding me, in my employ—and he was Franca's father. I had to get him down.

Damn the Baron and his friend! They were responsible for this. They were holding us up. They were keeping us from where we wanted to be most of all. Their trap had detained us; only their truck could make up for it.

I told Nicolosi and Edoardo to wait where they were. I would go down to the stone lodge and persuade the Baron to take us down in his truck.

They shook their heads to indicate that I would not be able to bring it off.

"I have a plan," I said. It was up to me; the Baron would ignore them.

I bent down and wrenched the iron trap from its burial place in the ground. I examined it closely. Through all the years I had never before seen a hunting trap. It was so like an anti-personnel mine. Plant in the ground, concealed, wait for your prey, for the hasty or the foolish move, then spring and explode. And it worked two ways. If you were on the other side, the hunted, proceed cautiously, unarm the mines, fool them instead. They could be the attackers, especially with game, but how good were they on the defensive, against a man?

I put my arm around Nicolosi's shoulder, holding him this way for the first time.

"You'll ride down in the truck," I said with assurance. "You're going to be okay. We'll have you in Brucia in a few hours, in your own bed."

"I'm feeling all right. Don't worry about me. It was just the shock of those damn irons. I never expected it."

"You just have to have the wound looked at, that's all. You'll be hopping around in a day or two. That sulfa will keep it clean until we get there."

"I don't want to hold up anyone."

"What do you mean anyone?" I said. "We're here together." He looked at me gratefully.

"Anyway, this will get us down sooner. You'll see."

"How can that be?" Edoardo asked. "We have to move. The lava is not standing still."

"They have to move, too, don't they?" I said. "They've got a truck. Right?"

"There's no chance that they'll share it with us," Edoardo said. "They're loading it with their own stuff. There's plenty in the lodge to take down. It's in danger up here."

"Leave it to me," I heard myself saying boldly. "We'll all be on that truck when it goes."

"You, maybe, an American," Edoardo said, "but we'll be left behind. You heard him speaking to me—there's nothing he'd like better than to see me stuck here. And Nicolosi's no better off if he can't help the Baron in some way."

"Not only am I going to see that we're on that truck," I said resolutely, "but I'm going to show those people."

"Who, that guest with him? What do you mean?"

"Yes, the German hunter and the Baron, they're the same to me."

I looked down the trail toward the stone house. There was no sign of human life stirring, no movement toward the truck. I knew what I had to do. It was necessary. I felt a tightness in my chest as I stared at the scene below, the comfortable place surrounded by barbed wire, and my eyes narrowed in anger, long contained, long recalled.

I said, "I'm going to straighten out those people in the bargain."

Edoardo said, "Don't do anything that'll get you in trouble."

"Why shouldn't I?"

"You can't fight those people on their home grounds."

"This is my home grounds, too. I know what I'm doing."

"Be careful."

"You'll see."

I took a last look at Nicolosi, stretched out on the ground, and picked up the iron trap. I said, "Cover me," and Edoardo asked plaintively, "With what?" and I said, "With your eyes." They both looked at me strangely, and I smiled reassuringly. I put my finger to my lips signaling silence, and then turned away.

I crouched along the posted fence, down and around to the Baron's stone house. There was no one in sight. The caretaker must have been up early to let out the hunting dogs. The large beasts still played with foolish malice near the entranceway, baring their teeth and pawing each other. Now it was my turn to be hunter. I had to get close to the doorway without being detected. Surprise was an element; that was ground into my mind as a combat engineer. The guile of stalking an enemy on a hillside began to flash back. I edged along the fence, dropping to the ground where there were openings, letting the iron trap trail silently after me. I was going good. I knew how to reconnoiter the situation, to move in daylight, taking advantage of natural cover, advance from a prepared position by crawls and bounds. My face grimaced into the glazed dumbness of an animal's in the presence of an enemy, and I slowly began to snake forward, toward the entrance that was my objective, and now I was less than a hundred feet away, brought to fever pitch by the anger of the harm that had befallen a companion, determined upon retribution in my own way, opening wounded memories of other years here, going good, closing in. . . .

There was a narrow defilade along the road, and the treacherous soft shoulders were mined and somewhere ahead a lone 88 was zeroed-in and firing with terrible accuracy every ten minutes on a forward turn in the road. This was on the main roadway to Palermo, one of those glory roads of war that had been traveled many times before by many armed men in the past, past ruins of Greek temples and princely modern catacombs, where grisly skeletons preserved by monks were killed anew by bombs, this time bloodlessly. We had come up that July from the beaches of Gela and Licata and moved quickly into the low mountains and tangerine groves, and there was a classic pattern to the fighting: probe, attack, dig in, counterattack, patrol, over hastily built iron Bailey bridges and around the broken posts of the wooden bridges, single file and spread out, walking. The infantrymen walked low and bent over by round-shouldering packs, looking smaller than life, like the poor; there were no rich infantrymen, yet they were spirited under their deformed shapes.

And this was in the first half of the fourth decade of the twentieth Christian century of the fighting Christian man, in a summer of war, coming out of the Mediterranean Sea in a historic armada of a thousand ships that could have swamped Jason's fleet in its backwash, up the shores with our impregnated clothing and into the carob trees, dust choking our lungs. Some may still be there, unfound, under our numbered hills.

The shoulders were mined and the roadway had to be cleared and, once again, I heard the cry, "Engineers!"

I was one. I came forward to the Infantry lieutenant leading a company of riflemen who were held up here and said, "Only three men in my platoon."

The lieutenant said, "Where's the rest? Clapped up?"

I said, "Casualties."

We were attached to these forward Infantry companies, called for wherever mines needed clearing. We went forward with our clicking iron brooms, sweeping the ground, listening for the telltale sounds of buried metal. We unarmed mines.

The lieutenant said, "Take some of these jokers with you."

154

There was a handful of eager young Sicilians who were dying to fight. I looked them over. They carried red Italian hand grenades. Some wore German jackboots. Their leader's name was Dinucci, and he was about my age. He had been an officer in the Italian army but had run away when the Germans had shoveled his unit into their abandoned foxholes. Dinucci had the usual relatives in Brooklyn, Jersey City and Detroit, like all good Sicilians, and he spoke in torrents of his hatred for the Germans. I believed him.

He knew we were discussing his reliability among ourselves. Sometimes the sergeants and lieutenants made battlefield decisions the generals never heard of.

"*J'ai toujours saboté la guerre, Signor,*" Dinucci said, speaking the lingua franca of schoolboy French, Italian, English and handsign that greased Allied communications on the lower levels. "*Vraiment, toujours saboté Fascisti* son-of-a-bitch."

"All right, Dinucci," I said. "Get some of your boys together and I'll show you what has to be done."

They gathered round and we showed them how to sweep the ground ahead of us. None of them had mine experience and they didn't seem enthusiastic.

"We want to kill Tedeschi," the eager boys shouted. "*Boom boom.*" They pointed at the air with imaginary triggers and went through the motions of operatic death. "Give us guns to shoot."

The lieutenant said, "You jokers want to be heroes? No *boom boom* yet. First you go with sergeant to clear mines." The lingua franca also included baby talk.

The youthful Sicilians did not take to the mine-sweeping methods, and I told the lieutenant that it was better not to have them walking haphazardly in the mine fields or it would be our ass in a sling.

"All right, heroes," the lieutenant said. "Dismissed. Goombye. Everybody can go home now."

Some of the Sicilians drifted away, but Dinucci stood fast with two of his friends.

"I'll go with you, sergeant," he said. "You tell me what to do and I'll do it. Then I'll tell my boys."

I translated to the lieutenant that it was okay with me for Dinucci to come along.

The lieutenant, who was an American-Japanese from Hawaii, said, "It's your funeral." He added that he would send along two of his Nisei riflemen to cover us while we unarmed the land in front of us and set out the tapes for the Infantry.

I said to Dinucci, "Follow me, in my footsteps."

So a small team of us started walking slowly, sweeping the ground. I led the way. I could not help laughing when I turned around and saw Dinucci's attire: in his belt was a German potato masher, a wooden grenade, and he carried a Sten MK II. He wore the tops of Italian motorcyclist's boots over a pair of wingtip brown-and-white sports shoes. It was the shoes that got me, so highly polished, so mocking war gear. He was very natty, a fine figure of a partisan.

I laughed and pointed at his shoes and he grinned and waved his Sten in the air.

We rolled out the tapes where the land was clear. This was still our side of the forking road, and we were not a visible target. Behind us the Infantrymen from Hawaii were spread out along the road, relaxed, bunched here and there in groups around Coleman stoves, heating coffee.

The German 88 kept up its fire, but by now the riflemen had determined the pattern and had moved inside a protective ridge. One shell landed close. We heard it start and heard it come to a stop like a train screeching into the back of a caboose and crashing down an embankment, wheels still churning and smoke coming out. We knew we were getting closer to their mine field when a machine gun splayed a tracer warning across the sky.

Dinucci came up closer behind me where I crouched on the ground. The Nisei riflemen were on their stomachs, their eyes sweeping the terrain for enemy telltales, their bodies as still as fallen trees.

156

"This is where it begins," he said. "Here we saw them putting in the mines two days ago." He pointed out the turns in the road where the mines were strewn carefully by the Germans.

"Where are the Tedeschi?" the Hawaiians asked him.

Dinucci's hand swept the northern hills before us.

"Where's the eighty-eight?"

He crossed his arm muscle obscenely, pointing to the hills in the same motion.

"This joker's a calm one," the riflemen said admiringly.

The machine gun choked its rasping sputter, but it was far away.

Dinucci pointed to his chest with his finger and then to the ground ahead. He meant for us to follow him. I looked at the riflemen and wondered the same thing they did: trap. But if this was a trap he was in it, too.

"Take a chance on him?" one of the riflemen asked.

"Son-of-a-bitch Hitler-Mussolini," Dinucci said, his eyes afire.

"Okay," I said. "You go first."

"Hey, joker," one of the Hawaiians said to the Sicilian. "See this?" He shook his rifle threateningly in his hand.

"Good, *boom boom,* Joe," Dinucci replied. He didn't comprehend that the M-1 might be pointing at his back, just in case. He was a calm one, all right.

Dinucci walked ahead of us, peering at the ground. At a point where the roadway turned he motioned the mine locations. I spotted where the Teller mines were buried, waiting for our vehicles to come along, and signaled to my engineers. They moved in professionally and dug out the mines. Dinucci kept walking ahead of me, stopping only to point out the loosened earth. We kept this up for a half hour. So did the German 88, but it was far over our heads and off to the left. They had the turn in the road in range, but ironically, as we came closer to the gun's position in the hills it became safer. I no longer heard the machine gun. By the end of the afternoon, we had cleared a marked pathway, thanks to Dinucci's ability to detect the German mines.

He was almost a hundred feet ahead of us when the machine gun opened up. It was dug in behind boulders on a high ridge, and we saw the flashes but lost the location in an instant as we fell to the ground, keeping our heads down. The Nisei riflemen were firing back in the flattest prone position before the rest of us raised our heads. The machine gun was itself pinned down by our answering rifles. I looked around, real low, and counted heads. My three engineers were all right and the two Nisei riflemen lay still but taut with life. Up ahead of us, Dinucci lay twisted, his body knotted in anguish.

A sudden silence descended on the small battlefield. We lay in the ditches on the side of the roadway, low and pointing toward the motionless ridge with our rifles. I measured the distance between us and Dinucci's heaving form. He needed help. He was worth saving.

One of the Nisei riflemen said to his buddy, "Cover me." He began to crawl forward, toward the Sicilian partisan. I started after him.

Before he had advanced ten feet, the lumpy human form that was Dinucci untwisted itself with final agonizing effort and stood erect in the face of the danger from the ridge. He took the German potato masher from his belt and, in a brave and foolish gesture, threw it with the remaining strength in his body toward the ridge, toward the Nazis. It shattered against the rocks.

Dinucci screamed aloud, *"Viva Americani!"*

He said no more. The hidden machine gunner cut him down in a burst of fire. The Nisei riflemen fired rapidly on the ridge held by the Germans. They were exposed on the roadway and I yelled to them to crawl back to the ditches. The machine gun kept still, not wasting a round on the flattened figures. The riflemen joined us, covering one another in low leaps, and we held a council.

158

It was no use staying here. We had unarmed the mines up to the ridge. The rest was risk. The machine gun called for a different flanking assault. From our position we could not surprise the efficient Germans ahead. I ordered the men back around the curve in the road.

Dinucci was spread-eagled on the ground ahead of us, lifeless.

There was no place to go but back. We joined the lieutenant and the rest of his company of Hawaiians on a glory road in Sicily.

I reported that we had cleared the mines. He told his radio man to inform the battalion commander. Then he asked what had happened. We told him.

Our explanation was punctuated by the 88, which still churned great mounds of earth near the turn in the road. Some of the Sicilian boys came up who had been unwilling to go out with us before, and they asked where Dinucci was. One of the Nisei motioned with his thumb toward the road ahead and said, "*Kaput.*" Death mixed up all the languages. The Sicilians cried out at the news. The Nisei said, "Paisan brave, *capish?*" and added in explanation, "Your buddy, he was good soldier, brave." They nodded and sobbed, "Dinucci, Dinucci," and walked tearfully back to their village.

Dusk fell on the minor battle area. The 88 was still in business. Our artillery had not silenced it. The machine gun was poised in its lair. We were stuck here, waiting for word on what to do next from battalion.

The quartermaster trucks rolled up with ammunition and gasoline and food cartons. They came every evening from a unit attached to regimental headquarters. There were two trucks that followed this company. Sometimes one of the newer riflemen who came up as replacements would say to the Negro truck drivers, "How are things in the rear—any three-day passes?" But the older riflemen just kept their silence. There was envy at the front but no time for elaborate sarcasm. After a while, rear and front were divided mentally among all the troops; the breaks were held responsible. Anyway, the QM trucks were always a welcome sight—the touch of regimental home and authority.

There was a new driver on one of the trucks. He leaped off the cab and came toward me quickly, calling out my name loudly. I recognized him immediately: Willie Harmon.

I got off the ground quickly and we pummeled each other.

"What the hell you doing in Sicily?"

"Looking for a game," he said, grinning. "You got a hard ball?"

We hadn't seen each other since college. We had played baseball together. He was a beautiful second baseman the season I held down first. The major leagues were after him when he was inducted into the Army and I hadn't seen him since.

"I came across your name at regiment," Willie said. "So I hightailed here as a driver. How's the war treating you?"

I said all right.

"See you made sergeant."

"You last long enough, it'll happen to you."

"Not here, not in this man's army."

I knew what he meant. The Negro QM outfits were off by themselves then.

"Lucky you don't have to be lugging an M-1," I said, and, as soon as the words came out I knew I had made a slip.

"They wouldn't let me even if I wanted to," he said plainly.

Changing the subject, I said, "You keeping your arm in shape for the double-play pivot?" He could really get a ball off fast over sliding spikes.

"I haven't touched a ball in two years."

"Maybe we can get some gloves around here, Willie. Like old times."

He said, "I'm not interested in ball for the duration plus six months. I can hardly read a box score any more. Don't know half the players." He paused. "They think we're all

160

yellow, afraid of combat. That's why we drive trucks. Dammit, I'd give anything to get into a line outfit."

"It's no fun," I said. "These boys have had a lot of casualties. A lot of guys think of nothing but ways of getting as far back as regiment. Plenty of them would trade with you."

"You sure?"

He looked at me meaningfully for a second.

Come to think of it, I wasn't sure at all.

It was getting dark and the Coleman stoves heated the rations and the coffee for supper, small fires that could not be seen, and the 88 on the other side of the hills only fired sporadically now to harass.

I asked Willie to eat with us. The other QM truck returned to regiment.

We sat around on the ground, protected by the rock ledges and the lowering night, and we must have appeared to be strange conquerors to these first Europeans: Nisei infantrymen, Negro truck drivers, dust-pocked engineers—not looking like the ideal image of the Sons of the American Revolution.

One group of Sicilian kids watched us as we ate. We tossed rations at their feet, but most of the stuff they pocketed, without eating, for later.

The Nisei lieutenant came over to Willie and myself.

"My boys are saying they'd like to bring him down after dark," he said.

"I'd better go along," I said. "I know where the pathway is cleared."

"Up to you," the lieutenant said. "Four on the stretcher is easier."

Willie looked puzzled.

"A Sicilian in sports shoes," I explained, and told him what had happened when Dinucci had led us around the bend in the road.

"That guy had guts," the lieutenant said. "He was no joker."

"You know what he yelled when he got it?" I said to Willie. "The guy said, 'Long live the Americans!' "

Willie said, "Let me help you bring him down."

Immediately I answered, "It's not your show. No use your going out there when you don't have to. Stay here—we'll be back in ten minutes. Just had to wait till it got dark."

"You got any objections if I go?" Willie asked the lieutenant.

"Me? I don't care who goes, just so it's four." He laughed. "Your funeral."

"Okay, then," Willie said, excited. "I'm going out there with you. Let me have one of the rifles. Hell, wait a minute, I've got my own Springfield in the truck."

He ran off to get his rifle that had never been fired in combat and joined us.

The lieutenant said to us, "Never spoke to you, never saw him, in case anyone asks. Right?"

"Okay by me," Willie said happily. He slung his rifle over his shoulder and practiced aiming it a few times and then held it across his body.

There were four of us who moved out, Willie, me and the same Nisei riflemen who had accompanied us earlier in the day. The clouds covered the moon and we walked head up, unseen and safe. I led the way, along the strung-out tapes, and let them catch up with me when we came to the turn in the road where the machine gun had first fired on us.

"It's about one hundred and fifty feet ahead," I whispered. "Keep it low. They can't see us and we can't see them, but they can hear us if we make too much noise. The tapes end, but everyone walk Indian file, keeping in touch with the man in front. We put him on the stretcher and come right back here without stopping. Okay?"

They nodded.

I said, "Willie, you stay behind me. Stick close."

The moon came out for a minute only; then clouds blackened the roadway to Dinucci again. I walked quickly and surely on the path that he had followed. There was no sign of any German activity here. For all I knew, they had left their position and moved on to the next high ground, waiting patiently for us. Twenty-five feet ahead I spotted Dinucci. I waited until my companions closed up and pointed at the body on the ground. They nodded. The moon came out again for a moment and we lay low until it disappeared.

We came up to the crumpled form. The riflemen set out the stretcher. I got near Dinucci's shoulders and Willie got his legs. Just as we lifted the body off the ground, there was a flash of smoke and fiery metal.

I was blinded for a moment by the flashing gunpowder and a startled cry of pain. Willie lay on his side, contorted in his wounds. The ground was sticky with blood. And the whole scene was once again terribly, ominously quiet.

"Anti-personnel mine," I said. "The bastards wired Dinucci's body!" Dinucci had only half a body now; the lower half of him below his knees was missing. No more sports shoes. I called to Willie, but he was out from shock. He had been hit by the exploding metal.

"Load him on the stretcher," I whispered. "Careful. Keep him straight."

We placed the Negro in the place intended for the Sicilian partisan, and carried him down. The medics came and took over professionally. He lay silent most of the time. There was a battalion aid station at a crossroads a mile back, and their ambulance came and took Willie. I went along, waiting for him to come out of the morphine. The medical administrative officer asked how he had got hit and I said by an anti-person-nel mine, without going into details. I didn't want any questions asked about why he was in a front-line position away from his truck.

The next day I returned to the battalion aid station and visited with Willie for an hour. The medics came down the aisle and told him that they had taken out most of the shrapnel and that the rest would work its way out by itself. Willie asked them when he would be able to return to his outfit and they told him that he'd have to go back to a station hospital outside of Algiers. I walked out with one of the doctors and asked him what gave, and he said that the colored boy was out of this war for good. Then I returned to Willie's bedside and he asked what the doctor had really said. I told him that they said he was going to be in great shape soon. I told him I'd see him the next day, but we were moving fast toward Palermo and I couldn't see him for five days because they kept calling for combat engineers and we kept going forward, sweeping the roads of Sicily. When I returned to the aid station of battalion, he had been tagged and shipped south and across the sea to North Africa again. I wrote him, and my V-mail chased him back to some big Veterans Administration hospital outside Boston. Months later, I received a brief letter from him saying very little: he was still convalescing and getting better, but they wouldn't allow him out of the hospital. The letter didn't sound like him; it was too impersonal and formal. I wondered if he was sore at me.

I didn't hear from Willie again for the rest of the war. He didn't answer my letters; I don't know why. The war after Palermo was a newsreel of sudden names of quickly forgotten villages and mountain peaks with numbers instead of names. But every once in a while, whenever I saw the Quartermaster trucks driving up to the front, I thought of the rotten luck Willie had that night he wanted to see some action in a war he wasn't regularly permitted to shoot in. And I relived often the nightmare of Nazi barbarism—the grisly ingenuity of the German mind—when Dinucci's dead body was wired for a new victim. If only I had not asked my friend to accompany me; or had he asked me? The event over the years blurred in guilt and anger and apology. And the flensing knives of memory stripped nostalgia to expose the torn flesh of war beneath: an 88 firing regularly and a machine gun buried unseen on a hill of rock . . . partisan with guts (what was his name?) and sports shoes . . . but long live the Americans! . . . a Negro second baseman with shrapnel, reduced to bitter silences . . . and hurrah for the great marvelous splendid Germans you've got to give them credit for their recovery and their industrial swastikas unlike the lazy British and French and Italians who do not have the mechanical ingenuity and willingness to work and make mines that go off so methodically. . . .

Closing in, angered by the harm that had befallen Nicolosi from the cleverly hidden animal trap, I shook off the memory of the iron mine detectors sweeping the dreadful hills of war, when all the world was divided into soldiers and civilians. One of the Baron's hunting dogs turned its huge head toward me, sniffing. I froze. The lava on the eruptive mountain burned its nauseating smell and it was an ally upwind. The dogs rushed away out of sight behind the Baron's lodge. The way was clear.

I stood up and walked silently to the entrance of the lodge. Not a sound came from inside. I placed the Baron's trap at the doorstep. The truck was half loaded with stuff about to be taken down to safety in the valley. Nobody was inside. I lifted the hood quietly. There used to be a small rotor on jeeps that could be removed to immobilize them to prevent theft; I looked for one in this strange vehicle. I did not recall where it was; it had been years since I had studied the insides of a car. I traced the line of spark plugs leading to a small cover, and wrenched it aside. There was something that resembled what I was after. It twisted off. I slipped it into my pocket quickly. Still no one stirred inside the Baron's lodge. I shut the hood, but it banged loudly in the still morning. I kept my head low. Then I glanced toward the ridge to see if Edoardo was watching me, covering me: I wanted them to know where I stood. But there was no sign of activity on the rock ledge near the fence. Carefully, I began to retrace my steps. I avoided the entranceway and edged my way along the stone fence above the lodge. Keeping my eyes down, I watched for animal traps cautiously. Then I knelt on the ground a hundred feet from the trap I had set, waiting for it to be sprung. From here, I turned

165

my gaze up the ridge line and saw Nicolosi. I waved my hand.

I had taken a stand and I lay in wait, taut and suddenly nervous.

Over the protective stone fence, a few pebbles slid. I froze. Something was on the other side. A few more pebbles came down, deliberately.

I waited to stand up to see the cause, puzzled.

A head appeared over the stone fence and looked down on me.

It was the German, Wernher. He carried one of the Baron's shotguns. Its twin barrels shone. The gun pointed to the ground.

"Good morning," he said quietly.

I was startled but I did not want to show it.

"Hello," I replied.

He offered me a cigarette, and I refused. I said, "Did you have a pleasant night?" He had stood by when his friend the Baron had kicked us out of the lodge.

He nodded. I waited for his next move.

"I'm an early riser," he said. "Like yourself, Mr. Borken."

"I suppose your friend is still asleep?"

"He should be getting out of the lodge soon." He looked around. "Where are your companions?"

"One is laid out on the ground up there. He was caught in your friend's animal trap."

He nodded. "The same one you placed on the doorstep?"

I did not answer him.

"We must all get down quickly," he said. "It's dangerous up here."

"Nicolosi has to be driven down in that truck. He cannot walk."

"Why should he? Or any of you? There's plenty of room in the back of the truck."

"If the Baron wouldn't let them sleep in his place last night, why do you think he'll let them ride with him? The truck is loaded with his stuff. Do you think he'd take some off? You don't know your friend very well."

"What do you propose? To catch his leg in a trap—is that the way to get them down? It will only make the Baron angrier."

"It might wake him up to the fact that we mean to get down. It's just insurance."

"Like tampering with the truck's motor?"

He had been watching me all along.

"That's right. One way or another, we'll get down in that truck."

Wernher laughed. "Maybe you're right. Okay." So okay was in his language, too. "The Baron likes to make deals. Maybe he'll have to now."

He seemed to find this very amusing. Who the hell's side was he on, anyway?

"Enough of this," he said suddenly. "You had better remove that trap. It is liable to hurt someone. You wouldn't want that to happen."

I didn't make a move. I didn't trust him, before or now.

"Come now," he said. "What if the Baron's caretaker is the first one out that door? You have no reason to harm him."

"It could be the Baron himself. Or one of his dogs. Nicolosi is stretched out from the fangs of that damn iron trap."

"The dogs are dumb beasts. It is only a fifty-fifty chance you have on the Baron. Figure your plan. It doesn't work out very well."

Not with him up here. That was one less chance of catching an enemy. The percentages were lower.

When I still stood there, watching the trap, he said, almost pleading with me, "I think it best to remove it. Let's not have more pain. Someone will get hurt and we'll all be sorry."

I said, "If you want, you can remove it."

He said, "It doesn't matter as long as no one gets hurt."

He set the shotgun down on the stone fence, next to me. I

picked it up and examined its inlaid-silver stock. "It's a nice gun, isn't it?" he said. He had put it down deliberately.

He turned and ran along the fence toward the threshold of the lodge. He kneeled carefully and examined it for a moment. Then he held the chain length that extended from the trap and slowly pulled it away from the door and out of sight.

I wondered how he had seen me and where he was while I was moving around the lodge. I had stalked them while he stalked me, and now the trap was gone.

He entered the lodge by the front door. A few minutes later, I saw him emerge with the Baron and the caretaker. All were fully dressed. The Baron and his man were carrying some of their stuff and loading it into the back of the truck.

I rushed down the hill and confronted them.

The Baron saw me and said to Wernher, scarcely looking at me, "Well, it's the American."

Wernher said, "Good morning," as if for the first time.

I shouted, "One of your traps caught Nicolosi."

He said, "The fool—doesn't he know enough to stay off posted land?"

I stepped toward him and said menacingly, "Nicolosi can't move because of you."

"Please, not because of me—because of himself. I did not put him in the trap. I did not tell him to travel up the mountain this way. He is not working for me, you know. If you wish, I can make room for you, Mr. Borken."

He turned his back and told Wernher and his caretaker to get the rest of their stuff and climb into the truck.

I ran around in front of him and shouted in his face, "Nicolosi has to be brought down. This truck won't move without him."

"Please, out of my way," he said, walking around me.

He ordered the caretaker into the driver's seat and told him to warm up the motor. Then he turned to Wernher and said, "Have you my other shotgun?"

"Yes, just a moment," he said. He trotted up the hill and brought it down. "I left it on the fence," he said.

"You should not have done that," the Baron said. "It's very valuable. Anyone running around these parts would have been glad to take it away as a souvenir."

Wernher said, "It's good only for hunting."

The shifting wind on the mountain fanned the volcanic vapors in our direction, and we could smell the steaming, sulphurous ashes blown into a convoluted mass of bubbling cloud, mud and rock.

The Baron called to get the motor started. But his man could only turn over the froggy-throated battery. The motor would not catch. The Baron climbed into the cab of the truck and told Wernher to hop on. He announced that he would drive down the mountain himself.

The Baron began to step on the starter and pump the accelerator and use foul language as fuel, but the truck would not budge. He ordered Wernher and the caretaker to push. The old man pushed hard, but Wernher did not. The Baron dared not ask me. He got out of the cab, exasperated, and began to curse Bardi, blaming him for not taking care of the vehicle. The caretaker stood by silently, as if part of his job was to be maligned by his employer, suffering whim gladly.

The Baron turned to Wernher and said, "Do you know anything about motors?"

Wernher replied, "Not truck motors."

"I know they're not as good as your German motors."

Wernher said, "Americans are supposed to know about automobiles. Maybe Mr. Borken can fix the motor."

The Baron faced me. "Can you do anything about it?"

I said, "Maybe."

"I'll pay you for fixing the motor—if you can. Here, I've got an American five-dollar bill for you." He pulled one from a money clip.

Wernher was watching me, concealing amusement.

"I can try to fix it," I said, "but the first thing I'll need is a mattress—unless you have a stretcher."

The Baron knew what I meant. He told Bardi to go inside the lodge and get something. In a moment, the man returned with a low cot. I told him to come with me.

We trudged up the hill in the direction of my companions.

I said, when we were out of earshot, "Your employer stinks worse than this lava. Do you know that?"

He replied, "*Beh,* he's the Baron. What can I do?"

Centuries of primitivism and oppression died slowly.

We came upon Nicolosi and Edoardo, and I knelt and asked how he felt.

"Like a caught rabbit," Nicolosi said, forcing a smile.

"Let's put him on," I said. Bardi lowered the cot and we lifted Nicolosi on it. We began to walk downhill toward the lodge.

I waited for Edoardo to utter some word of gratitude.

"Did you cover me?" I asked him.

"I watched you," he said. "What happened to the trap? Did you manage to get any of the bastards?"

"I didn't have to use it." We walked in silence, and then I said, "Well, at least Nicolosi will be getting a ride down." I said it loud enough for Nicolosi to hear. He turned on the cot and smiled.

Nicolosi said, "Franca must be worried. She, about us here, and we, about her in Brucia. That's why I want to get down— so she won't be so concerned."

Edoardo said, "Joseph must be in a hurry to get down, too."

He kept blowing hot and cold toward me.

"Yes, I am in a big hurry. There's work for me to do."

Nicolosi said, "Franca must be worried about all of us. She is so considerate. She worries about the whole world, but especially during these volcanic trials. She gets frightened. Like a young girl."

He turned to Edoardo and said, "Joseph has shown he's on our side, on the mountain and now again."

170

Edoardo said, "Yes, isn't he?"

When we came near the truck, I told them to lift the cot, and we placed it on the back with Nicolosi inside. It hung over slightly. I motioned to the Baron that some of his precious stuff would have to be taken off to make room, and he told his caretaker to remove a carton and rope it onto the fender.

"All right," the Baron said officiously. "Let's see what all your boasting is about."

"You're mistaken," I said. "I never made any claims that I could fix the motor." I thought I'd let him squirm a little.

"What's this all about? A trick? First you trespass, then you move in on my truck. It won't do you any good unless you can get the truck moving."

It was his dilemma, not mine.

"I'm willing to take a look under the hood," I said confidently.

I moved around to the front of the truck and said, "How does the hood open?"

The Baron came around and opened the hood. He watched me as I peered inside.

"If you don't mind, please—I would prefer it if you would not look over my shoulder while I'm working."

They walked away and the Baron stood next to Wernher, muttering about American crudeness.

Quickly, I bent over, uncapped the spark line, and slipped the rotor out of my pocket and back in position. I took a quick look around the rest of the parts; not that I would have known if anything else was missing. That would be the final irony. Anyway, I had to play out the game to the last. The bastard would pay for putting us out in the rain, for setting his traps.

I clapped shut the hood and went around to the front of the truck.

"Try it now," I said.

The Baron walked toward the cab and the driver's seat.

"Wait a minute," I said. "Not you." I got up near the steering post, then slid over, leaving the wheel empty.

"You," I said to the German. He came over. "You start it."

Wernher stepped up and got behind the wheel. "All set?" he said. I nodded. He turned over the battery once and it caught, rasping loudly. A few holes in the muffler, but otherwise the truck's motor ran smoothly and noisily.

"Everybody on?" I inquired. Edoardo got in next to Nicolosi in the back. So did the caretaker.

The Baron slid in next to me, demoralized.

"How did you fix it?" Wernher inquired. "I thought they'd wear out the battery before this thing turned over."

I said, "I didn't do anything—you did. You're the one who stepped on the gas and made it catch."

The German had played out the game against the Baron.

"I can drive down," he said.

"You've driven on these hills before."

"Haven't you?"

He backed up, and then swung the truck onto the highway leading down past the lodge. The Baron suffered in silence until, after a few moments, Wernher suddenly began laughing.

"You owe him five dollars American," he said to the Baron. He grinned a Nordic death's-head, at once cruel and humorous—at least to my eyes.

"That wasn't the proposition," the Baron said, sulking.

"I was the witness, Baron," Wernher said.

The Baron reached into his pocket, but I said, "You're right —it was a different deal. Wouldn't you say, though, that five dollars American is just about the right amount for the trip down the mountain for myself and my companions in your truck?"

The Baron recovered his coolness. "As you wish," he said. He fought for his composure. "Keep your eye on the road," he said to Wernher. "You've got a precious cargo here." As if to underline his meaning, his hunting dogs barked.

High above us, the lava stream pushed itself forward; the rock and mud and bubbling liquid earth began to race its forestream down the volcanic mountain. The roadway was safe but the vineyards and the woods in the lower regions were in the path of the eruption in some places. As the truck rolled on, my mind wandered: away from my companions on the climb, from my samples of this rock that could contain the new lodestones, from the conflicts and associations with these people; there was an odd mingling of thoughts of the Professor talking into the night in his observatory where he could see more distantly than men less detached, and of Franca, her voice recollected in the sounds of the wheels spinning and the mountain spuming and the chance of recapturing love in a resurgent new time.

Part Three

CHAPTER EIGHT

THE TOWNSPEOPLE of Brucia appeared to be indoors. Coming down from Mount Etna, the roadway turned away from the coursing lava stream. The impending danger dissolved against the familiar sights of the valley. The regional cathedral at the edge of Brucia was reassuring; more than religion, it meant continuity of civilization over the impermanence of life on the slopes. A gentle wind blew in from the Ionian Sea, lightly caressing the brow. Under the skillful hands of the German, the Baron's truck sped downhill and into the town square.

Word spread that the truck had just come off the mountain and a crowd formed. The Baron placed one hand on his hip and spoke authoritatively. He recovered his composure quickly here. Several officials came over and bowed and scraped for information from him; they pointed at one another's chests and then in the direction of the mountain. A map was brought out and the Baron was asked to locate the lava stream on it. He hesitated and then waved his finger here and there positively.

I interrupted the Baron's discourse and said that Nicolosi and Edoardo actually had seen the lava and could locate it precisely. The Baron glared at me and then announced to all that he had rescued everyone he could in his truck. The ring of people now moved to Nicolosi. Willing hands lifted him down from the truck; he became the center of attention. I looked in the crowd for Franca.

"We were actually above the lava on a shelf of rock," Nicolosi said. He raised himself on an elbow. "This was early in the morning when the rest of you were asleep in your beds, unaware of the eruption. We were waiting for the sunrise because the party I was guiding was intent on seeing it. Suddenly, instead of the view we were confronted by the sight of this gash in the earth. The lava poured from it—I don't have to tell you what it looked like, my friends. We were safe ourselves. In fact, we could not have been in a safer place anywhere in Sicily than above the Osservatorio. Nobody has ever seen lava flowing up the mountain, am I right?" The crowd nodded. "But this American gentleman saw our concern for families and friends here in Brucia. He put his own desire to see the summit out of his thoughts and insisted that we all come down for warning. I had a little accident—nothing to speak of—but here we are anyway."

She was still not in sight.

Brucia's police chief placed a map in front of Nicolosi. "Tell me, where is the exact direction of the flow and the position?"

Nicolosi called me closer, and the three of us examined the map. The police chief, a surprisingly young man, asked Nicolosi if I understood what they were saying, and Nicolosi nodded. The contours of the map showed a ridge line falling away in a parabola toward the villages on the western side of the Valley of the Bove.

"This is where it was," Nicolosi said.

"Where is it by now?"

That was hard to say. It meant judging the rate of flow on the incline, and neither Nicolosi nor Edoardo offered accurate

176

information. I looked around; the Baron and his truck were speeding off in the direction of Catania. But Wernher was still here. He moved in closer to the map.

The police chief turned to me. I took out a pencil and began to make some calculations. There was a way to figure this precisely, the way artillerymen calculated target distances from information passed back by forward observation posts. I made some tentative notes, trying to recall the formulas. Wernher watched me, checking, and the others looked on, puzzled.

"The azimuth," Wernher said.

The simple formula came back from some hidden resources of memory, and I took into account the unknowns of height, distance, slope, even the wind. Finally, I arrived at a figure and gave it to the chief. I wasn't sure of it until Wernher said, "That's close enough." Then the German walked away, out of our sight, still faceless to me.

From what I could make out, it was clear that unless something interrupted the flow on the terrain or the lava's crawling force became spent, by nightfall the forestream would reach the edge of Brucia. The chief took down the information carefully. He handed orders to one of his men and directed him to inform higher provincial authorities in Catania. The crowd began to disperse after the chief told them to return to their homes; he said that the officials of Brucia would protect the town.

Several of Nicolosi's guide friends took the corners of the cot and began to carry him home. I started to follow them.

"Is a doctor being called?" I asked Edoardo.

"Don't you worry," he said. "We can take care of our own." His manner was brusque. Now that we were off the mountain, it was no longer the carnotite that disturbed him but something else. I controlled my anger.

"He should have a doctor look at the dressing," I said. "It's got to be kept clean. That trap was rusty."

I moved in front of the group carrying Nicolosi.

"Promise me that you'll call a doctor," I said to him. "My

company will foot the bill—you were with me on the job."

I had already put an envelope in his pocket with the pay for himself and Edoardo.

"I'll have Franca call when she returns from her classes at the school," he said.

"I'll take care of it," Edoardo declared.

"You must have a lot of work to do, Joseph," Nicolosi said. "I don't want to hold you up any longer. I'll see you tomorrow and we can straighten everything out."

"If not before tomorrow," I said, glancing at Edoardo.

I was dragging the pack with the samples of rock and the Geiger counter; exhaustion suddenly gripped my neck and shoulders.

"He's studying our mountain for certain minerals," Nicolosi told his friends as they carried him, and I was sorry he did so. "A very important piece of work."

At least he did not consider the search too reprehensible now.

"A busy few days, but not bad. Right, Joseph?"

"Better than not bad, Nicolosi."

I said goodbye, and Edoardo could spare only a nod and they turned down the alleyways of Brucia and were out of sight.

I was hungry and unwashed and loaded down and I walked back again to the center of town, turning to look at the ominous mountain, and the disturbed groups of people moving tensely through the streets, and then toward the waterfront hotel. I sniffed the air, feeling the noisome lava lingering in my nostrils.

The lobby of the Trinacria was almost empty when I walked up to my room. The few Americans in the hotel had moved on to the mainland when word reached here that the mountain was kicking up. I was glad that strange American youth with his spidery Volkswagen from the expatriate colony —so beat in Taormina—was not working the Trinacria's lobby again.

I unlocked the door of my room and stretched out on the high bed with my clothes on. I lay still, my feet on the bed, alone and quietly forlorn. I tried to kick off my shoes against the iron posts, disgusted at the mud marks I imprinted on the bedspread. I got off the bed and opened the laces of my shoes and walked barefoot over to my suitcase. There was a pint of bourbon that Subito had packed inside at the Company's villa in Palermo. I poured a drink into the thick hotel glass. I stripped down to my underwear and threw myself on the bed again. I sipped the bourbon slowly, allowing the burning sensation to heat my raw throat.

Looking up, I saw visions taking shape on the ornately plastered high ceiling. I saw the coastal breakers riding the rolling surf of Brucia and the whitened ridges near the Osservatorio and the seismographic styli writing endlessly and the fissures spewing the forestream of lava and the undulations of the mountain road coming down, but I could not find the faces, I could not visualize Franca whole, her face and form in lovely details, and the serpentine patterns in the plaster returned to their still places in the ceiling.

I was exhausted and caked with the layers of habitation on the mountain. The water in the bathtub was ice cold, but then it turned steaming hot; the sounds were still of kettledrums clanked by ghostly iron staves somewhere deep in the basement of the Trinacria. The warm water cushioned my body and the weight of the packs on the mountain began to slide away. After a half hour my muscles were loose again. I dried my body, and the room was cool and I went toward the tall window door to look out over the town.

I hardly heard the tapping, it was so tentative. But no more; and yet it was not imagination calling. A tapping, gentle but voiceless, on the door of a room.

I quickly turned away from the windows and walked to the doorway and listened, and the tapping now was audible.

I could think of nothing to say but "Who is it?"

"Joseph," the voice said. It was whispering softly.

179

I looked down at myself, half dressed, and stepped toward the closet and put on my bathrobe, but I still felt embarrassed.

I unlatched the door. She stood there, smiling the half smile as when I had seen her waving to us starting out to climb the mountain. She was alone. I looked both ways down the hallway.

"Nobody is here," she said, anticipating my anxiety. Strange that it should be mine. "You may invite me in."

"Of course," I said, still startled. "Come in, Franca, please."

"I'm not interrupting?"

"Oh, no."

"I am. You were dressing to go somewhere."

"No. I'm sorry I didn't hear you. I was trying to take the chill out of the room after a bath."

"Poor cold Joseph," she said.

And we both laughed, standing there inside the threshold of the room. It broke my tenseness.

I held out my hand for her hand, and our palms locked, our fingers squeezing tightly. With my other hand I guided her toward a soft chair in the room.

"My God," I said, "you're here. I had to call you from the Osservatorio."

"We are both here," she said. "I'm here and I've never been inside this place before."

"The Trinacria?"

"Yes, in Brucia, and I've never even seen what the lobby looked like."

"I've been in the hotel more than in Brucia. Except for a few hours."

I moved away from the chair, sat down on the edge of the bed, and gazed at her. She seemed slight and self-consciously straight within the chair's high wings. She wore thong sandals on her bare, sun-tanned feet and a yellow cotton dress. Her hair was adorned with a wide riband of green, and it fell loosely over her ears. I stared separately at each feature of her face: almond-brown hair and delicate nose and, magnetically,

180

into her deep gray eyes, with their dark rings below brightening them by contrast. Her eyes were at once shining and sad.

"What do you see?" she asked, returning my stare.

"You, Franca."

"You think I'm different-looking."

"All I can do is look at you. It's unbelievable—I have nothing to say that's as important."

"I came to see you. As you asked."

"Is that all?"

"Yes," she said softly.

I got up and walked toward the door and closed it from the inside, listening for sounds in the hallway. Then I sat down on the bed again.

"It's quiet here," I said. I continued looking at her impolitely, without once blinking my eyes.

"My face is older," she said. "I'm not bothered by that. Don't you think, Joseph?"

"Your face is lovelier than I remember it. You're only a few days older to me."

"I mean, from before. You saw me in the evening and only for a little while the next morning. This is a harsher light. The sunlight of Sicily is very bright. Is the sunlight this bright in New York?"

"That depends on whom it shines on. Sometimes it's difficult to reach everybody there. I'd like you to see it."

"The sun must be rationed in New York, I think. Like cow meat in Brucia, there is not enough for everybody." She tapped her sandal on the ground and said, "Stop me from talking about nonsense."

We moved our words carefully across the barrier of long-separated time, speaking the language that pleases unsurely but without evasion. There was a distance beyond the distance between the chair and bed.

I said, "Is your father feeling all right now?"

She said, "The doctor came and bandaged his foot. The sulfa powder you put on kept it clean. It is not serious. He was walking around the house when I returned from my classes at the school."

"Nicolosi is impatient. He is a fine guide."

"Hearing you talk about Father is so farfetched that I could never imagine its happening a week ago."

"He's very different from the way—"

"From me?"

"No, from the way I had imagined him to be. You seem somehow more serious than your father. He's lighthearted."

"Maybe resigned. His life is hard here. And I'm not serious, Joseph, don't say that," she said petulantly.

"I'm sorry," I said, and when she smiled I realized that she mocked me. "What I meant is that your personalities seem different for father and daughter. I couldn't help thinking as we went up the mountain, This is Franca's father; I had avoided him once for six months. Somehow I expected him to be stern with me and suspicious. Instead, we were more like friends. I felt as if I were fooling him until we established our own link."

"He told me about your search on the mountain. And still he said he liked you."

"Yes, my work," I said, suddenly thinking for the first time of what that could mean to Franca. "Do you know, I had a feeling once or twice that your father suspected that you and I knew each other. It seemed so deliberate for me to seek him out of all the guides."

"You said nothing—about us—before?"

"No. I couldn't possibly. I couldn't share that with anyone, not even my oldest friends. I hoarded our relationship. I always kept you reserved in a private corner of my mind. I wouldn't share the memory of you with anyone."

She smiled shyly. She gazed around the room.

I asked her what she was thinking, but she shook her head without saying a word. My eyes followed hers to the high ceiling, to the dresser, the closet, the washbasin, my bag and the equipment. She took them all in, the things around me.

I got up from the bed, carefully covering myself in the enfolding robe. I lifted out the bottle of bourbon from the bag and walked to the basin. I poured some into the thick glass and added a little water. I took a sip. Then, with a playful bow, I turned to Franca.

"A cognac-and-vermouth, Signorina?"

She reacted swiftly, breaking the mood.

"Oh, Joseph, I'm fed up with nostalgia," she cried.

I looked at her in shocked surprise. She placed her face in the small palms of her hands and began to weep softly to herself.

"Franca, Franca," I said. "What is it?"

I stepped toward her and reached down into the chair. She came to me eagerly, and I drew her face to my body and cradled her in my arms.

Except in the sobbing ecstasy of our love, I had never heard her whimper or voice unhappiness. I held her head in my shoulder and comforted her with endearing words. She unburdened herself, and when I tried to raise her face, she kept it down and only her hair met my lips. After a few minutes, she moved away from me and dried her eyes. She looked up and smiled, almost childishly, as if expecting to be reprimanded.

"That was foolish," she said. "I don't know why I cried, it just had been stored up."

"Don't explain your feelings, darling, not with me."

"I thought of the Flower Bar when you said that. And you wanted me to, didn't you?" she said. "And of all the times I recalled our days together. The memory of the long nights of recollection more than of the months you were in Sicily. Those were of love—it was the times alone afterward that were difficult. In the last few years, I've made an effort to wipe the slate clean. I've tried to keep each time in its place and all the people in each time separated."

"Nostalgia is not always troublesome. It's one reason why I'm back in Sicily." I looked into her face intently. "It has brought us together here, alone."

We moved toward each other, and our arms and bodies drew together with all the magnetic yearnings of love. Our lips touched and sucked hotly at the flesh of parted mouths, and the curve of her slender body extended and stretched along mine; our loins locked intimately, and we were warmly entwined in the embrace of a known love. Memory and desire linked past and present.

Still I trembled; in love, a phantom cold shook my body when desire broke out. Franca brought herself within the folds of my robe, and I felt the warmth returning slowly. I opened my eyes slightly and brushed my lips across her closed lids. My hand moved slowly down her throat and the bareness of her shoulder, and I touched her, and she leaped under my hand breathlessly. Love overwhelmed us, arousing a deeply imbedded, wartime passion; and simultaneously we moved toward the waiting bed. For a moment we drew away from each other, eyes opening, regarding ourselves bared of pretense, skin taut and minds firm in the right. Our fingers reached out eagerly, and, sightless, we rediscovered our intimate selves, awed by our own presence and silence. Forge heated and anvil struck, slowly quickening into rhythmical strokes of passion.

Then at last, after the violent excitation, the explosions of youth ignited and fused into the bluer flame of mature love. I extended my hand, and our fingers met, and she drew my knuckles to her lips; and we lay there, in the afternoon darkness of the room, without a thought of the vastnesses beyond here, whispering endearments.

In the half light, emboldened by the shadings of delicious intimacies, I said, "I love you, Franca."

She said, "I love loving you, Joseph. I had to come here, to be with you this way again."

"It was a dream. Love only comes once at a time. I lived

184

with the illusion of you all these years. I had to see if it were possible. Is it?"

"Let's not talk about possible things," she said. "So many of them in my life have been within my grasp and then have slipped away. All my life I've been too weak to reach hard for what I wanted, to run after things. My desires have begun to melt away. I have started to become reconciled, knowing that I should be struggling and thinking and reaching. For people and for other less important things. That is why I came here, unashamed, doing what no nice woman does without scandal —I wanted to see how many second chances I am allowed. If I could break loose from the conventions of my life. I have, at least for an hour. That is enough for now."

"But there will be an after-now. We're here now and it's more wonderful than it ever was. I'm thinking of beyond this room."

She searched my face thoughtfully. I looked at her outlines, the curve of her body next to mine. I brought her cheek toward me, and again we sought each other's arms, and I whispered my love, and yet Franca was silent in my embrace.

I drew away and said, "You have not said it."

She said, "This moment is what matters most of all. Nothing is more important."

"It won't go on forever, darling."

"It is more than I had wished—more than I thought would happen while you were on the mountain."

"Do you find it so hard to say it?"

"No. That's not it," she said. "Why is it that the words are important? They have not meant much. . . ."

I reached across and stroked her hair. "In the past? Yes, I know. All the words, the meaningless letters I wrote."

"It wasn't the letters, Joseph. You know that."

"What else?" I asked.

And I thought back to then, when I had sent CARE packages of food to an intermediary, arranged understandingly through their offices, so that Franca could receive them without her family and friends knowing too much about the American soldier she once knew during the war that touched Sicily. It was a subterfuge born of confusion, at first, and indecision, toward the end when I had stopped writing altogether. Our love was nurtured in the hidden back entrances and exits of wartime Palermo, and it had winked out as the war and the postwar years themselves had dissolved into a continuous smoke screen, the quiet demise of a broken generation's idealism.

But those were matters on the world outside the skin. They had no right to cut short the lives of lovers, to shatter the dreams: the outside enemy, they.

"I've forgotten the letters, Joseph. The packages helped for trading. Did I ever tell you about them? One contained only tins of sardines—and that was one thing we had plenty of here."

She looked amused, and we both laughed at that until we heard footsteps going down the hotel corridor and lapsed into silence in the room. The fear of discovery brought all our past Saturdays to mind.

"It was fun," I said, "and then it slowly became much more."

She nodded, and I saw myself in the center of her eyes. Looking closely, I saw the maturing expression that had grown gracefully in her face and had changed the lovely features into womanhood.

She said, "I love being here with you."

I said, "That's close, but it's not the same. I don't want to press you to say something you cannot. You give love but you cannot say it—why?"

"Joseph, Joseph, why should we prepare for more disappointment? What if I said that I did love you? Where would that lead us? Is there a direction away from this room?"

"Of course there is—that's why I'm here, Franca. But I think the first way to continue what we have here is to will it—to say it."

She shook her head sorrowfully. I was puzzled; and hurt.

"If this is embarrassing to you," I said after a minute, "don't say anything. I can understand. I know what you're driving at. And I wouldn't want to hurt you again."

She threw herself at me and put the flesh of her lips on mine violently.

"Don't say that, darling," she said, pulling away intensely. "There was no hurt—no harm done except to the heart." She smiled and said, "What we had were the most beautiful months of my life. I have no anger about that time. Please, please do not think so. Ours was not an unrequited love—it was unfinished. Almost as if the war itself did not have an ending."

I was still looking for a clue. "You said something the night before we went up the mountain. It has remained with me. You said your body was unfulfilled, and I wondered—"

"No, that was it—my body felt barren. Many of the girls in Palermo married and had children with soldiers."

"Or had children and married."

"Yes, it was the dread at the time. The shame is different in Europe than in America, isn't it?"

I said that it was not too different.

She said, "But as the years passed, the children seemed the most natural outgrowth of those days. Nothing is evil conceived in real love."

"I don't think that is the popular view. Even children born of marriage are not very popular sometimes in many corners of America."

"Maybe for a different reason, there or here. Too many children are born not from a union of love but of passion, even of a hatred and a revengeful feeling. Those poor children should be spared. But all over Europe where the church decides morality, without knowing of love, there is only scorn and a lack of sympathy. They rule on death but not on life."

I said, "Your sister was so angry with me when I saw her

in Palermo that, as I walked with my thoughts on the mountain, I wondered if she was voicing your—"

"Can I tell you?" She hesitated and then said, "Dorotea was hurt once herself. She knows what trouble can be. She wanted to see me spared. An older sister does not think of her younger sister as following her wrongs, only of profiting by her mistakes. She did not want me humiliated. I tried to tell her of our love and what it meant to me, but she saw only her own image. She expected more of you than I did."

I sought her eyes with curiosity and said, "What did you expect?"

"The thing I hoped for was continuation," she said.

Footsteps hurried down the hallway again, and we lowered our voices until the sound disappeared. No matter how natural it was for us to be here, alone and loving, a furtive air permeated the room.

"That is what I am talking about now," I said, "continuing what we had. Am I dreaming? Tell me, Franca."

She wrinkled her brow, and I waited for her to give me the answer, but she was silent. I had to bring his name into our room, clouding our consciences.

"I know," I said. "Edoardo. Are you in love with him?"

She said, "I like Edoardo. Love? That is just what we were talking about. The more we pledge ourselves ardently, the more disappointments we have. Edoardo wants me to marry him when he finishes his special courses. I am no longer a girl. I've had one brief marriage and it was a mischance. Now I am in my thirties. I want children of my own, Joseph, but my time is beginning to slip away. Don't you see?" she said, biting her lip. "I want you to know what I am thinking, my most intimate thoughts—I haven't voiced them to anyone for years. Not even to Edoardo."

"Darling," I said, moving closer. "Are you saying that your mind is not yet made up?"

"Joseph, Joseph," she whispered, responding to my touch,

188

"I will have to go soon. It is late. I don't want to leave this room."

Her face came over mine and she caressed me. Again our bodies stroked in one rhythmical line, voices moaned, and our yearning flesh was empressed in rapture. Afterward, we lay still together, close enough to hear only our hearts beating.

When again the sighs of breathlessness tolled, we moved away and returned to our own selves. Franca dressed quickly, and in a moment her sandals were on her bare feet. I reached into the closet and began to put on my clothes, and Franca watched me dress, and that, too, as before, was part of our love-making.

I flicked on the light over the bed, but she walked over and turned it off. It was dark in the room, and she went over to the window door of the hotel and opened it slightly, and we faded back, in the shadowed room, so that nobody in the street below saw us. We stood, hand in hand, looking over the town of Brucia. The yellow lights began to twinkle on behind the store fronts and restaurants along the waterfront, as if nothing had happened, unaware of the tremors in our room.

"It's a beautiful view from here," Franca said softly. "It's the first time I have ever seen Brucia from this height. So different from living in Palermo."

"What made you leave there?" I asked.

"An opportunity to teach here. I came ahead of my father. I love teaching the children."

"Often, at night, before I'd go to sleep, I'd try to make out the shape of your nose, the look in your eyes, trying to reconstruct your face all at once. In the middle of the night, I would put on the light and look at this small snapshot."

I took the wartime photograph from my wallet, and she tilted it toward the faintly reflected light from the street. It was dark, and she slipped toward the bathroom and put on the light there. A moment later, she emerged, laughing.

"That's so funny," she said. "My hair was so long and my

189

dress so short. And those crazy shoes with the cork heels. Please throw it away, Joseph—how horrible I look."

"So horrible that it brought me here," I said, laughing, teasing her. I reached for her hand, but she held the picture against her chest, and I tickled her and she twisted in my arms and I kissed her long and the picture fell to the floor. We looked out contemplatively toward the town below, holding each other.

"Do you remember when that picture was taken?" she asked. "You and another sergeant were at the beach at Mondello. I was visiting a friend of mine near there. You saw me walking with her, and we all climbed into the little jeep car and drove to the Flower Bar when it was near the opera. That was really the beginning of our Saturdays."

"Oh, no, darling. Somehow, whenever I put on that funny little soldier's cap and tilted it, I became bold. You were my prey weeks before we first went to the Flower Bar. Remember Berlitz?"

"Oui, Monsieur."

"I saw you one day—our headquarters was in a requisitioned building near by. With your ugly cork heels, going so efficiently to the school. And I—"

"How did I look then, Joseph?"

"As you appear to me now. With a look of loveliness. And kindness. I knew when I planned to meet you that you wouldn't turn and run. That's how I planned it—or have you forgotten?"

"No, Joseph. I remember it well. I like to hear you tell all over how you first saw me. It's very flattering for an old schoolteacher to hear how a young man ran after her."

"An aging young man would be more like it. What were our first words? I think I said, 'Good day, miss.' And you answered, 'How do you do, gentleman?' And I asked, 'What is your name?' And you replied, 'My name is Franca.' "

"You said it must be a boy's name," Franca said, laughing softly.

"How many times I mouthed your name."

"Franca, Franca," she said, pronouncing her name twice, mocking me, and I kissed her, and she said, "You made dreams of all my Saturdays afterward."

"I know," I said. "For all the years afterward, Saturday afternoon meant a time for love-making. Or thoughts of love."

We would meet at the Flower Bar, away from the excitement of Palermo, and I would select a pink camellia for her, and we would walk through the pulsating streets, carried on the tide of Allied humanity, taking new turns and always exploring, first the byways of the small side streets and then ourselves, talking of nothing in particular and laughing—oh, there was so much laughter in the streets—and we were purposeful: at the end of the aimless walk we would always, somehow, find ourselves going down the Via della Libertà, past tropical gardens concealing stone villas through the trees, and there was one lovely place through a bower, where the city meandered into a suburb. I had an arrangement there for a secret suite, in a villina occupied by a gay old contessa, who enjoyed conspiring for love, and she would leave when we arrived and we would be alone. The room was huge, the doors concealed in the walls by *trompe-l'oeil* wallpaper and paintings, and the bed a monument to baroque vulgarity. The rich fabric of the heavy spread, folded back lovingly by the conspiratorial contessa, heightened the splendor. Between the coolness of the sheets we would shiver in anticipation, groping for each other and warming our bodies. The room was an echo chamber, repeating our whispering laughter. We did what we wanted.

In the shadows of this later room, we savored the memories. Then Franca said, "Why didn't you ever marry?"

And I replied, "Maybe because I pursued the wrong things after the war. I really tried hard to get ahead in my work, almost to the exclusion of everything else."

Franca said, "But you had girl friends—maybe you have one now?"

I told her, "In passing, but I was never even engaged."

She laughed softly and said, "Who would want you, anyway?"

"I was so occupied with my work—"

"You work too hard in New York," she said. "You must think more of your life."

I wondered if she was hinting about my particular mission here, or if I was becoming sensitive on the subject. "Did your father tell you about my work here?"

"Edoardo, too," she said. "He was quite agitated about it."

"Damn, what right has he to tell you about my business? He was trying to make trouble. To prejudice you against me."

"Don't be angry at Edoardo. He is no different than many of the politically minded people here. I don't have to tell you that some are very anti-American. Not everybody, as they would have you believe, but some are worried about another war. Every peasant in Sicily has heard of fall-out and radiation—the world has closed in. Everybody was so hurt in the war that they don't care what the consequences are, they just don't want another one."

I asked, "Has anti-Americanism touched you?"

"You mean am I against Americans?" She laughed. "I don't think of politics or Hollywood or the Grand Canyon when I think of America. All I think of is an American—the one I know, the one I came here to be with."

"I love you, Franca," I said tenderly.

We found each other's lips and kissed hard and long. She withdrew suddenly.

"What can we do?" she cried out, more to herself than to me.

Then she murmured that she had to run home, and before I could think of the next day she was slipping away quietly and gone down the stairway of the Trinacria.

A chill came into the room, and on its slight wind I detected the odor of the smoking fissure on Mount Etna. There was a more hurried movement by the vehicles in the square below; they looked loaded with evacuated goods and furniture. The

192

lava could be sliding closer to the sea, closer to Brucia; I wondered how accurate the calculations were that I had made for the police chief. I had a desire to see for myself, to be a man engaged against danger to the civilization on the slopes. I peered toward the square but I could not catch a glimpse of her departing. The vibrancy of life was coursing through me again, and it was a strange feeling, a renewal with the desires of youth in Sicily.

CHAPTER NINE

WHEN I OPENED MY EYES early the next morning, pleasing cloudy images floated gently over the plaster designs on the ceiling above our bed. My mind shook out the evening, and daylight entered harshly: Etna's volcanic ash had sent its noxious heralds ahead. The stench of sulphuric gases and molten rock rolled through the newspaper-patched crack in the window door of the Trinacria and entered my nostrils. Barefoot, I stepped out upon the balustrade. Below me I saw Brucia's townspeople rudely in motion.

I dressed quickly and went downstairs to breakfast. There were not many tourists around. The few stuck here because they could not get rooms in Taormina had departed at the first word of danger; only those who could not help it remained. The desk clerk greeted me cheerily, going through the motions of the hostelry's professional air of optimism no matter what. He said that everything would be all right. I threw his words back at him and asked, "Isn't everything all right?" and he smiled toothily and said he liked Americans because they had such a sense of humor, and I didn't believe him.

As I was walking out, the officious clerk called to me. "Sir, do you want to look at your mail now or later?"

I don't know why but he antagonized me; I would not allow just anyone to throw his anti-Americanism at me. His manner said it; it was patronizing and cool.

"I'll pick it up after breakfast," I said casually, and continued through the door. I went into the bar next door to the hotel and ordered some coffee and a roll. The place was empty, but the smell of the mountain had reached here, too. I wondered which one of my lives was involved in the letter. I gulped down the bitter coffee and went back to the hotel desk and demanded my mail. The clerk handed it to me with elaborate politeness.

There was only one piece. It was a telegraph from Palermo. I walked off into a corner and sat down with it:

BY THE TIME THIS REACHES YOU YOU SHOULD BE DOWN. HAVE NOT RECEIVED SAMPLES FROM YOUR SECTOR. HAVE RECEIVED RUMORS OF SOME UNPLEASANTNESS. WHAT GIVES. EXPECT YOU BACK PALERMO TOMORROW WITH STUFF. WE'RE MOVING ON NEXT PLACE. TABBERT.

What the hell did he mean by the rumors? Was it something to do with the Company and myself or any of the people encountered on the mountain? It couldn't be that, I thought; maybe he meant the volcanic reports. Those must have reached Mediterranean American's monitors in Palermo. So they were moving on again, our good old team. I reread the brief telegram. Nothing said that I would or would not be going to the next place with the Company or what the home office thought. Well, I had a few questions to ask him, too. I had conflicting thoughts about the chips of rocks I had picked up on Etna; professional pride and the hope of discovery against a hostility toward Mediterranean American because of the Von Loesches it so willingly used and glorified. But I had nothing against Tabbert, who was trying to beat the Company his own way and help me if he could. I didn't want to let him down. The telegram was dated yesterday, late, and he expected me back today. But I couldn't walk out on what was happening here in Brucia. I had my samples. Tomorrow, first thing, would be only a day after and soon enough. By then I'd know where I was going.

I walked past the hotel, along the waterfront, toward where the town, the plain and the mountain met casually, looking for the center of activity. I asked a cleaning man brushing the cobbles where the school was located and he pointed over his shoulder with his broom. I wanted to see the building where she taught. And I also wanted to know what was happening about the course of the volcanic fissure, and if there was a way to help. Wernher—he was a strange one, checking the artillery-range formula and then disappearing afterward; I was puzzled about his behavior. But I was glad to walk alone again, away from everybody, in the stillness of the morning, trying to sort out my thoughts.

A light wind blowing in from the Ionian Sea stirred the sullen air. I turned a corner and came face to face with an assembly of vehicles over which flew a bright banner—the Something-Something Parco Divertimento. Of all the weird things to run across here, the least likely was a traveling carnival show, but it was unrolling its wheels, tents, platforms, floorings and attractions of human beings and small animals. A man dressed frantically in satin, including satin trousers, did setting-up exercises with dumbbells, and he had a satin shirt imprinted with a bicycle wheel, with the word *Licata* interwoven in its spokes, and I asked him, "*Licata?*" because that was one of the beachhead towns we first had stormed in Sicily, and he replied in English, "Yes, *boom-boom*, Americans." The war had brought his town fame, brevetted it with honor by accident. I pushed past a row of booths, a vendor of cooked octopus slicing rubbery pink-purple tentacles, a vicious loop-the-loop whose seats were made from the bodies of dismantled jeeps.

An enormous roulette wheel was being set up in the center

of the carnival midway. The wheel was adorned with a painting of a nude with heroic proportions, and numbers were placed all over her to bet on. A smell of animals permeated the area. I asked a man wearing a tie if he knew that there was an eruption on Etna and that lava was rolling toward the sea. He replied that he did but that Brucia was one of the regular stops this week in the year and the carnival never deviated from its itinerary; unless they kept their bizarre attractions wheeling and turning steadily the performers and animals would not eat. So it went on in the midst of threatening disaster.

I walked through the carnival, suddenly eager to get away from its queer sideshows, and hurried to a group of people in the middle of town. The streets began to fill: the women of Sicily in mourning garments and bent men in short striped jackets and still-barefoot children. There seemed to be a confusion about whether to evacuate or continue working normally. The people carried cheap cardboard cartons with their possessions inside, but some tenant farmers shouldered hoes and sickles. They waited around for a voice to tell them what next to do.

There was a new sound of carbines clacking on the cobblestones. The garrison in Catania had sent a company of soldiers to stand by in case of any trouble and to prevent others from looting what they, as men in uniform in the service of the state, lawfully deemed theirs first. It was traditional and expected in the Mediterranean countries. A handful of young boys, carrying a monkey as a mascot, ran between the ranks of the soldiers. The boys played their own monkey game, dragging their arms below their knees and imitating the squealing sounds. They found tails on one another's backs and tugged and grabbed at their genitals, and the soldiers watching them grinned.

The commanding officer of the garrison walked his troop to the town building and consulted on the steps with Brucia's mayor and police chief. The mayor wore a purple sash of office across his chest. I stood on the edge of the crowd that

197

gathered. There were not many kids around, and when I asked about them someone said they were in school. Franca's classes still went on. We had made no plans to meet again. In the crowd I saw Nicolosi.

"Joseph," he called out. He motioned a pathway through the crowd importantly. I came up and shook his hand and asked him how he was. "As good as ever," he said, hopping around. I said that he recovered quickly, and he replied, "One has to around here," and then he asked me if I was all right and added, "I want you to know that you're a friend." The friendship went both ways, I said, and he said, "Everything that happened on the mountain proved that," and I nodded, but he did not mention the hoped-for carnotite chips I had assembled quietly.

He moved with me closer to the mayor and the officer in charge of the Catania troops, who studied a map of Brucia. They had the lava flow line zeroed-in and were receiving telephoned reports regularly from the Professor up at the Osservatorio and from the central volcanic headquarters in Catania. It now was a case of how the lava struck the outer hills and became diverted in the downhill run. The forestream of lava had not miraculously evaporated but was a living, fearful thing.

The roar of a cut-out exhaust echoed in the square, and brakes screeched. A black Mercedes-Benz brushed against the crowd and a familiar figure emerged. The Baron was in sports tweeds and highly polished boots. Wernher was not with him now.

Nicolosi whispered slyly, "There's your old friend."

At the same time the Baron caught sight of Nicolosi and myself. He sprang toward us with outspread arms and gesticulated back and forth between ourselves and the town officials.

"Borken and Nicolosi! I was thinking about you. Nicolosi, your foot is okay?" The okay was for my sake, a gesture toward America. "Everything is all right with you both?" He

198

turned to the officials. "I gave these gentlemen a ride down the mountain in my truck." He tapped me playfully and addressed himself loudly to the group around the maps. "They probably would still be up there if I had not picked them up. Correct?" His charm oozed like hot tallow.

I thought to myself, He must think he has these people in his back pocket.

The Baron turned to the officials and said, "We were all on Etna together and we're all in the same boat now. The first thing we must think about is the preservation of our property. We must all help one another—that's why I returned from Catania this early."

The young mayor said, "Thank you. We will call upon your services, Baron. We may need vehicles to evacuate."

The Baron said, "My personal property is in danger of being overrun. It must be moved and I shall need some assistance. You," he said to the commander of the troops, "I will need some of the soldiers to carry down my possessions."

The captain of the troops seemed uncertain and looked to the mayor. The Baron drove a wedge in the hesitancy. "It's perfectly proper, you need not concern yourself about that. I know your commander in Catania. An old friend."

The mayor shook his head. "I'm sorry, Baron. We need these men and their vehicles to stand by here."

"My property is in danger of being overrun and damaged," the Baron said, trying to sound reasonable. "There are books up there which will eventually be of use to the library. There are trophies, valuable porcelain, and heirlooms. These things are a part of our life in Brucia. Can't you see the benefit to everybody? What good will they do buried under lava? We need a big truck up there immediately."

The mayor said, "If we could spare it, we would. I assure you we treat your property as anyone else's. But we cannot take chances with the vehicle or with the soldiers."

"I'm willing to pay the entire cost of the truck and soldiers," the Baron insisted. "I don't have to. It is an obligation of the

199

province to take care of the property of its citizens. That's why we pay taxes, and I pay plenty. What if my property was being looted? Would you not send someone up there to protect it?"

Nicolosi said to me, "This mayor has it in for him. He's one of us—elected on the Independents party ticket last year." The mayor was a young attorney who had returned to practice in his home area after having been graduated from the law school in Palermo. "Listen to him talk. The boy has a golden tongue."

"My job, Baron, is not to answer hypothetical questions. Here we are faced with realities which give us enough of a problem. The first is the flow of lava and how to prepare for it. The second is how to evacuate people. The third is property. If you wish me to pursue this, let me explain it this way: If you were on the mountain now, I would be obliged to send up one of the vehicles to rescue you. For your silverware, et cetera, the answer is, I am sorry."

The Baron turned his back on the mayor and strode toward us. "You saw the conditions, you came down in my truck. And you, Nicolosi, we old-timers know each other. Tell them what a waste it would be for my property to be ruined. You've seen it. Both of you. You, you're an American, you can reason with these people."

The crowd turned to me, waiting for my reaction. The words in Tabbert's wire flashed across my mind: rumors of some unpleasantness.

I said resolutely, "It's up to the mayor to decide."

Nicolosi gave me an approving look. I wanted his approval.

But I was not finished. I said to the Baron, "I speak for myself, not as an American or for America, when I say the mayor is right."

The Baron looked at me with hatred and muttered under his breath. Then he turned on his heel, and a path was cleared for him to his car. He accelerated his car and it coughed noisily and sped away in the direction of Catania.

The mayor said, "Let's get back to work. Enough of this nonsense."

Everybody bent over the maps. One of the group was a vulcanologist-in-training from Catania who had come to observe on the spot how a town handled such an eruption. The vulcanologist said he needed information from the Institute, and the officials and some of the townspeople crowded indoors. I hung back; this was their business. But the mayor signaled me to come along, and I nodded eagerly and followed them into his office.

The mayor got on the telephone to the central relay point in Catania which assembled the information about the path of the threatening lava stream for all the towns in the shadow of Etna. He repeated aloud for our ears, ". . . one thousand yards from here and headed toward the Saint's Ridge . . . correct . . . strikes a glance at the edges toward the sea . . . trucks for equipment . . . interested in the evacuation and how many can be accommodated . . . the man from your Institute is here and he says one of the streams surely is on its way."

I glanced at the studious young man making notes; he was self-absorbed.

". . . of course you have our permission to do so. . . . I'm the authority approving it as long as that is the recommendation . . . there's nothing to lose by trying . . . speed speed speed . . . yes, you speak to him yourself."

The mayor handed the telephone to the scientist from the Institute. In a serious tone, he said, "Director, this is the opportunity for which we have waited. If the Army plane is available, we can put the experiment to the test in the next thirty minutes. The mayor is correct—we must move quickly. The aircraft is arranged for and the pilot follows his instructions as rehearsed. Are you in favor? Yes, of course, I am also. Yes, sir, you arrange for the aircraft. I will forward the exact position from the spotter map as soon as he takes to the air."

For the first time the vulcanologist smiled. He spoke triumphantly, as if he had just made an important scientific discovery.

"My director at the Institute is agreeable," he said. "At this moment he is arranging with the military commandant in Catania to send up an aircraft. The pilot will release bombs or dynamite charges at the lava stream, splitting it into weaker and ineffectual streams which can then be diverted easily."

The mayor agreed. This was the first time dynamite charges released from an airplane would try to change the course of lava from Etna's eruptions. I had never heard of the technique, but the Sicilian vulcanologist said that the method had been used successfully in the American territory of Hawaii during an eruption at Manualoa. The iron wisdom of scientific opinion prevailed in the room.

Runners dashed into the office every few minutes to report the position of the lava. A spotter stationed in the cathedral's campanile at the edge of Brucia relayed the shifting mutiny of the descending forestream of rock and spewing lava. The direction had not changed on the marked map; the peril was greater and nearer.

The vulcanologist began to call off the positions over the telephone to the Catania headquarters: "Location on scale of 50,000 to one . . . bombing on the top quarter, fifty yards . . . area evacuated . . . ready on this end . . ."

Suddenly his voice lowered. He listened and we strained into the telephone with him. Something was not happening. He hung up the receiver; despair turned to anger.

The mayor sensed what was wrong ahead of the rest of us. "No airplane," he said.

"They cannot spare an Army plane to divert the lava from the town," the vulcanologist said.

"The hell you say!" Nicolosi spoke up. "It's that bastard of a Baron who put them up to this."

"I don't think so," the mayor said. He addressed the troop captain. "We do not ask for a squadron, all we need is one plane." The captain shrugged and pointed to the air, saying that he had nothing to do with what flew.

"They say the Catania air squadrons go on maneuvers," the vulcanologist said. "Tomorrow they have a big air review over Rome with the North Atlantic forces. The director has been told that if one plane was taken out of the fly-by it would break up the formation of two others. If the plane flies on a lava mission today, they say it might not be operational tomorrow. Besides, they have written orders."

"What is more important," the mayor said, "a damn formation or Brucia?"

"I know which is," the vulcanologist said. "So does my director. I'm sure the air commander in Catania knows, too— he's from around here somewhere. We worked out the plan to bomb the forestream with him originally and he was very enthusiastic. We have just run into a blank wall."

"There is no excuse in an emergency," Nicolosi said pointedly, looking at the troop captain. "They are not interested in our welfare."

The mayor said calmly, "Who is the *they?*"

"Whoever prevents the plane from going up to bomb the lava," Nicolosi muttered.

"Let's not turn on one another," the mayor said. "There is work to do. Forget the damn plane. There is still a chance that by some stroke of luck the lava may bypass us and run off into the sea." He turned to his assistants and to the troop captain. "All right, let us have the evacuation trucks, the automobiles and wagons assembled in the square. Nobody drives out with an empty car or wagon. Spotters to stay at their posts—the records must be kept up. Vulcanologist, I delegate you to take care of that, and you can have my office staff. We know how to do things for ourselves, we have done so before."

The police officer on the open line with the spotter in the cathedral at the edge of Brucia broke in to say that the distance was a quarter of a mile now, but there was a slight bend in the forestream. I moved closer to the maps to see how the contour rose and fell northeast of Brucia. If the lava stream only kept curving on the low ridge that formed a natural wall for the town, Brucia could be spared.

Nicolosi and I went outside the mayor's office. The word had reached the townspeople that no outside help was coming from Catania. Trucks and cars lined up. Soldiers assigned to the vehicles stood by importantly. The carnival's trucks were ordered unhitched from their exhibitions, but some could not be, and I saw tarpaulins covering the wagons, lowered like the curtains around a house canary's cage, and behind them shapeless animals bumped and growled. The square filled with women and children too young for school.

"When does Franca return from her classes?" I asked Nicolosi, unafraid to reveal myself.

"Normally a few hours from now she would come home to eat," Nicolosi said. "The school is on the high ground away from danger. Maybe they will keep the students there—it's safer."

"I'm worried about Franca," I said.

Nicolosi looked at me intently and said, "*Beh,* she knows how to take care of herself. She is very independent."

I paused, thinking how right he was, that she did what she wanted to do without fear.

"I haven't seen Edoardo this morning."

"Joseph, I can't tell you where he is—a private matter."

I said nothing and Nicolosi changed the subject quickly.

"Look at them," he said, pointing to a group of old women in their church mourning dresses. Slowly they marched in the direction of the cathedral chanting hymns, led by a priest. Other townspeople formed behind them. From within the cathedral I heard the murmur of prayers and a voice passionately shouting, "Saint Agatha! Saint Agatha! She will save us!"

Two men who had joined the procession suddenly ran to the altar and grabbed a three-foot plaster statue of the Catania patroness. The sight of Saint Agatha's statue gave the

204

women in black an actual presence they could appeal to, unlike the morality enveloping ordinary prayers to unseen deities. Here was a graven image; therefore, a real god.

But Nicolosi, who had prayed here alone, refused to join this group.

The two men adjusted the statue between them and began to walk out of the cathedral. The priest followed, carrying an ivory crucifix. The women rose and formed a line behind the standard-bearers. They walked as if at a funeral, heads bent, and soon passed the unfurled tents of the carnival.

On a tower of the cathedral, I saw the posted spotter from the mayor's group. He was stationed so that he could see the stream of lava as it slid nearer Saint's Ridge. Behind and below him stood the town.

From the cathedral an old priest emerged. A path cleared for him as he moved to the head of the column of worshipers. He motioned the bearers of Saint Agatha to stand behind him and he took the ornate cross from the young priest's hands and knelt on the ground. The people fell to the earth. The old priest chanted, "Grant, we beseech Thee, O Lord, an answer to our heartfelt supplications. O Lord, Thy wrath being appeased, turn away from us this disaster, that the hearts of men may know that these scourges proceed from Thine anger with the sinning mortals beneath Thy hand, and cease by Thy mercy."

The kneeling people shook and cried; the old women wailed. The air smelled strongly of incense and lava. The wind had swept the sulphur vapors in this direction, and now, as a harbinger of catastrophe, the nauseous smell invaded our throats, mixing with the holy perfumes. The praying people sensed the nearness of the lava stream and rose in confusion, seeking guidance. Some left the priests and started to run toward the evacuation trucks, revealing pink and white underclothes as they lifted their black skirts to move swiftly.

But the old priest continued. "Hear us, O Lord, who cry unto Thee, and grant us, Thy suppliant servants, that we who are justly afflicted for our sins, may by Thy preventing find mercy. O Almighty, who hast compassion on all, and wouldst not that any should perish, favorably look down upon all those who are seduced by the deceit and impudence of Satan, that all heretical impiety being removed, the hearts of such as err may repent and return to the one true faith. O Lord, Thy wrath being appeased, turn away from us this disaster, O Lord, Thy wrath being appeased, turn away from the one true faith this disaster."

The old man passed the cross to the young priest and slowly returned to the cathedral. The people ran frightened to the center of the town. The young priest shook his statuary at them in admonition.

The spotter was still at his post in the tower. I asked the priest how to get up there and he pointed to a circular stairway behind the altar. It was narrow and dark and perhaps something could be done, being a forward observer here, and I wanted to play this out. Nicolosi and I climbed the stout flooring, up to the campanile. The spotter lay on a ledge with his telephone next to him.

"How does it look?" I asked.

"Five minutes will tell," the spotter said.

We peered into the sunlight streaming through the openings in the bell tower. Prone upon a wooden crossbeam, the cathedral's bells above our heads, we saw the lava forestream again as we had first seen it on Mount Etna.

The narrowed lava boiled along the edges of Saint's Ridge. Its thick bed was now reduced to a sharply cutting wall of rock and steam the height of a farmer's fence. The thinned column was powerful enough to climb the stone barrier on the distant side of the cathedral instead of turning toward the sea. Slowly it dragged its life force, crawling like a soldier with a gut wound, toward the cemetery grounds bordering the church. The first evidences of destruction we saw were the tumbling tombstones. The gray-black lava of burning, moving earth buried the carved granite and marble and filled in the undug but marked places reserved for future generations here. Broken headstones stuck up jaggedly through the rivulets of molten earth as the stream moved to encircle its commemorated victims. The dead were reburied, and new graves outlined.

The stream passed beneath us, its force diminishing, with no harm to the buildings, and moved onward to the next natural depression where the carnival, with its exhibits of animals and freaks and other wondrous sights, was parked. One of the wagons, covered with tarpaulin, contained a circus of trick dogs. As we watched the stream near the wagon we heard, above the hissing noise, the sounds of screaming of the overbred animals. Then screams turned to whimpering. But now the rise in the land outside Brucia was too formidable a barrier for the spent stream, dissipated down thousands of feet of winding mountain, down the slopes of the formidable volcano and the ash and earth curled alongside the ridge and, feeding itself with huge weight, it retched a hissing, burning path into the beach next to Brucia, into the Ionian Sea.

Nicolosi and I listened to the spotter report the news on the telephone strung to the young mayor with the purple sash of office. We climbed down the winding stairway of the cathedral. I heard the animals in the carnival truck weeping pathetically. A trainer rushed up and said that some of his best animals had died of fright, as the overbred do.

The area where the lava had struck near the cathedral was roped off and the local police were posted there. Soldiers from the Catania garrison were ordered back, but a few were not to be found when they counted off in the square. Someone sugested that they might be found in the local bordello, but, after a search, they were discovered drunk behind the bar along the waterfront, having slept through the whole danger period.

The old priest appeared, carrying another Saint Agatha, this one only a foot high, and the townspeople touched it as he passed among them. Some of the people declared, "A miracle."

207

Other people said, "Is it not a miracle?" The young priest modestly said miracles were not that easily made; that what had happened was that the flow of lava had changed its course when it neared the cemetery and that some damage had been caused to the sanctified monuments. But the legend was there to grow.

I watched the people of Brucia go their own ways after the crisis had passed, and the mayor and the vulcanologist from Catania asked me to join them in a drink in the mayor's office because I had helped them chart the lava's course. "It is too bad you could not try out the airplane," I said to the vulcanologist, and he said the Professor at the Osservatorio would be disappointed because he was the one who had suggested the idea. "I know your Professor," I said enthusiastically. "I met him up there," and the vulcanologist said he was a great scholar, and I nodded.

While we were talking, a young photographer from Catania entered the mayor's office. He was crisscrossed with Leicas and Rolleis and he eagerly said he had just arrived to take photographs of the damage but that the local police would not permit him to do so unless he received written permission from the mayor. The photographer said he was anxious to take these pictures not only for the local publications in Catania but also for American magazines. "My goal is to have a beautiful picture in your *Life* magazine," the photographer said, after the mayor mentioned that I was an American.

The mayor smiled and handed him written permission. "Do not be too disappointed if they do not buy your beautiful picture," the mayor called out. Then he turned to me and said, "This eruption is not successful enough for *Life,* is it?"

I said that I didn't know much about the contents of the magazine and recalled only the covers with movie starlets from all the world.

"Anyway," the mayor said, "Brucia is too unimportant to concern people outside."

208

In the afternoon, I called downstairs for some sandwiches and coffee and ate alone in the Trinacria. I stretched out on the bed afterward and listened to the noises of the town below the balustrade. I strained for the sound of the gentle tapping on the door of Franca. I visualized her outlined in the high-winged chair, sitting demurely in her thonged sandals, and sought her body next to mine on the bed. But there was only a private silence here.

· I reached for the telephone and thumbed through a memorandum book with some notes and addresses. I asked the operator for Mr. Tabbert at the Mediterranean American Development Company in Palermo. I wanted to cover myself because I'd be a day late, and besides, I wanted to be straight with him. The operator said she was having some line trouble going through Catania on the circuit to Palermo. I told her to keep trying and leave a message that Joseph Borken was calling. I took my rock samples from the pack in the closet and laid them out on the bedspread. Each was tagged and identified and I rearranged the chips carefully. I liked this testing and sorting, the sense of discovery.

I reached for the phone again and called Franca's number. The rasping noise on the other end went unanswered. It was no use waiting; this was my move again. I hurried into the street. I heard the desk clerk call out my name but I continued without turning. Nothing he could tell me was as important as seeing Franca.

The streets began to swell with people returning from tilled fields and near-by quarries. It seemed as if a huge sigh of relief had lightened the countenances of the Bruciesi. With the town spared, they had recaptured their vitality. Many headed in the direction of the Something-Something Parco Divertimento to play and be entertained. The carnival unrolled its exhibits again.

I stepped along briskly toward the school on the far side of town where Franca taught. I got lost on one street but recovered by following the departing line of students in reverse, going where they came from. Finally I saw a handsome brick-and-glass building. Late students still streamed through the doors. Occasionally a teacher appeared, mounted on a bicycle, and pedaled off. I asked one of the women if Miss Florio had left yet, and she pointed to the school, shook her head and rode away. Franca stepped through the school door at the same moment.

She saw me and came running up. She seemed concerned.

"What are you doing here, Joseph?"

"Looking for a Miss Florio who teaches here. Have you seen her?"

"Please, Joseph."

"I shouldn't have come to the school—it's too open. I'm sorry."

"No, dear," she said, and I smiled and reached beneath her books for her hand, and she returned the pressure.

"What is it?"

"An obligation. I am in a hurry. I just received a message from my father and Edoardo. I must join them for a while. I don't know how long it will take."

"It's private, isn't it? Your father hinted at something this morning."

"You were with him through it all? That makes me feel good."

"I like Nicolosi. I'd like him even if he didn't have a daughter with beautiful eyes."

"Joseph. No, really, this is important. I can tell you—they are going to take possession of the Baron's farmland this afternoon. It was timed this way. A meeting is on now. Many people must be present, of all classes and occupations in the town."

I hesitated. "It's not just Edoardo's show, is it?"

She replied, "It's the whole town's show, if you wish to call it that. This is something Grandpa and the others have talked about here for a year. The Baron owns most of the good culti-

210

vated land. The peasants who rent want an opportunity to break their old indentures. They want a chance to buy."

"That sounds like free enterprise to me," I said. "I'm here until the early train tomorrow. Can I give you some moral support?"

She paused. "I do not know if they would want an outsider. Joseph, it is up to them. But what of your company and your work? Have you thought of—"

"My work is completed, darling. The rest is personal."

"Come if you wish. If they do not want an outsider there, Grandpa and the others will say so. But it is your decision first."

"I'm with you."

We walked through the crowds of Brucia and turned in at a basement of a small building near the waterfront. A crowd of roughly dressed townspeople and tenant farmers milled around. Among them were Nicolosi, Edoardo, and the old man. And I recognized big-featured Cousin Vittorio, at whose house we had stopped briefly.

Vittorio came up and shook my hand. "Mr. Borken," he said, "I see you got down off my mountain in one piece. Remember what I told you?" I nodded. "The time has come—we are going to seize the Baron's tenant holdings."

Edoardo spoke. I could not make out what he was saying; the dialect was deliberately obscure. But I gathered from the looks on the faces of Nicolosi and Franca that he was questioning my right to be here, in the middle of their planning.

"You are too damn anti-American," Vittorio said. "The question is not high politics but only one man's belief in our cause."

They turned toward me. I said, "Don't get into an argument about it. I am not part of your action. Edoardo is right, I'd better leave."

"That's nonsense," Vittorio said. "The more support we get,

the more people we have from all over, the more successful our job will be." He faced me. "Are you for us or not?"

Franca and I exchanged glances. I said resolutely, "I'm on your side."

The people in the room nodded their heads. A smile played around the corners of Franca's mouth.

"Let us get on with it," Vittorio said. It was clear that forcefulness had made him the leader of the local Peasant party. "Our activist committee thinks this is the hour to take possession—to strike out while any organized opposition still has the eruption in their noses. The Catania garrison has left Brucia. The way is clear. Let us use democratic procedure. All those in favor of seizing immediately raise their hands."

More than half the men and women in the room, including Nicolosi and Edoardo, raised their hands. But not everyone was geared to immediate action.

"Now all those who are disagreeable enough to ignore the will of the majority and vote the other way, raise your hands."

Not a hand went up.

"In that case," Vittorio said, "we are unanimous for seizure now."

The people filed out, determined to speed the wheels of history for Brucia, too.

Franca walked with her father and a girl friend, also a teacher. Edoardo walked next to Vittorio, as his lieutenant in command of the seizure by virtue of his special hatred for the Baron. Grandfather marched with two of his cronies—old swaybacked farmers like himself; pinned on their sweaters were World War I victory medals from the House of Savoy. I trailed along behind Nicolosi. That was close enough; I was part of it and yet outside.

There were fifty or sixty men marching with pitchforks, spades, rods, shovels and even sticks. They were joined by wives and older children and the curious who followed as if this were a religious procession. At the head of the crowd Vittorio strode, followed by some of his lieutenants rolling bicycles. We passed the young mayor's office, but, if he was around, he did not notice the marching people. Nor did the town police in front of the mayor's building. Sympathizing local authority vanished before the growing phalanx of townspeople and peasants.

Nicolosi called to me to walk beside him and I did, avoiding Franca and her girl friend. "A stick is good enough," he said. I said that I would come along but carry nothing. "We must," he said. "One of the peasants whose son lives in Calabria, where they pulled off a seizure last month, said that to make it legal in the Government's eyes, the land must be turned over a few times. That shows a legitimate working claim on the land of an absentee landlord." He winked. "That makes illegal work legal."

We reached the cathedral. Vittorio raised his hand to halt the marchers. He conferred with his lieutenants, and a delegation entered the church. A hush fell over the crowd. Nicolosi whispered that they were trying to get a blessing.

The old priest was asleep at this hour in the afternoon. But in a few moments the young priest came out. He surveyed the crowd which had gathered without entering the cathedral. He began to speak slowly. He said that the delegation before him had come to the church for blessings for conduct against other individuals, the landlords who were not tilling their own soil but leaving choice areas only for everlasting indenture. Not only could the church not sanction the setting of one group against another, he said, but it was forced to condemn such behavior. On the other hand, he suddenly continued, there were equally strong words in the Holy Laws favoring honest toilers and that the workingmen should receive the fruits of their labors.

"Listen to him," Nicolosi said, encouraged by the priest's sympathetic words. The young priest spoke with Jesuitical reasoning, logical, viable and appropriate to the occasion.

" . . . acting against the landowners is prohibited by all laws, legal and moral. But it has come to my attention that in

213

some regions of the Latium, the peasants have moved against the land itself. That, of course, can be another matter worthy of reflection. Man cannot judge man. But man can husband the soil for his own needs. That is a blessed thing—"

"Do you or do you not give your blessings to our group?" Edoardo interrupted. "My party and these people came here for approval. Do you give it or not?"

The young priest looked at Edoardo without emotion and replied that he could neither bless nor condemn the mission against the land. But, he added, since so many of his parishioners were involved, would it be possible for him to accompany them? The people motioned and smiled. He said softly that they would be less inclined to get into trouble with him present.

It looked as if he was with them himself but could not come out and say so officially. But he knew the rationale of his church.

The parade started up the mountain roadway. Besides the Etna hunting land we had been on, the Baron held thousands of choice acres outside Brucia, less than a half hour by foot. I glanced at Franca and caught her eye several times. Her girl friend noticed our little game and I saw her twitting Franca. Up ahead, Edoardo stuck to the road without turning. It was best that we did not walk together now.

Around a ridge, and past a crossroads, the group reached a long strip of cultivated land. The tenant farmers were called to the head of the procession. Standing on a rocky ledge, Vittorio studied the terrain before him. He was a natural commander. The farmers pointed out the parts of the land they had broken and tilled all their lives for feudal pay. This was their one chance.

The land was ringed with new barbed wire strung on the piled stone—a warning to peasants with ideas. Nicolosi said the wire had been put up a month ago, after the land seizures in Calabria had been given tacit approval by Rome. Across

214

the field, I heard the Baron's dogs barking. I knew that their master could not be too far away. I smelled trouble.

Vittorio led the group up to the edge of the barbed wire. He ordered everyone to spread out along the fence's waiting barbs. Then the peasant leader turned to the priest. "A prayer, please," he said.

It came more as command than request. The priest lowered his head and prayed. While he did so, on the opposite side of the field the roar of a motor fired the air. An eight-wheeled truck, far more powerful than the one which had taken us down Etna, tore across a narrow pathway in the tilled field, crushing olive branches beneath its rubber treads and churning the earth. When the truck reached the little pitchfork army, it turned sharply about, its tailgate facing us. Everyone on our side of the barbed wire instinctively moved back.

The tailgate of the truck banged down. A score of armed men, strangers to Brucia, jumped out professionally. They wore no uniform other than street clothes bulging with small arms and carbines and bandoliers. They looked tough as they stared, blank-eyed, at their compatriots across the fence. They knew what they were up to, these strangers who formed a private individual's private armed force. It would be suicide to try to wrest the land from these hired guns.

Vittorio called a council of his lieutenants a dozen yards behind the barbed wire, facing the gunmen. He walked the length of the fence, sorting out the women and children and sending them to the rear. Some of the women refused to leave their husbands, and these were forced back together with their men. A shadow of fear fell across Franca's face. But she went with the others, obeying Vittorio's firm orders. I stood close alongside Nicolosi.

The priest came over to Vittorio, and I overheard them talking. "Call off the raid, Vittorio," he pleaded.

"There is greater reason not to," Vittorio declared. "If we back off now we will never be able to strike here again."

The priest shook his head, saying, "You need not try to be brave in front of armed men—bloodshed does not help your cause."

Edoardo interrupted. "This is our crusade," he shouted.

The priest said patiently, "Let us try to reason with them, at least."

The next move on either side counted. It came from Edoardo. He leaped upon the barbed stone wall. He stood high above the others, looking down on the gunmen. "This land belongs to the people of Brucia who have worked it," he shouted. "That is the new law of the land here. We abide by it. So must you. We are all on the side of the tenant farmers in this struggle. You are Sicilians, too—these men are not your enemies. The only enemies we have are poverty and greed."

Across the field, an automobile turned over its motor and started toward us. Its outlines marked it as the Baron's Mercedes-Benz. There were two people riding inside it. Call it off, I said to myself; the priest is right, more bloodshed in our time will prove nothing. But the pitch of events could not be halted.

The gunmen began to take shape as individuals, no less grotesque, and among them I detected their leader. He was a man of the city with a pencil-thin mustache and a bluish, unshaven face. He stood at attention and snapped his fingers stiffly at his sides. It was not nervousness but a gesture of command. Immediately two of his gunmen sprang onto the truck. They dug beneath tarpaulins and uncovered a light machine gun. One grabbed the handle and the other the feed belt. It was already loaded. A 30-caliber, American-made. They pushed the gun up to the dropped tailgate and crouched on the floor.

The 30-caliber and the men became as one haunched piece of assembled, obedient machinery: bolts, feeder, stand, barrel, firing mechanism and the fingers and eyes of the killers locked in place. The barrel of the gun swiveled until Edoardo was fixed in its sights.

216

A terrible silence descended on both sides of the barbed wire. The peasants were frozen into indecision by the unsmiling gunmen before them. Halfway down the field the Baron's car idled. Far behind us the women stood.

Vittorio measured the armed enemy. They were not playing; these men were capable of obeying orders given by those who placed the weapons in their hands. The cause they fought for as hirelings did not matter. Vittorio sensed the futility of fighting machine weapons with pitchforks and began to fall back. But Edoardo taunted the gunmen from his dangerous perch on the fence.

He was a man aflame. He told them they had a stake in this land redistribution—he did not call it a seizure. That this kind of action from the bottom upward was part of a great movement around the whole province to help everyone, including the landowners; that by tilling the soil as men with spine, increased productivity would result. He appealed to the gunmen to join in the aspirations of the peasants. He said there was no difference between the men who worked the soil and those who guarded it.

Vittorio watched the stone-eared men and their leader. The words fell away. Nothing had changed.

"Edoardo!" Vittorio called out. "Come here next to me."

Edoardo turned and motioned negatively. As he did so he slipped to avoid the barbed stones beneath his feet and fell to the ground on the Baron's land. Or did he jump deliberately, defiantly?—I could not tell.

The mustached leader raised his arms quickly and snapped his fingers. The machine gunners followed Edoardo down to the ground. For a moment they hesitated, looking for further orders from their leader. "Fire, damn you!" he screamed.

A burst of flame tore out of the barrel of a machine gun. The bullets struck the fallen body and ricocheted against the stones. Edoardo's form shuddered and lay lifeless.

The shock of the exploding bullets froze us to the ground. Not a sound came from either side. Nobody here, certainly

217

not myself, had seen a man machine-gunned to death in cold anger this way for years—not since the Panzer divisions fought here.

I looked up and saw someone running past the Baron's car, which began to move slowly toward us. The figure loomed up as Wernher. Before the armed men knew what was happening, he had leaped up on the truck and wrenched the smoking machine gun from the hands of the killer. Then, raising the machine gun in his arms, he leveled it at the mustached leader and ordered him to drop his arms. The leader, confused because he had seen Wernher coming from the Baron's direction, did as he was told. The others threw their carbines to the ground. I picked one up, helping to cover them.

Now Vittorio awoke to action. He yelled to the townspeople and peasants to follow him. They smashed a hole in the stone wall with their pitchforks and hoes, and came tearing through the opening. Vittorio knelt over Edoardo's body and called to the priest. Then he boldly struck the leader of the gunmen across the face. The unarmed gunmen shrank before Vittorio's forcefulness. They retreated toward the Baron's car. Vittorio ordered, "Spread out! Work the land!" His people scattered over the fields, staking out their claims. But they were not festive.

The Baron pulled up before the people invading his land. He saw Wernher still cradling the machine gun. He saw Edoardo on the ground, the priest praying over the body. The crowd pressed in. He was surrounded.

"This is your doing," Vittorio shouted, pointing at Edoardo's body. "Your men did it. We did not touch the land until your thugs killed him."

"Those men were told not to use their arms," the Baron argued, addressing himself to the group around him. "I specifically told them there was to be no shooting. I was protecting my land. Is that illegal?"

The group pointed their fingers accusingly toward Edoardo's body.

218

"I did not hire them; they forced me to employ them. I have never seen them before. I do not know where they came from. Their leader came to me and volunteered his services. I could not get aid from the town. This is a terrible calamity. I will compensate his family."

He saw me standing near his barbed fence.

"Borken, you know it is not my fault, mine is private property which must be protected—in my country as in yours."

"In any country," I said angrily, "you would be held responsible for the acts of your gunmen."

He appealed to Wernher. "I tried to stop them, you heard me tell the men to behave themselves. They were here to guard the land—"

"You are mistaken, Baron," Wernher said. "This machine gun is your property." He threw it to the ground.

Two jeeploads of police from the province arrived. Behind them came the mayor. They herded the Baron's gunmen in his own truck, stacked their carbines, and drove off. The mayor spoke quietly to Vittorio, and in a few moments the peasants in the fields were called in. Vittorio told them that they had achieved what they were after. The Baron began to protest to the mayor, saying that the provincial courts would guard his rights. Many of the peasants remained on the land, among them Franca's grandfather. Soon the townspeople dispersed. The mayor and the Baron stood in animated conversation. Then the Baron raced the motor of his car and drove away.

I searched for Franca, but someone said she had left with her father. I saw her girl friend walking back with some others and asked, "How is Franca?"

"Edoardo was her friend," she explained, needlessly.

I nodded and said I knew. "Did she cry?" I asked her.

"Franca does not cry very much but she feels," her friend said quietly.

The late sun glowed over the seized fields. Wernher and I began to walk back to Brucia together. Nearly everybody but

219

the peasants in possession had left. Friends had wheeled away Edoardo's body in a decorated cart. The land turned blood-pink under the reflected light from the surrounding hills. We stepped slowly along the worn pathway where the different sides had fought for many centuries, including ours, hurling polished thunderbolts.

I looked at this German, wondering what made him behave the way he did.

"You know this part of Sicily well," I said.

"As you no doubt do—from the war. I ate plenty of dust that summer. We were here only a few months but I never got a chance to see anything after I was hit. My division was in the line below here."

"The Goering Division? We first saw you in North Africa."

"In Sicily we faced the British on this side of the front," Wernher said.

"Why did you return here, anyway?"

"To keep a resolution. This mountain was behind and then in front of us—I think I have dug holes on three sides of it! I told myself that if I ever came out of the war alive, I would see what this mountain really looked like from above. Sentiment, nothing more."

"A lot of Germans revisit these old battlefields, I hear. Trying to relive the old glories—"

"Forget that," he said curtly. "I went through it all. There was no more glory to war by the time we were in Sicily."

On an impulse, I asked him, "Did you ever know a Colonel Von Loesch?"

"Von Loesch? The rocket expert, wasn't he? Did the Russians or the Americans get him?"

I dropped the subject and asked him how he spoke English so well, and he said he had studied it and now taught high-school students in his native Bonn. I listened to him suspiciously; there was still his unexplained association with the Baron.

"Do you think he'll get away with the shooting?" I asked.

220

"Yes, his breed knows how to survive. They can even get away with murder. No matter what country they come from."

"Then why did you associate with him?" I asked loudly.

He stopped short and gripped my arm. The muscles in his hand thickened. I looked at him squarely, demanding an answer, not hiding my pent-up feelings. We stood alone on the still pathway in the twilight. He was angry; I was on guard. And then his grip loosened and he dropped his arms to his sides.

"I was deceived," Wernher said. His voice lowered. "I had not touched a gun all these years. Then when I came to this part of Sicily, I had a sudden desire to try my skill on a target. Why, I do not know. Sentiment, too, perhaps. My consulate in Catania suggested the Baron's hunting preserve on Etna. That coincided with my wish to see the mountain. I held the shotgun but could not shoot the doves. My consul is a good friend of the Baron's—but that is his business."

The lights were coming on in Brucia above a ridge. I could see the Trinacria from here.

"You moved like lightning to grab that machine gun from them," I said. "The Baron won't recommend an Iron Cross to your consulate for that."

"Are you making a joke?"

I said, of course.

"I hated to touch that damn machine gun. It made me animal-like again. But I had to take it away from those children. Stupid fools that they are—that foolhardy young man's life was taken needlessly."

"It took bravery to stand up before the gunmen."

"I suppose," he said, almost disinterested. "What angered me was the deception. The Baron said he had a skeet shooting range back there. I did not realize what was going on until it was too late. It was necessary to disarm those ruffians. There has been enough death in Sicily."

"Anyway," I said, "you helped to open the way for the people to take possession of the land from the Baron."

"I did not mean to. That is politics, and not my concern." Almost in fear, he added, "You do not think there will be trouble with the authorities?"

"For you? No. You're probably one of the first Germans passing through here they—" I hesitated over the words.

"I know, I can see it on their faces. German tourists, they say, are only soldiers out of uniform. It is in too deep."

"For this generation it is difficult to be unprejudiced."

We walked into town together, and he turned off toward the main square to rent a taxicab that would take him back to his hotel in Catania.

At the last minute he asked, "Would you care to have dinner with me?"

He noticed my hesitation and added quickly that perhaps I had another engagement. Then he put out his hand and left for Catania.

He appeared, at last, a little less faceless to me.

There was another wire from Tabbert waiting at the reception desk of the Trinacria. It said what I had expected. What was keeping me and didn't I know he was waiting to see the results of my trip and why was I not back right away? Sure I knew: the job and my name were at stake. But there were more important things than the world of Mediterranean American. I checked the timetable obediently. There were no flights that night; the rapid train early the next morning would do. I wasn't jumping up and clicking my heels for the Company: I was in better shape.

I washed and went downstairs again to the place near the hotel. Some of the steam that had built up in Brucia in the past couple of days was being let off—a double celebration for the "miracle" which had spared the town from the lava and the successful land seizure. There were toasts to Edoardo for his courage. I overheard a discussion about the machine gun that had killed him—whether it was American surplus or stolen contraband—but they quieted down as I approached.

Some of the Bruciesi at the bar welcomed me as the American who had joined them.

I sat and ate alone. Soon a voice behind me said jokingly, "Guess who? No fair looking." I turned around and there, smiling audaciously, was that American clothes designer (or whatever he was) who lived at Taormina. He had a good friend with him, and he said, "Aren't you going to invite us to sit down?" and I said, "Sure, do that." He introduced his tightly jeaned friend, who was much younger, as a traveling fellowship scholar named Tab or Shad, one of those all-American nicknames I never could quite catch, and he added, "You're not the only pebble on the beach." They were in high spirits, having come down from a party among the American colony in Taormina to replenish their food and wine supplies in Brucia. "Come on along and meet the crowd," the designer said. "We're having a ball." That tickled his friend.

I said thanks but I couldn't because I had to wake up early to catch the train to Palermo, and they went through the doors with their arms loaded with stuff and into their Volkswagen, laughing privately.

After dinner I took the direction toward Franca's house. The streets were familiar by now. Here stood the courtyards on her side and the row of newer houses across the way. I walked up to the small door within the wooden portal and lifted the knocker. It made a hollow, meaningless noise that echoed down the street. I knew what I had to say to her.

Heavy footsteps came down the stone hallway and into the courtyard; someone was unlocking the latch, unhinging the door.

Nicolosi stood before me in the pale light.

"Joseph. It is so late. What are you doing here?"

"I came to say goodbye. I leave before breakfast tomorrow."

"Well, come in then."

I hesitated. "You're right, Nicolosi, it is late. You all must be so tired."

He said, "Yes. Franca is asleep. You know—it has been a sad day. But come in, have a last drink with me."

"No, no. I've disturbed you enough. I didn't realize how late it was." I stood there, not saying anything for a moment, and then I asked, "Is she very unhappy?"

"*Beh*, who knows what is going through her mind? Edoardo came to the house often, he was a good friend. We thought that when he got on his feet someday, they would be married. She has had too much hard luck, and she is not a young girl any longer. First, it was the damn war, then all the uncertainties afterward. Her father had to scratch for a living—I wish I could have done more for my daughters."

"Nicolosi," I said, "did Franca say anything else?"

I meant about myself, but he continued, "She is a fatalist, like all her friends—all those around here. When Edoardo jumped over the stone fence onto the Baron's land, he took a bold step. Franca said that he always wanted to do something brave, poor soul. It was a noble act for the tenant farmers and the ideas we all believe in. No, it was not wasted. The people are still on the Baron's land."

I held out my hand. "Thank you for all the help on the mountain."

"*Beh*, all I did was carry part of the load and then I caused trouble by getting my foot caught in that damn trap. By the way, if any of your associates need a guide—"

I smiled and said I'd tell them I knew of an excellent one.

It was cool outside, standing in this half-open door where she had stood, and I said to him, "Will you say goodbye to Franca?"

Nicolosi nodded, and looked at me closely.

"Don't forget what you saw here," he said.

"It's all inside," I said.

Outside, there was the mountain, hovering over Brucia and the towns in the valley, where the foothills and the Ionian Sea slid gently together, momentarily undisturbed. But there were old scars still visible.

224

CHAPTER TEN

THERE ARE TWO WAYS to enter Palermo. Oh, there are no doubt different routes and many means of transportation, from the donkey-drawn carretta of the primitives and the poor to the cushioned, many-motored Constellations braking over the harbor's golden shell and landing on a mountainous airstrip, which once cradled the broken bodies of Mustangs and Spitfires and Junkers and Messerschmitts. No, I am thinking now of the two ways I have come in because time merges dream and incident against the walls of memory, nostalgia alters fact, but the embellishments are arrived at honestly, deep down all the living sequences of day and night are continuations, nothing is lost.

You can come in as I did that summer of invasion in the forties, up the dusty roads from the southern invasion beaches that we called beachheads, but they were not beachheads (I now realize), they were places where sand, dirt, brush and tree unceremoniously met the Mediterranean. Also, there were homes and gardens, country lanes and farms, granaries and vines and markets. Up the beachheads, then, and past the staring townspeople extending grapes as noble as Roman laurels, past the temples of heroic gods from eras long dead and rekindled into rubbled hiding places. The dust forming a terribly fierce-looking gray armor upon the faces of the kindly, embarrassed warriors from across the Mediterranean Sea. The love grasped quickly in the groves and in the purple shadows of the new catacombs. (You speak me, Joe.) The kaleidoscope stops for an instant in the places called bivouacs but which were villages and cities: Sciacca, Agrigento, Castelvetrano, Partinico—hail the new legions for Rome!—and the hills with numbers on their summits, finally, the hills of Monreale and the hills of Palermo.

It was a time to walk with the angels. The authority in uniform, when all the world was divided between soldier and civilian, called out, Engineers, engineers. I was one. But there was no need to call. We knew that where the earth was soft and newly dug, around the edges of the blown bridges where the riflemen had to walk in detour, here the cunning mines waited. Here vines of steel could bloom in bursting red explosions. And we went forward to unarm the coiled terror, planted so affectionately, one by one, by the hard-working, oh-so-mechanically-minded German burghers in battle dress. This was the way to Palermo the first time.

The second way to enter Palermo is this way, in the fifties, a gentleman, a businessman, perhaps a geologist. Beachheads are beaches, bivouacs are towns, permanent bridges of delicate tracery ford the rivers. The train's tracks lead from destination to destination. The car is first class. There are stops for breakfast across the island. The train slices like a scythe's blade across the ancient fields of Sicily. Late in the morning, the incongruously modern *ràpido* hurls itself into Julius Caesar Square in Palermo. Steam and crowds pour through the arcades. Fleets of taxis maneuver between the walkers in the square, motor scooters bark arrogance, the tangerine vendors pull hired carts by hand, temporizing the onrushing civilization. The news ark is overloaded with movie and television magazines, but the headlines on the *Giornale di Sicilia* resemble those of the Rome *Daily American:* the threat of radioactive peace. Situation normal, the story unchanging.

I asked the driver to turn around, past the street called the Course of the Thousand, and I looked at No. 72, laughing to myself, and the driver knew his neighborhood because he said there were some fine girls there. The street was foreign now. I told him that it was too early in the morning, and to head down Via della Libertà to the villa of the Mediterranean American Development Company. The driver grinned and said it was not so good on an empty stomach, anyway.

Subito hurried down the steps of the villa and reached for my bags, grabbing them from the taxi driver. It was comfortable to be known and protected by the sub-lieutenants of the Company.

It seemed as if I had barely left. The American secretary at the reception desk of the villa greeted me heartily.

"A pleasant sojourn, Mr. Borken?" she inquired.

"More like work than a vacation," I said, remembering my Company manners.

You never could tell in this atmosphere when the careless language would be conveyed to those in authority. I had learned to wear the veneer of caution.

"Here's something for you," she said, handing me my mail. "And here's a note from Mr. Tabbert."

"A note?" I said. "Isn't he here?"

"Oh, my, yes," she said. "He's been asking about you. All the others on the team have already returned from their assignments." She was very efficient, an office girl who had carried America with her overseas.

I took my stuff and returned to my assigned room. Subito opened the hinges on my bags, and in a moment he slipped a drink into my hand. I asked him what was up, and he shrugged.

I tore open Tabbert's note. It was brief: "Don't bother phoning. I'm waiting in my room."

Dated that morning, timed to the rapid train's arrival, and initialed with a bold *T* in green ink.

I didn't like the meaning of its terseness. But maybe I was being sensitive.

I took out my samples from Mount Etna and arranged them, one each, in labeled little cases. I liked my work shown neatly. I lay down on the bed, the soothing drink in my hand. The telephone rang next to my head. I watched it ring with dulled fascination, the machinery of bell, cradle and receiver vibrating. I heard it ring itself out after an incessant minute, defying the summoning noise. Then I took my good time, moving at my own pace, the hell with you, Tabbert, and I changed carefully into loose clothing and walked down the hall.

I lighted a cigarette of confidence before knocking.

"Push in the door, Borken," his voice said.

He was seated at a desk, his eyes focused in a microscope. He moved fragments of stone on and off the glass platform without looking up. Finally, he shook his head in disgust and waved hello.

"This junk from Trapani and Agrigento is all right for putting tile around fancy toilets, but for our purposes it doesn't mean a penny. Some of the people they send me are not geologists, they're plumbers. No goddamn craftsmen around any more. Well, it's their buck, not mine." He held out his hand for my samples. "How did you make out?"

I placed my labeled cases carefully on the brocaded spread on his bed.

He packed a fat-bowled pipe and inserted it in his mouth, drawing the corners of his face. He avoided touching my samples, and I made no comment about them.

"How was it in Taormina?"

"You tell me," I answered antagonistically.

"So near and you didn't make it? Foolish. The boys and girls playing ring-around-the-rosie together there—all three sexes. Whatever were you doing all week?"

"Playing, having fun. Is that what I'm supposed to say?"

Tabbert laughed, and then he asked me to sit down.

"All right, let's begin again. First I ask you how you are. That's the way the charm is laid on by the bow-wows in the New York office, isn't it? You like to be formal, I'll play along. How are you, Borken?"

I said I was okay.

"Well, now that the formalities are over, let's get down to business. I'm asking you, how do your samples look to you?"

I said that I wouldn't want to guess and why didn't he see for himself.

"Well, you're not giving very much, are you?"

I didn't say anything.

He went on. "Maybe we'd better talk about you first. Did you get my wire about returning sooner?"

I said I had but it had been delayed because I was delayed on the mountain.

"I heard about that," Tabbert said. "That's why I wanted you back here *subito*. You became involved in something political down there. I got a signal from one of our sources in Catania."

I interrupted to ask who checked up on me there and signaled him.

"I don't mind telling you. Our consul in Catania. We work together closely. That's why they're here—to service American interests abroad. Don't look so shocked."

"What the hell has the consulate got to do with our activities—especially mine?"

"Look, Borken, I don't know every last detail of what happened. All I heard was that there was some trouble down there, the consul got wind of it because that's his job, and that you were involved in some way. What way is important to him more than myself. I don't give a good damn about politics—haven't voted in years. All I care about is what affects Mediterranean American here and the people working for me. You can carouse your ass off as long as it's done after

229

hours. But getting mixed up in some local politics or whatever, that's something else."

"Your informant was wrong," I said. "I wasn't involved in anyone's politics. If you want to know what happened, I can give you my version. But only if you think someone working for you should have a say."

"Don't be so touchy. Sure, go ahead."

"There was a land seizure in the countryside around this little town I stayed in. Maybe you've been reading about them. The tenant farmers go out and occupy the land that has been tied up by absentee owners—situations of that nature. You know Sicily better than I do and what exists here for most of these people."

"What's that got to do with your getting back here?"

"The people who guided me on Etna participated. I went along and watched."

He did not have to know all the nuances and details. He wanted it straight, he said.

"That all? You didn't take part, help them do this act?"

"No. It was their show, something that had been brewing long before I ever went to Brucia."

"How did the farmers make out?" he asked, relighting his pipe.

"I think they scored."

He nodded and said, "Must take some moxie to do that. Anyone get hurt?"

"One casualty."

"Well, that's not our affair now, is it?" he said, testing me.

I didn't say anything. In a way he was right: Mediterranean American did not meddle on these lower levels.

"Let's get back to the business at hand," he continued. "As far as I'm concerned, this other thing in Brucia is a closed book. You got a little too close, but you didn't implicate the Company. That's your version. I believe you."

"Thanks, Tabbert," I said.

"Now, let's have a look at your carnotite," he said.

I moved the samples over to his desk, and he fingered them and studied my markings for ten minutes. I could read the satisfaction in his face.

"Some of this stuff looks pretty good to me," he said, "especially this group you picked up between three and four thousand feet. My map lines help any?"

I said they had. I had tried to cover the predetermined pattern carefully.

"Glad you went off the positions, too," he said, "on your own initiative."

I told him I had to because of lava accretions I wanted to avoid which might give a false reading. He nodded. He took some of the rock chips and rolled them like dice in his cupped hands. The ones which looked hot he re-examined closely with a jeweler's loupe, fixed to his eye like a Cyclops.

"I won't know for a few days exactly how all this stuff will pan out," he said, "but it's certainly worth getting back to New York for assaying. By the time we get the answers back here, we'll be on our way."

"I'd like to know how I made out on the mountain," I said. "As a pro."

"You are one," Tabbert said. Then, enthusiastically, "We're moving fast. The whole team. Arranged for us through Washington. Central Africa, then up to the Blue Atlas in French Morocco. We swing a lot of weight in that part of the world. British and French move out, we move in, alone, or on co-production arrangements. It's virtually new territory, crying to be explored in a real way. Those countries had their chance in the first half of the century, we'll take a whack at it in this half."

"But what if there are deposits here in Sicily?"

"Won't matter to us at all. In the first place, I've got orders to get packed and go in two days, regardless of the possibilities. Second, my job running these teams out here is to explore, not to exploit. Hit and run—let the drones follow me. I'd die of boredom if I ever had to stay put too long and do the drilling."

"It seems like a terrible rush," I said. "I don't get it. There's still work to do here. A geologist can't just jump this way—you have to get the look and feel of a place by studying it awhile."

Tabbert laughed. "You sound as if this is child's play, Borken. This is the big leagues. Haven't you been reading the papers lately?"

I said the headlines hadn't changed in years.

"It's damn big," he said. "The other side has found a vein of pitchblende in one of their areas. It's supposed to be second only to ours up around Hudson's Bay. No, that's not the kind of news you'll find on the front page or on your television screen. Newspaper editors don't receive free passes to scientific laboratories like they do to baseball games. There aren't as many press agents for scientists as there are for entertainers. That's why you don't read much about these things."

I asked him where he got his information, and he said he played it mostly by ear from different places—the home office, friends passing through, the consulates, scientific journals, once in a while from an astute correspondent.

"This all ties up with Mediterranean American's program. We are in one hell of a race. The investment alone for looking for the resources surpasses all your gold rushes." He got up from his desk and walked over to a wall safe and dialed it open. "Here's another reason we've got to be pitching our tents on the other side of the Mediterranean," he said, handing me a flimsy carbon of a confidential communication. It was a new directive from Kurt Von Loesch. "Just read the heading, that's all," he said, withdrawing the carbon. "That's what we're going to be after as well—the so-called exotic fuels. You know, for the missiles and rockets. Some of the components are going to have to come out of the ground. It opens up a whole new field of exploration and laboratory work."

Tabbert's eyes shone as he spoke; he was a born adventurer. That, plus the per diem and fat bonuses and avoiding of taxes which sweetened the dirty work of so many men from many lands abroad. There was no question that the stakes in our work were as high as they came. The other side did not stand short; and morality never disturbed them. The thought of the end products was frightening: of picking away at the tired earth for more fiery brimstone.

"How does it hit you?" Tabbert asked. "All the boys are excited."

"I want to bring up one thing before I forget," I said, changing the subject. "If you don't mind my asking you—"

He nodded assent.

"You said that I was still hot in the Company and that you were supposed to file a report on me. Have you written it yet?"

He glanced at me quickly and said, "No."

I asked, "Are you going to write it in Sicily? Before moving on?"

"I'm supposed to. They've asked for it after you return from your first trip. But I told you not to worry about that. What counts with me is what's in the kitty. Dammit, that's all that counts with the home office, too. It's a business, not a popularity contest. You don't have to be lovable."

"But what about this loyalty they want you to report on?" I asked. "What is the test there?"

"The same one. Don't you get the message? You don't know very much about how these big corporations work. I told you all they're interested in is production. Each year the statement must show a little better than the year before for the bankers and the investors. You may have to juggle it around, sell off certain stuff, cut out some of the hired help, whatever, you have to look good on paper—including, in the Company's own paper."

I smiled easily for the first time since entering his room.

"The loyalty is as simple as you say it is, really, isn't it? No matter how you slice it, it's still to the buck. I was looking for some high-powered notion."

"Mediterranean American is incorporated to do business at a profit. The officers in charge may not like Von Loesch any more than you do. Yes, they would find a way to cut him down, too, if it became necessary. You give the Company too much credit. You show increased revenue from this part of the world and they'll get right behind you."

"Just like that," I said aloud.

"Damn right."

He got up and walked toward the door.

"Most of the boys are knocking off this afternoon. Tying up loose odds and ends before the Africa move. I suggest you do the same." He gave me a friendly tap on the elbow. "I need a good geologist like you with my team."

He walked out of his room, and I followed him down the steps, and he drove off in one of the Company's cars.

I went downstairs to the big living room with the high ceiling. Subito was pouring wine for some of the others. We greeted one another and sat down to eat together. Harris and Hill, the two young fellows who had transferred because they couldn't stand the perverted Arab ruler on the Gulf of Aden, were in fine spirits.

"I'm going to hate to leave Palermo," Harris said. "You going with us?"

"Why do you ask?"

"Because you got connections here, friend."

He said this almost in admiration, and I looked puzzled.

"It was really something," Hill explained. "I've been in joints here and there but this was the living end."

He lowered his voice as the American secretary with the haughty manner passed our corner of the room and sat down at the far end. Then he took out the madam's card I had given him and flashed it in front of me.

"Oh," I said. "How did you make out?"

"It was so great it got us back here a day early." Harris laughed. "We were there again last night—a dusk-to-dawn job."

"I'm getting horny again just thinking of her," Hill said.

"Down, boy," I said. "Who's she?"

"The one they call the Whistler there," Hill replied. "Come on, don't look so innocent. She said she knew you."

"Me? That's nice, but I'm afraid I haven't had the pleasure."

Harris said, "She doesn't know one customer from the next. Chances are that if you mention any American-sounding name, it's fifty-fifty that they've asked for her."

"If you really haven't," Hill said, "you've got to try a piece of that. I don't know her name but just purse your lips and they'll know who you mean. This dame whistles while she does it! Man, it gives you the shivers! It's the eeriest feeling to hear this sound at first—you don't know where it's coming from. You're going along and you hear this low-pitched sound creeping all over you and it becomes a musical accompaniment. At the end it's all piccolos and flutes."

"You're making it all up," I said. "But, anyway, you boys can't say I didn't help you in your hour of need."

"How did you make out?" Harris asked. "Anything on that side of the island?"

"I brought back a lot of samples—"

"Come on, I'm not talking about that, friend. We can guess why you switched there. Taormina must be loaded with that tourist white meat now."

"I didn't get there, fellows."

"Too bad," Harris said. "Man, if we could teach her to do the same thing," he said, thumbing toward the American secretary, "we could probably sell it at a hundred a shot in the States."

"Fat chance," Hill said. "She can't even whistle."

Then they both burst out laughing, and the American girl looked up in our direction and smiled like a good sport.

Harris and Hill left after lunch, destination known, and I walked across the room to the girl because she looked lonely.

"Are you going on to Africa with them?" I asked, making conversation.

"Oh, yes," she said. "It should be loads of fun. Mr. Tabbert said you did very well, Mr. Borken."

"Did he?"

"Gosh, I get the shivers just listening to Mr. Tabbert talk about the Company's next project in Central Africa and Morocco. He's the only one who can make fuel sound exotic."

"It'll take you to the moon," I said, "if that's where you want to go."

"Each one of us gets assigned two servants," she said. "It beats sharing a room with two other girls in Greenwich Village. I'll have a cook and a houseboy for myself, and I'll share a cleaning woman. Forty dollars a month including servants. I wonder what my houseboy does?"

"I hear they come in handy," I said. "Hope you get everything your heart desires in Africa."

"Aren't you coming along with the team?"

"No," I said.

"Oh. But Mr. Tabbert has you down on the Company manifest—"

"Do you know where Tabbert is now?"

"He said he was going over to the U.S. consulate."

"I might just walk over there," I said.

I left her and slipped out through the English garden behind the Company's villa, and circled the deliberately crowded flowers and shrubs slowly. Then I turned and walked along the Via della Libertà, taking my time, certain of what I had to tell him. A taxi honked toward me, spotting a live customer, but I shook off the driver. I blended into the crowd, going my own way, until I reached the marble consulate building.

236

Tabbert's car was parked in front of the curving driveway and he stepped into it just as I walked by. I ran up and rapped on the window.

"Hey, Borken! What are you doing here? Jump in."

"I was looking for you," I said. "Thanks, I don't feel like sitting down. Have you got a minute?"

"Sure. But make yourself comfortable."

"No, that's okay." I paused for a moment. "I forgot to tell you something this morning," I said. "I'm leaving."

Tabbert got out of the Company limousine and walked around toward me. He leaned against the great shield of the United States on the consulate building.

"So you've decided," he said. He lighted his pipe. "Why?"

"I've had it with Mediterranean American."

"As simple as that?"

"No, it's not as simple as that."

"You're not mad at me, are you?"

I shook my head.

"I suspected something. I knew when you came back a day late that you had some doubt about sticking it out—that you softened up on our mission out here. But I still say what I said this morning—I could use a good geologist with me in Africa and you're one. I'm not conning you."

"Nothing personal," I said.

"Matter of fact," he continued, "I permitted myself to do something I seldom do with my men: I allowed myself to sympathize with your troubles."

"I have no troubles," I said. "I'm feeling great now, Tabbert. I've decided to get Mediterranean American and all its world-wide operations and vice-presidents in charge of personnel and new developments off my back."

"This is the place to beat the system, Borken. Out here, with me. Away from all that nonsense. Here we can do our work and make a score uninterrupted by the administrative hecklers."

"Maybe some can. I can't any more. I've just reached a cut-off point for myself."

"That's what I guessed, Borken. Somewhere along the line you lost heart in the work."

I searched his face, but it was without rancor.

"Maybe Mediterranean American kicked it out of you. Maybe you were atrophying in the home office too long. Maybe someone filled your head with all that crud about nice scientists not dirtying their hands with atomic materials. Why the hell you got involved with that land-seizure nonsense —that's never going to change things out this way."

"At least they're trying," I said. "They might be able to pull it off."

"Maybe you fancy yourself a boy philosopher. Come off it."

"That's right. You can call it a clash of conscience between Borken the boy philosopher and Mediterranean American the savior corporation of our way of life."

He laughed, and stared at me over the smoke from his pipe.

"Borken, you're a dumb bastard all right, but you got moxie, I'll say that. Okay, do what you want. I'm not one to try and mix in your personal life. Just remember that whether you're in there digging or not, somebody is going to do it for the Company. You're not the first one to leave under his own head of steam and you won't be the last. You, friend, are expendable."

"Oh, I don't think they'll go out of business because I leave. I tell you, Tabbert, I'm not even saying someone else shouldn't be doing the work, much as I despise most of the purposes to which the stuff is put by Mediterranean American. But to me, with Von Loesch one of the honored members of the so-called team, the rottenness of the whole operation began to fall into place. It's a little too corrupting to be on his side. I haven't been able to make that full peacetime leap yet where I'll work with ex-Nazis. I'm queer—I can't rid myself of the old wartime attitudes and dreams even in the fifties. But I'm not condemning others who stay—I'm just telling you that I've reached the point where it's not for me."

He looked thoughtful. "You really mean it, don't you? I'm not going to try to make you change your mind—don't think I could. If you don't mind my asking, what do you think you'll do?"

"You really want to know?"

He nodded.

"Well, I intend to do something independently where I won't have to rationalize the work. Research, maybe some teaching. Even my own testing office. There's a demand for small independent operations. There are plenty of good uses for what we were searching for out here. And I don't mean M.A.D.'s rocket fuels. Corny as it sounds, I mean the peacetime uses, from agriculture to medicine. I know my field, I know testing, and there must be decent ways to work."

"It's a ball-breaker trying to stay independent," Tabbert said. "But that's your worry."

He extended his hand and I shook it.

"For the record," Tabbert said, "I'll put you down as resigning. That way there won't be any trouble caused by Mediterranean American. You know, they have their finger in a lot of pies in the States. You wouldn't want them to louse you up. That okay with you?"

"Thanks, Tabbert," I said. "Nothing personal in what I've been saying. Straightening myself out—"

"Check," he said, running around to his car. He started up the motor, signaled and waved to me, and drove off quickly.

Then it was time, in the still full autumn of the Sicilian afternoon, to go again to the Flower Bar in Mondello. At last to free myself of the binds of years, to kiss these scars of long ago. . . .

A venerable taxi stood in front of the consulate building,

and I stepped inside. The driver took the long way outside the city and past the unchanged low mountain on the right, past the flowering oleander, the palm trees sweeping the tiled roofs of the small villas lining the shore. The driver assumed that I was going to the beach club jutting out into the water on wooden piers, and I did not protest when he stopped there. The striped beach cabins were as still as sentries on the sand. Tea was being served on the terrace of the club—tea and Coca-Cola. Foreign tourists were around, Americans and Germans and English and Scandinavians, even Italians from across the seas.

I got out and walked past the tourist palace, along the street facing the cove of Mondello, past the undisturbed water and the leather-faced fishermen sloping at their tillers. Up the hill behind me women strung wash of wet sails and old men regenerated their bodies and children danced again between the nets and cork imported from the other end of the Mediterranean. At the tip of Mondello small shops were framed by a gently banking promontory. The gold "Costanza" sign gleamed.

I entered the Flower Bar. This time the bent bartender remembered me; it was only a week ago that I had been there. We shook hands and he poured the vermouth first, but I restrained his hand when he reached for the cognac.

"Enough of that nonsense," I said, laughing.

"Agreed," he said. "That mixture was for war stomachs."

I asked him if I might use his telephone because I wanted to speak to the same Florio family he had helped me find. He led me to a small room behind a door behind the bar. It was filled with uncut fibrous leaves above which grew a panicle of white blossoms ready to be placed in the glass cases out front. I put the lire for the call on a counter, and then tried to explain to the operator what number I wanted: Yes, the town of Brucia, in the province of Catania.

I was tense with anticipation.

The voice on the other end was low, faraway.

"Franca . . ." I repeated.

"Joseph. Joseph! From where are you calling?"

"Darling . . ."

Her voice suddenly came through clearly, as if she were near by. "I thought you had left."

"I did. I'm in Mondello."

"At the Flower Bar?" She laughed lightly.

"Yes . . . It's good to hear you laugh."

"I'm sorry I could not say goodbye when you came here last night. My father told me. I was angry that you did not come into the house."

"Are you feeling all right? What happened was saddening."

"Sad and brave."

She paused and the phone was silent.

"Franca?"

"I'm still here, Joseph."

She laughed; she still could.

"Darling, I want you to come here this evening."

"You, Joseph, what are you saying?"

"This evening. On an island plane from Catania. You can be here by nine o'clock. I've looked at the schedule. I want you to come to me. There's nothing to keep you in Brucia."

"It's a dream." Her voice caught, and I could see her face.

"No longer. It's true, it's us again."

She did not answer, and the receiver hung still in my hand.

"I'm staying here at the Flower Bar until you get here. No matter when or how long it takes. I'm not leaving until you arrive."

"Joseph, I have classes to teach here."

"I love you, Franca. This time you're coming home with me to my country. I want you to marry me—here, if you wish— this week."

"I love you, Joseph—that is all that matters."

"You said it, dear, finally. I know, you have faith only in now. But this is now for us."

241

"Joseph . . . All right! I don't know what I'm saying, but you came to me again and I'll come to you."

"Forget everything but this. Pack a bag and rush here. I'll be at the Flower Bar even if I have to drink all the vermouth and eat camellia petals for dinner."

"Joseph, darling. Will you call and tell my sister? I'll need Dorotea to help us with our arrangements."

"Of course. It will happen this time, Franca."

"Joseph, if you say so, it is now. Goodbye . . ."

The time of dreaming was over, of visions formed on the ceilings in lonely hotel rooms and apartments and of love grasped without love. The courage of youth surged back that had been left on those terrible hills of war. I strolled past the tables and the bartender; he was pouring a Bavarian beer for a thickset tourist in leather pants. I took my drink outside and watched the fleet of small fishing boats coming in from the safe Mediterranean seas. Across the curving bay of Mondello, the dog-shaped mountain crouched still, as it must have in the time during the First Punic War when a foreign soldier looked across this hill toward Monte Pellegrino. (They killed so primitively then.) Still, when dusk began to cast purple on the mountain, it appeared as it once had that first late summer day: when the grapes handed the American soldiers were the Roman laurels for my time. We had rushed in as strangers, sweeping the ground for cunning mines, walking with the angels.

About the Author

HERBERT MITGANG is on the Sunday staff of *The New York Times*. He studied law and had just been admitted to the New York bar when, in 1942, he began three years of Army service which took him to North Africa, Sicily (the scene of his novel), Italy, and Greece. He became caught up in journalism, serving as a military correspondent in the Mediterranean Theater and as managing editor of *Stars and Stripes* in Sicily and Oran–Casablanca.

In addition to his writing for the *Times*, his work has appeared in *Harper's*, *Holiday*, and other magazines. He is the author of *Lincoln As They Saw Him*, a biography published in 1956. *The Return* is his first novel.

He lives with his wife and two children in Great Neck, New York.